# TO LOVE IS TO LIVE

# TO LOVE IS TO LIVE

### Denise Robins

## CHIVERS

British Library Cataloguing in Publication Data available

This Large Print edition published by AudioGO Ltd, Bath, 2012.
Published by arrangement with the Author's Estate

U.K. Hardcover    ISBN   978 1 4458 3038 4
U.K. Softcover    ISBN   978 1 4458 3040 7

Printed and bound in Great Britain by
MPG Books Group Limited

# ONE

It seemed to Gail Partner a significant fact that the very day on which she accepted Bill Cardew's offer of marriage, England declared war against Germany.

A war! Not only a World War, but a little private war within herself. Because only last night when Bill had made his sixth proposal within the month, Gail had said:

'What'll you do if there *is* a war, Bill?'

And he had flung back that golden, rather arrogant head of his; a familiar gesture with its faint suggestion of scorn, and answered:

'Be called up, of course. I'm a Territorial.'

She had looked at him a moment, aghast, for the Bill Cardew she had known for so many years, and whose home was only a stone's throw from her own, was junior partner in a City firm of electrical engineers. And to Gail he had never been anything except an habitually well-dressed young man with the stamp of London on him; interested in his job; mechanically-minded rather than artistic. Fond of tinkering with his old open Lagonda. Faithful to golf in the week-ends, and with his fair share of faults and virtues.

Although he had been in the Territorials since the crisis of 1938, and done his 'summer camp,' his occasional training, Gail could never really think of Bill as a soldier. And now she was facing the fact that he would, of course, be called up immediately. And that fact brought to her consciousness a train of memories connected not with Bill, but with another young man, who was in the Regular Army. A soldier born, not *made* as Bill would be, when he exchanged his striped trousers, his black suit, his bowler hat, for a uniform.

It was a very long time since Gail had allowed herself to remember Ian. (It must be three years, quite, since they had said good-bye in Paris.) During those years she had schooled herself sternly not to wince at the sight of a kilt, the skirl of a bagpipe, pictures of the Lowlands, and all the little heartbreaking things which had reminded her of a lieutenant in a Scottish regiment; a man whom she had once loved.

On the third of September, that Sunday when she stood in the drawing-room with the rest of the family listening to the Prime Minister's grave announcement, the whole thing seemed to her unreal and fantastic. And although the memory of Ian had leapt back to life and startled her by its very vividness, its potency to stir her to a faint wild thrill of pain, it was upon Bill she concentrated her thoughts.

Gail's young sister, Anne, still a schoolgirl of fifteen, and affectionately known in the Partner family as 'Scampie,' brought the thought of Bill right into their midst. When Mr. Partner turned off the radio, Scampie looked at Gail and exclaimed:

'I *say,* Gail . . . will Bill have to go and fight?'

Gail, still feeling mentally bruised and bewildered by that announcement which must have shocked millions, even while it had been expected, drew in her breath:

'I suppose so.'

Mrs. Partner, short, plump, grey-haired, but with a charm and vitality which made a young woman of her despite her forty-five years, looked slowly round the room, examining all her family with a mother's brooding anxiety. She thought:

'I've already lived through one war. Dear God, it'll be hard to get through another with the added responsibility of these dear ones of mine.'

Her gaze fell upon her eldest daughter, Gail, who was so lovely—much the best-looking of the family. Slender, with small bones like her father, and his delicately-cut features, but with her mother's colouring. The same burning beauty which had been Mary Partner's greatest asset in her youth. An almost passionate beauty with that red-brown hair, the sweep of dark lashes, the wide grey eyes with such big black pupils that they looked enormous, the red young mouth with an upper lip which seemed to challenge life. A lovely mouth when she was laughing, a slightly sad one in repose. Ever since her nineteenth year, there had been an almost brooding

3

sadness in the girl which, at times, had worried Mrs. Partner. An absorption into self. As though she had something on her mind. She'd been like that since she had returned from Lausanne where she had gone to study languages. She had never said anything, and Mrs. Partner was not the sort of woman to badger or demand confidence when it was not voluntarily given. And anyhow, lately there had seemed nothing to worry about in Gail. The thing that the family had always wanted was coming to pass. She was going to marry Bill Cardew.

In Mrs. Partner's opinion, for Gail to get married would be the very best thing that could happen. She was twenty-two now and the right age for marriage. They all knew Bill and liked him. He had a side to him which worried Mrs. Partner sometimes. There was a slight suggestion of the braggart, even the bully, in Bill. But that could be excused, because he was still young. Twenty-four and hopelessly spoiled. The only, idolised son of a widowed mother. But Gail had a forceful character. Yes, there was a lot of spirit and fire in that slip of a girl. Surely she would be able to 'manage' Bill when she was his wife! He obviously adored her.

Past Gail, Mrs. Partner's gaze swept to Anne. Nothing to worry about where Scampie was concerned. Plump, mischievous, crazy about games, gold band on her teeth, glasses because these big blue eyes were a little short-sighted, giggles, hockey, typical schoolgirl humour. And then Mary Partner's gaze came to rest upon Chris, her only son. And her heart gave a horrid jerk. It was upon him she focused, with all the concentration of her mother-love and purpose.

Chris, aged sixteen, due back at his public school at the end of the month. Safe enough now. Like Scampie, mad about games. A cricket enthusiast and in the Eleven. Could she ever forget how proud the family had been when they watched his innings—the white-flannelled hero of that summer's day! Darling Chris with his rough red-brown head, the same colour as Gail's. A snub-nose, freckles, and the fact that he was on the short side only just saved him from being too conspicuously handsome.

How long would this war last? In two years, Chris would be eighteen. In the last war they had taken the eighteen-year-olds.

Mrs. Partner crossed the room and stood beside her husband trying to steady her nerves. *He* had worn khaki in that other war. And she had been a nurse with a Red Cross on her apron when she had met him. Dear Charlie! After twenty-four years there was nothing much left of his figure or good looks. At fifty, he was bald and tired, an overworked solicitor who had had a struggle to make life what he had wanted for his family. But he had achieved it. And here they were in the big sunny house on Kingston Hill, full of the treasures they had collected together. At the back a good-sized garden and tennis court. They had had so many jolly week-end parties here, and considered themselves so lucky. A happy united family.

And now—war!

Mr. Partner looked up at his wife and smiled. He had a slow, reassuring smile. Twinkling eyes, comforting her over the rim of his glasses.

'Well, Mogs, I don't suppose they'll take me in the Army now. What about that Red Cross uniform of yours? Would it fit still, d'you think?'

'Certainly not. I'm much too fat and I got rid of it long ago.' She laughed. And she thought how foolish and sweet it was to be called 'Mogs' at her age, the mother of a grown-up family. The sound of her pet-name from Charlie, and his matter-of-fact speech, dissipated some of her dreads concerning Chris. Not that there weren't other terrors. The fear of air-raids! Not for herself but for these young things who were just beginning life . . .

'Mum,' said Scampie, 'can I cut out some more black paper for the windows?'

'Yes,' put in Chris, 'you'd jolly well better not show any lights tonight.'

'We'll get busy on it directly after lunch,'

said Mrs. Partner.

Then Gail turned to her mother.

'I must ring up Bill,' she said breathlessly.

'Are you going to become engaged?' asked Scampie with a child's tactlessness.

Gail answered without looking round from the door. She said:

'Married, I expect.'

The family broke into a hum of discussion as she left.

She only got as far as the hall. Bill had just opened the front door, letting himself in with the air of one who was privileged to walk in and out the house as he wanted.

She looked at him. She remembered that they had been going to play tennis this morning, if it was fine. But he had not brought a racket. He wore grey flannels. She liked him in those better than in his dark City clothes. They made him look younger, more appealing. Sometimes Bill was so cocksure of himself. 'Bossy,' Scampie had once called him when he had annoyed her. And Gail never cared for him in his bossy moods. But this morning she saw him only as Bill who would shortly be joining up, and who might be swept from her, suddenly, into the vortex of a dreadful war.

She could not look at him through ordinary eyes. Everything had changed in this last hour since the Prime Minister's speech. Their whole world, that happy, secure little world in which they had all been living in Kingston, was rocking on its foundations.

Gail was over-excited, thrilled, afraid, a great many things rolled into one.

Somehow she found herself walking straight into his arms.

'Oh, Bill,' she said.

The touch of superiority which always marked Bill Cardew's entrances and exits, vanished entirely from the young man's face as he held her. It was the first time she had ever allowed him to do more than kiss her cheek or touch her hair, her hands. But now her lips were warm and yielding, and he kissed them with an intensity which had always been within himself waiting for Gail.

'At last,' he thought. 'It's taken a war to shake Gail into my arms . . .'

He said:

'Darling, I'm crazy about you. And you're going to marry me. At once. I'm not going to wait. I'm chucking the office and going straight into the Army. And you'll go with me as long as I'm on British soil, I *hope*'

She did not answer verbally. Her hands were clasped about his neck. She looked at him with eyes full of tears. She could not possibly have explained her sensations in that moment. Only one thing was clear to her, her love for Bill. He had always attracted her in a way with that very golden head of his, the well-shaped mouth under the slight, fair moustache, the healthy glow of skin, the blue eyes which could blaze

8

with temper or be soft and passionate as they were today. And in this hour she believed that she loved him and it was no use holding back any longer. No use allowing that other love to chain her, or any memory of Ian to creep like a destructive shadow across the eager fire of her imagination.

Ian *was* a ghost. She would never see him again. She didn't even know where he was. And, anyhow, he didn't even love her. But Bill did. And she wanted to be loved. Wanted to be taken out of her loneliness, wooed from repressions, from inhibitions, lulled into the acceptance of a concrete devotion such as Bill had shown her for the last three years.

They stood in a soundless embrace for a few moments, murmuring to each other between their kisses. Bill said:

'You really mean it? You aren't just carried away by Mr. Chamberlain and this idea that I'm a hero going into battle, and all that?'

She laughed and shook her head.

'No. I know my own mind. I've been a long time making it up, but I know it now. I love you, Bill.'

'It's grand to hear you say that,' he said, then took one of her small white ears between his fingers and pinched it a little. 'And about time too, young woman . . .'

At any other time that gesture, those words, would have annoyed her. They were just slightly patronising. Bill was like that at times, and if there was one thing Gail hated, it was being patronised. But this morning she laughed. She was carried away on a tide of enthusiasm for him and for marriage with him. If that ghost of Ian lingered at all to refute the statement she had just made when she told Bill that she loved him, she banished it once and for all. Just as she had long since banished the memory of a foolish, very young Gail, crying, crying desolately . . . on the deck of a cross-Channel steamer, for an Ian who had just said good-bye to her.

She clung to Bill in bliss, listening to his plans for an immediate marriage. His mother would be delighted, he said, and he knew that her people would give permission. They couldn't afford to wait in these times. Financially they were all right. He had his father's money. It was *time* that was dear and precious. They must save every scrap of that in case he got sent to France at an early date.

She was happier, more content than she had felt for a very long time. It was good to be treated in this possessive manner; to be held and kissed and adored and dictated to by Bill. And she wanted to agree to all his suggestions. Yet it seemed unreal, still, like the thought of the war.

Nothing had really changed her, so far, in this home wherein she had lived for the last sixteen years and where both Chris and Scampie had been born.

10

In this very hall everything was the same. That big oil painting of Daddy's uncle, with his scarlet face, his side-whiskers, in Dickens-like collar and cravat. The stand with Daddy's hat on it, and Chris's school scarf, Scampie's old mack, Mummy's umbrella. The semi-circular table up against the wall, bearing a china bowl of flowers. The family clothes-brush which was never there when Daddy wanted it.

Ever since Gail could remember, they had had to chase that clothes-brush before Daddy went to his office in the morning. And either Chris had it up in his room, or Scampie had been using it to brush the rabbits which she kept in her home-made cage at the bottom of the garden.

The sight of the familiar things was comforting to Gail. Like the close pressure of Bill's arms; the roughness of the little fair moustache against her lips.

'Darling, darling Bill,' she murmured.

'Come back with me and tell Mother,' he said abruptly, releasing her.

'Let's tell the family first.'

'All right.'

They walked arm-in-arm into the drawing-room. Gail's eyes swept round the room, challenging her family, gay, proud, pleased.

'Mum. Daddy . . . all of you. Bill and I are going to be married.'

There was a rush, Scampie knocking off her glasses in the effort at a frenzied hug.

11

Mr. and Mrs. Partner quick with kisses and congratulations for their eldest daughter, with handshakes and congratulations for Bill. Only Chris refrained from any energetic display of enthusiasm. He stuck his hands in his pockets and gave a quick, frowning glance past his sister at the arrogant, fair young man beside her.

'Congratters,' he said, muttering to himself rather than voicing his emotions aloud.

Gail took no notice of that lukewarm response. She knew Chris did not care for Bill, and that Bill was not on the best of terms with her young brother. They just did not 'get on.' But what did that matter? The rest of the family liked Bill enormously.

Mr. Partner went down to the cellar to find a bottle of champagne. He had one or two put aside for family celebrations.

Gail and Bill were toasted, and the possibilities of a hasty marriage discussed. And after that Bill took Gail down the hill to his mother's house.

When she emerged from it, an hour later, flushed and smiling, it was with Mrs. Cardew's blessing, and a diamond ring—one of Mrs. Cardew's rings—on her finger.

The first day of war marked the first day of Gail's brief engagement to Bill. An engagement which was to last barely a fortnight before her marriage to him, and his obtaining a commission in the Territorials,

12

soon to be classed as one with the whole Army.

But on the very day of her wedding Gail was troubled by the old searing memories of Ian. Memories that not even the feverish excitement of this precipitous marriage with Bill could destroy.

## TWO

Gail was not a person who cared much for ostentation or fuss. And because of the past she would have liked a very quiet little wedding, after which she could just creep away with Bill for their honeymoon and give herself up to the peace and happiness of this new and concrete devotion which he had offered her.

But Bill had other plans. In his masterful fashion—he was exerting that arrogance of his rather more strenuously now that they were officially engaged—he demanded what he called 'a good show.'

'I wish to let the world know that you're mine,' he said, 'and even if it is war-time, we'll show Kingston what we can do.'

Gail felt that too much of a celebration was not only undesirable to her personally, but rather hard lines on her parents who, like everybody else, were financially hit by the times. But Bill was not to be put off.

'What I want, I get,' appeared to be his motto, and his mother had no say in the matter at all.

Mrs. Cardew was kind and sweet to Gail and kind and sweet to Bill. An elderly, rather stupid woman, who had had her son late in life, and now, nearing sixty-five, was insanely devoted to him. She encouraged him to think himself a young god, and would have been shocked if Gail had expressed an opinion that he was anything less than god-like.

Bill ruled her with a rod of iron, and there were moments when Gail disliked to see any woman so completely under a man's thumb. But rushing headlong into this marriage, she was given little or no time to analyse her feelings or dissect them in the cold clear light of reason. There was a war on. Bill might be killed. They might all be killed in air-raids. She, who had been quiet and introspective for so long, was flung into a state of neurotic excitement, and she allowed Bill to sweep her along on the tide of his particular enthusiasms.

They were married at the Kingston Church at which the Partner family worshipped. Gail had no time to deck herself out in white satin and orange-blossom, but she found a long chiffon dress of lovely mist-blue, and a little hat which was nothing but a handful of blue flowers perched on top of her red- brown curls, a soft veil across her face. Bill sent expensive pink tiger-lilies for her bouquet. She did not like tiger-lilies and had expressed a fancy for more simple flowers, but he had said:

'They are rather exotic. I like *you* to be exotic. It amuses me.'

That sort of remark gave her a curious mental chill, but at the time she forgot it. There was so little time for thinking in the rush and excitement of getting her clothes and preparing for the ceremony.

When she finally stood at the altar beside Bill and took the solemn vows, she tried also to offer him her whole heart and to blot out that other love and stamp it for ever from her memory.

But she could not. It was a dreadful fact that the ghost of Ian was there again in the very church, close to her, looking at her with dark, reproachful eyes. She hardly heard the little sermon which the vicar was giving them. She felt faint, weary, anxious that it should all be over. And when at length she walked out of the church beside Bill into the sunshine she breathed a sigh of relief.

There was a rush from Scampie to shower her with confetti and rice. Cheers from the little crowd which had assembled, eager to see a war wedding. The bride was an exquisite girl. Bill looked handsome and glamorous in his new uniform. An old woman called out:

'God bless you both . . .

Gail said:

'Thank you so much,' with a catch in her voice.

But Bill frowned and said:

15

'What cheek these people have!'

In the car, driving back home where the family had a big white cake and champagne ready, Bill took his wife in his arms and kissed her repeatedly.

'Mrs. William Cardew,' he said between the kisses. 'Well, you belong to me at last, my darling, and I enjoyed every moment of that wedding. Didn't you? Look at me. Tell me you're glad that I'm your husband.'

She looked at him, feeling slightly dazed.

'Of course . . .'

'Kiss me, Gail.'

'Darling, wait . . . you're crushing my dress . . . my flowers . . .'

He drew back with a little laugh.

'Better not crush them, perhaps. They cost a packet.'

That jarred her. She found herself instinctively thinking:

'Ian wouldn't have said that. He never spoke about money. He couldn't.

No! Ian had bought her so many flowers in Paris. She had never been without them. But what they had cost did not matter. Anyhow, he preferred the simple flowers, as she did. Violets . . . Dear God, why *must* she remember that day when she had worn violets which he had sent, and when they had met he had held her close, so close, and when she had warned him to take care of the flowers, he had answered:

16

'What does it matter! I'll buy you some more.'

'Yes, I enjoyed every minute of the ceremony,' repeated Bill, sitting back in his corner of the car, stroking his little fair moustache, and adding in a very soft voice:

' *"With my body I thee worship . . ."* '

She sat still. Unable to make any kind of response. But her heart was jerking and she knew that it was not with excitement and happiness, but with fear. Fear of these strange, unaccountable feelings which were sweeping over her within ten minutes of her wedding with Bill. Terrified because *something* had leapt like a menace out of nothing and nowhere to make her ask herself why she had done this thing. She ought to react rapturously to what Bill had just said. To the look in his eyes. To the touch of his hand. But a coldness had come across her which made her tremble as she sat there even though the warm September sun was beating through the thin chiffon of her bridal dress.

*'With my body I thee worship.'* That was how Bill felt about her. That was how she ought to feel about him. Yet she didn't like the way he had said it. And if those same words had been whispered to her by Ian, her heart would have leapt in sheer ecstasy.

She began to pray dumbly, furiously, that this feeling would pass from her. Otherwise she had made the greatest mistake of her life in marrying Bill today. She began to pray, too, that Bill would be at his very best and draw out the best in her, as he had done on that day that war was declared.

But he was not at his best. Once they got back to the house and he had drunk some champagne, he was flushed and overbearing in his manner toward everyone.

He ignored his own mother who hung round timidly, waiting for him to say a word to her. He had little to say to his new father- and mother-in-law. He paid attention only to two people in the room, beside his wife. To Sir Reginald Pakin who was the one man he knew with a title; the head of his old firm who had condescended to attend the wedding. And to Gail's godmother, old Mrs. Latchett, who was supposed to have a great deal of money and who the Partner family had once said might leave Gail a bit of it.

Gail had had a restless night with little sleep and she was tired before the day commenced. Now she felt exhausted. Curious, for as a rule she was strong and alert. She did not want any of these people who were gathered here. She only wanted her own family. She longed to take Mummy into a corner and talk to her, or to wake her brother Chris out of his 'mood.' Christopher didn't like Bill. There was no doubt about that, and neither did he like the wedding. And Scampie was in tears. She was a mischief-loving little girl and she had played

18

an innocent practical joke on her new brother-in-law. She had fixed up a device so that when he entered the room an old slipper fell upon him. It was a soft one, but it had not produced the laugh and the compliment which the child had expected. In front of everybody he had icily snubbed her, showing his disapproval.

At one time during the party Gail heard her young brother say to Scampie:

'I shouldn't cry over him if I were you. Don't let him see you care. He's a conceited prig, anyhow.'

The colour stung Gail's cheeks and she moved away rather than let Chris know she had heard. *'A conceited prig.'* Was that true? Certainly Bill wasn't showing up in the best light just now. But she sought desperately to make allowances.

'When we're alone, it'll be all right. He isn't so good in a crowd,' she tried to console herself. 'And he is so thrilled over me, he can't think of anybody else's feelings.'

(But Ian would have thought of those things. Ian was so extraordinarily sensitive, where Bill was blunt. Bill took things as his due. Ian, never. She knew that if poor little Scampie had tried that joke on Ian he would have roared with laughter. What a gorgeous sense of humour he had had! A way of flinging back his head and laughing when he was amused. And he adored children. She used to talk to him about Scampie, and he had often

19

said how much he wished he could meet her little sister. He would have been interested in Chris, too.)

The strange wedding day came to an end.

Gone was Kingston, now, the old home, the family and the friends. Gail was alone with her newly married husband. Anxious to please him, longing to be pleased. Ready to make excuses for his early blunders. Striving her uttermost to get into real touch with him . . . into tune and sympathy.

She could hot help being as thrilled as any girl about her new status as a wife. It was fun being 'Mrs. Cardew'; calling this young, khaki-clad officer 'my husband.' A thrill to share the big double room in the lovely hotel by the river which Bill had chosen because he was fond of rowing and wanted to show her what he could do with the oars.

The weather was kind and the late summer had become suddenly perfect as if in defiance of the dark shadow which had spread across Europe. There was every chance that they could bathe, spend long, delightful hours on the river, and enjoy that beautiful garden which sloped to the water's edge.

Gail wanted passionately for this marriage to be a success, and her idea was to spend this first night alone with him, wandering across the bridge in the moonlight maybe, or in a punt, drifting down the starlit river, just holding his hand.

But Bill had other ideas, and he was not long in showing Gail that it was *his* ideas which counted and not his wife's.

When she was unpacking he saw a new evening dress in her trunk. Emerald-green with a wide sequin belt. He picked it up and said:

'Ah! This ought to suit you. Put it on, darling, and we'll go and dance in Maidenhead. I'm going to show you off.'

Her heart sank a little.

'Darling, let's just be by ourselves, and—'

'Oh, nonsense,' he broke in, pulling her ear (already that habit annoyed her), 'you'll be fine after a drink or two. I want to show my wife to the world.'

Gail bit her lip. *Show! Show!* Must it always be 'show' with Bill? Could he never do anything without an audience to tell him how good he was at everything?

She began to protest:

'But, Bill, darling . . .'

He cut her short with kisses. He was in a high state of excitement and intent upon having his own way. To please him she gave in, put on the green dress, and they danced until Gail looked so white that even Bill noticed it.

'I'm going to take you home now,' he said.

He was astonished when she burst into tears in the taxi.

'Good Lord, you can't cry on our wedding day. What on earth's the matter?'

She knew that her nerves were getting the better of her and that if she couldn't get some rest and quiet she would scream. She tried hard to control herself. Between her sobs she said:

'It's . . . nothing . . . just . . . sheer . . . exhaustion.'

He was all concern and patted her on the back.

'I know what it is, my darling. Just a little nervy like any bride would be. Poor darling! But you know you're O.K. with *me*. *I'll* be good to you.'

She relaxed in his arms for a moment.

'Oh, Bill, I hope you will . . .'

'There's no question about it,' he said in his haughty manner.

But in Gail's mind there was a very serious question as to how far that 'goodness' went with Bill. She had always known when they were friends that he was wrapped up in himself, but it took marriage to prove just how far his crass egotism could go.

She wanted someone to hold her gently, to lull those jumping nerves of hers to sleep, to woo her cleverly and slowly into acquiescence, into a state when she would respond, and offer a grateful surrender.

But that night was to be a revelation which shattered any hope which she might have entertained that Bill would ever understand her—or any sensitive woman. His love-making was as crude as his methods of approach. He was exacting and insatiable and her tears roused resentment rather than understanding.

Finally he said:

'I don't understand you. Anybody would think you weren't in love with me.'

With all emotion dead in her now, and her only desire to sleep, *sleep* and cease doubting and endeavouring, she whispered:

'I'll be all right . . . tomorrow. Forgive me, please.'

He liked people to apologise. He accepted Gail's apology and added:

'I'm sure you will. But honestly, Gail, you're lucky to have *me* for a husband. You were always temperamental, but I know you so well, I understand you, my darling!'

And then he was completely shocked and upset because Gail burst into hysterical laughter.

Later when he was asleep, she lay sleepless. She watched with reddened eyes the pale light of dawn creep into the room, and knew something akin to despair. The complete failure of her marriage at its very outset appalled her. She had wanted so much to give heart and soul to Bill and with his blundering, his arrogance, his insensitiveness, he had placed an impassable barrier between them. But the ring was on her finger, and the vows she had taken were vows before God, so she must make the best of it. And she must blame

23

herself as well as Bill for the debacle.

But it was impossible that she should see this dawn break without remembering that other dawn . . . In Le Touquet with Ian, her heart's love, her first love. Ian who had *understood* and shown her the magic of love and passion as shared between perfect lovers.

Now, she did not even seek to banish memory. She let it flood upon her, enduring a hot, searing anguish of spirit. It was Bill who was blotted out, Bill her husband, this room, and this awakening. And Ian and the past lived again.

## THREE

She had written it all down in her diary and kept it under lock and key until last night. Last night, her wedding eve, she had torn the pages from that book and burned them without allowing herself the luxury of a tear or a regret. She had resolved so firmly to do her best to be happy with Bill.

But now every word that had been written was there in her mind, just as though she could see it written across the dawn-lit curtains of the window facing the bed. Extracts from it jogged her memory. Took her out of herself, out of this room, out of this country.

To Paris. Paris in that spring after her last term at Lausanne where she had been learning

French.

'When Simone asked me to stay with her in that lovely house in the Boulevard Suchet, I thought it a glorious opportunity not only to see Paris but to see life. It was grand exchanging my old clothes for the latest dresses, for chic little hats and high-heeled shoes. André, Simone's brother, says I have a ridiculously small foot. I only take a three. André is a little *épris* with me, I think, but I only like him as a friend. I couldn't ever kiss him. I have never met a boy yet who has really made my heart beat faster . . .'

*That was the beginning of the diary. But soon there was another entry:*

'Yesterday I met Ian Dalmuir. It's difficult for me to describe my feelings on first seeing him. He is six foot two, strikingly handsome. He has the most marvellous eyes, dark, sad, Celtic. Yet he is amusing, and when he laughs his eyes are brilliant and his mouth is gay. He has a faint, soft burr in his voice, the blackest hair, the most vivid imagination. When he looked down at me his first words were: 'Aren't you a *little* girl?' and then he took my hand. The electricity that ran between our fingers was something I have never before experienced.

'He was at Cambridge with André. Now he is a soldier. He told me he had just passed his Staff College exam. and was waiting orders for India. It is queer that he should be a soldier because he is at heart a poet and artist. But on talking to him I learned that the Dalmuirs set their heart on him being in the Army. I'm sure he's a good soldier because he's not a man who would do anything by halves. It's obvious he's heart and soul in his job.

'When I was in bed tonight, Simone came and told me that Ian told André he had quite 'fallen for me.' He said I had bewitching eyes and hair like the polished chestnuts in the trees on the Bois. I don't believe it. But I *want* to believe it.

'He attracts me too, *violently*.'

After that the diary held pages of reminiscences of those days with Ian. and Simone and André. Descriptions of the parties, the dances, the operas. Little intimate dinners, shopping in the Boulevards, picnics at Versailles, and long, lovely drives to Fontainebleau. Pages steeped in the careless gaiety and glamour of that poignant spring.

*Then one outstanding page:*

'I'm in love with Ian. I know that I am. Perhaps some people would say it is just because I'm young and it's my first affair, and Paris is intoxicating in the spring. But it's more than that. It's something deep down inside me. Something that makes me tremble when Ian comes into the room and feel a chill when he goes out of it. Something that catches me when he looks at me with those brooding Celtic eyes of his, or I hear his sweet, husky voice call me

26

by my name.

'A circle of enchantment is closing around me *and I don't want to get out.* I love him. I believe he loves me. All my life I shall never smell French coffee, or taste chestnuts without thinking of Ian and all the heavenly fun we had together.'

*The morning following:*

'Was there ever a girl so happy in the world as myself? For now I know that I'm loved just as much as I love. Ian took me to the opera. It was *Madam Butterfly.* We both loved it. I heard it once before in Lausanne and cried when poor little Butterfly was deserted by her lover. The music is so sad and lovely, and the theme is dear to every woman's heart. But last night I didn't cry. Ian took one of my hands and kept it fast locked in his, and I sat there close to him in the dark Opera House, feeling half suffocated with emotion.

'In between the acts we disregarded the gay crowd. We just drank in each other's eyes, and each other's voice. We told each other all that we hadn't already told. Ian now knows exactly what sort of a girl I am. The sheltered sort of life I've led. All about my family at Kingston. And I know all about him and his ambitions. He *is* ambitious, and he comes of a strict family full of Scottish tradition and convention. People, not rich, but who have given up everything in order that he should be in his present position. I know that one day

27

he will come into money because he is heir to an uncle who has a fortune and a castle in the Lowlands. I have listened to so many stories of Scotland, of Edinburgh where he was born, that I feel that I *know* the places. I can see the Castle, and Holyrood Palace, and Princes Street. I love it because it is his home, the background of his boyhood.

'When the curtain fell on the last act, I was conscious of his nearness to me—I mean we were very near to each other in spirit—not merely physically attracted.

'We walked out together into the soft starry night where the velvet darkness was bejewelled by the glittering lights of Paris. Ian found a taxi and ordered the man to drive . . . just to drive on and on.

'Then he kissed me. And I can't, I *can't* describe what that first long kiss was like. It was so blinding, so wonderful, and such a revelation.

'Locked in his arms, I realised that I could never be the same Gail Partner again. I would never more belong to myself, but only to him.

'That night he said nothing about the future. We neither of us did. We were just drunk with love. Later on we got out of the taxi and wandered along the Seine, hand in hand, enraptured with Paris and ourselves:

'Oh, God, I love him so . . . !'

*A week later:*

'What am I going to do? How am I going to

bear it? I've got to go home. Mummy's written to say Daddy can't afford for me to stay over here any longer, and I can't go on taking hospitality from Simone's people. It means good-bye to my Ian.

'Ever since that night when we heard *Madam Butterfly* together, I've been dreading that this would happen. Why, *why,* should I have fallen in love with a man who isn't in a position to marry me? Oh, Ian, it's so hard! And you've been so honest. You've never deceived me. You're only twenty-seven, and a subaltern and you've nothing but your pay. You've explained to me that in the Regular Army no marriage is recognised nor allowance granted until a man's thirtieth year. To marry now when he is doing so well would mean ruin for Ian. I understand that. He explained to me that his family wouldn't even consent to an engagement, and his Colonel would be dead against his marrying. He's got to go to India as a bachelor. It's hopeless for us to consider letting this love-affair go on. We've got to say good-bye finally and absolutely. Because we both realise that if we continue to meet, we would neither of us be strong enough to resist. Last night he said he felt like throwing up the Army and everything and marrying me. I can't do that to him. I *can't.*'

There were pages and pages of that sort of thing. A girl's heart poured out on paper. The echo of that futile and bitter struggle against the strongest thing that had ever entered her life. And she, the young inexperienced girl, had to try to be strong enough for them both.

*Then, two days before she left Paris:*

'I've done the maddest thing. And Simone is my ally. She has added to the temptation by making things possible. I'm supposed to be crossing the Channel tomorrow, but instead I'm going down to Boulogne with Simone, then Ian's driving me on to Le Touquet for the night.

'We're going to have twenty-four hours together. Madness! I know it. And he knows it. But I just can't resist. Perhaps I may never see him again. And I know that whatever happens I shall never regret having loved him, having known the heaven of his love.

'He's so different from other men. We have such glorious times together. *We understand each other.*

'Yesterday we spent the whole afternoon in the forest at Fontainebleau. We picked wild flowers like children, laughing, chasing each other in and out the trees. We had a divine picnic. Ian had brought lobster, chicken-pâtés and a bottle of red wine. And grapes, little purple juicy ones. I lay back on the rug, my arms laced behind my head and he threw grapes at me and I had to catch them with my lips. How we laughed when I missed them! That lovely sort of laughter that ends in a kiss, a sob of passionate surrender. The blood seems to drain out of my body, when Ian's heart beats close to mine. I can't think. I can only *feel*, and adore him.

'He told me that afternoon how he longed for the time when he could settle down and marry and have children. And he wanted me for his wife, and *my* children.

' "You're so little and lovely, Gail. I want to take care of you always. I'd give my soul to be able to run away with you now."

'But I didn't dare let him speak like that. I had to tease him out of the serious mood and make him laugh again. He's a very alive creature, my Ian, and terribly strong. A born leader of men. Yet so gentle and tender. Just before our afternoon ended, he thought I had a headache and he put my head on his knees and stroked my brow with his fingers. (Ian has incredibly nice hands, brown, slender, vital.) The touch of them drove all the pain from my forehead. It's strange that a man can take all pain out of you in one way, and yet break your heart in another.

'My poor Ian! He didn't mean to break my heart. It was the force of circumstances. And we were both to blame.

'After the sun went down, we walked until I was tired. And then he carried me back to the car which we had hired in Paris. I shall always remember that walk. Ian with his superb height, his muscular, tireless body. And myself rather like a small girl, weary, curled up in his arms. I knew beyond doubt and reason that I could never leave France tomorrow without stealing those twenty-four hours with Ian Dalmuir.'

*There were only a few chapters left in that diary. The final poignant words wrung out of her pen. A mixture of honey and anguish:*

'We've said good-bye. I'm writing this on the deck, watching Boulogne fade into the sunshine and wishing that I were dead. That I'd died last night in Ian's arms.

'From the time we left Simone in Boulogne to the time we left the hotel in Le Touquet and returned to Boulogne, I've been in a kind of daze. Not in this world at all. It's all been so glamorous, so intense, so gloriously happy and so hopelessly *unhappy,* that it's indescribable.

'Yet everything is clear to me and I believe that I shall live all the moments, the hours again, again and again, as long as I live.

'We left Simone in Boulogne. She had a girl friend there with whom she was to spend the night, and who was also 'in the know.' When I kissed Simone, her plump, charming face was a little solemn. She said:

' "Are you sure you'll be 'okay,' *cherie?*" '

'(I loved the way Simone used to say 'okay' with her delicious accent.)

'I hugged her and said:

'Indeed I shall and it's sweet of you to do this for me. It's all understood, isn't it? If your parents or André phone, you'll say I'm in the bath or something and take a message, then phone the Royal Picardy where we're staying.'

'She nodded.

' "*Tout comprendre* . . . etc. Maman and Papa won't telephone. They think we are together with Marie-Louise here. They'll never dream. It was understood we girls were having a party. And André is with my uncle on the Loire, attending to his vines." '

'I said:

' "Oh, Simone, I love him so, my Ian. Do you think me terribly wicked?"

'She shook her head.

' "No. It is mad, if you like, but what is life if we cannot be a little mad? It would be different if the handsome Scot could marry you. *Mon Dieu!* what a country is yours, *chérie*, if an officer may not marry until he is thirty. It would not do to be so in France." '

'I said:

' "It isn't altogether true to say he *must* not marry, Simone, but that he is not encouraged to do so, and gets no allowances, and in Ian's case, his regiment particularly discourage it. Besides it would be a great blow to his people.'

' "And even an engagement is impossible?" '

' "Yes," ' I answered. And I spoke with conviction then, because Ian had convinced me. He could not even ask me to wait for him. It would mean a lapse of three or four years while he was on foreign service in India. It would be unfair to me, he said, and to himself.

Too great a tax on us both, because we were young, pleasure-loving, passionate people, and he considered it a frightful mistake for such people to be tied down, when thousands and thousands of miles apart. His wish was for us to remain friends and see, later, what life had in store for us. And as for that night . . . well, we both chose to snatch it "from annihilation's waste."'

'Simone's last remarks encouraged me.

' "You remember the talks we used to have in Lausanne, *trés chère*. We used to discuss the unhappily married people we came across. My own parents, for instance. My poor Maman was madly in love with a young *chasseur* who was penniless, and, at her father's command, made a *mariage de convenance* with Papa who is a darling, but do they get on? Ppf! No! They fight all day. And look at our mutual friend, Therese, who married as an innocent girl, and was shocked on her honeymoon—so shocked she never recovered from it. Did we not always say, Gail, *chèrie*, that experience was worth gaining. I do not believe you will regret what you are doing tonight.'

'I answered in full agreement. And I wanted Ian of all men in the world to give me that experience, however mad and foolish it was.

'I ought to have thought of Mummy and Daddy and the others at home. I ought to have remembered all the creeds Mummy had taught me to believe, but I was not quite sane that

34

day, and I confess it. Ian and I were both swept away by something stronger than ourselves.

'We drove together from Boulogne to Le Touquet. The long drive in brilliant sunshine was heavenly. We hardly dared look at each other, but sat with our hands locked, looking at the fresh green of the budding trees, the spring flowers and the fruit blossom which was making France so fair a sight.

'Sometimes I had to pinch myself and ask myself if I was really and truly awake, Gail Partner, going off on a stolen honeymoon with a young man named Ian Dalmuir. It was so unlike me. Unlike anything I had anticipated doing in my wildest dreams.

'Ian knew Le Touquet. He had stayed there in a party, last Whitsun, and enjoyed it. He rode, played tennis during the day and gambled just a little at the Casino at night.

' "It was all very smart and amusing," ' he said, 'But not really my cup of tea.'

'I asked, mischievously, what was his cup of tea, just to receive that long, ardent look and the expected reply:

' "You, my sweet, and you alone. Just you and no gambling, no rushing round in sophisticated circles, talking nonsense to metallic blondes."

' "Don't you like blondes?" '

'He shook his head. Brunettes with reddish lights in their hair were his mania, he solemnly assured me. And they must have grey eyes and

35

lashes that curled upwards and cheeks like warm pink roses.

'I asked him to tell me truthfully if there had ever been another love in his life. He told me that there was one girl, when he was at Woolwich. He was twenty-three and she was older. She was not a raving beauty or anything like that, but lovely in a serene, dignified sort of way, and clever. She earned her own living. Ran a dress shop in London and worked hard to keep an invalid mother. She had had a tragic affair in her early twenties from which she had never really recovered. She met Ian at a dance and they were mutually attracted. Even had he asked her, she would not have dreamed of marrying a boy so much younger than herself, and in his position, but she made him very happy for a year—the year before he was drafted to Palestine. Then they drifted out of each other's life.

'I felt absurdly jealous of this first love who had given Ian such happiness, but he laughed at me and pressed my hand harder.

' "Darling, you needn't be. I never really loved Margaret. I admired her, and she stirred me in a kind of way. But you must thank her for one thing. She taught me something about women and it's good to have experience."

'I told him that that was just what Simone and I believed. He sighed and said:

' "Yes, but for a man perhaps rather more than for a woman, little darling. A fellow can

36

take care of himself so much better and there are so many things against it for a young girl. In my heart I don't approve of what I am allowing you to do, Gail, my sweetheart, but I'm weak about it. I want you more than I've ever wanted anything or anybody on earth, and I know it isn't just a selfish infatuation. It's the real thing. Too good, too marvellous, to miss."

'How my heart beat at those words. I couldn't speak, but just sat beside him in the car, squeezing his fingers convulsively, the landscape blotted out by a mist of emotional tears. I knew, too, that what I felt for him was terribly real and much too marvellous to be missed. I *couldn't* send him to India, perhaps lose him for ever without belonging to him utterly and absolutely. And nobody but my girl friends, Simone and Marie-Louise, would ever know. Nobody would be hurt. I argued with myself that one's life was one's own and that so long as one didn't hurt a third person by any rash action, that action was justified.

'Now, when I write this all down and I feel my heart breaking slowly in pieces, I wonder whether the hurt one does oneself in such a case *is* justified. I could never again be the Gail who had left home to go to Lausanne. Never that same happy, ignorant person who had giggled like a schoolgirl, danced, rushed around, thought a drive in a fast car or a party, and a harmless flirtation with a nice boy, the biggest thrill life could offer. God, how I've

37

changed!

'I know now that being with the man you love and who loves you, is the greatest thrill of all, and much, much more. Heaven on earth. And the end—the good-byes, sheer hell.

'I had never seen a lovelier hotel than the Royal Picardy, which was like a fairy castle with its many turrets and towers. Its glorious garden, flanked by dark pinewoods. And its terraces, brilliant with spring flowers of every hue.

'Ian pointed out the Casino, white and shining in the sunshine.

' "That's where the idle rich gather and fling their francs away, sweet. But not for us. We'll not waste time in crowds. We only want to be alone." '

'He spoke for me, as well as for himself. That was all that I desired. To be alone in this gorgeous place where the warm sun shone down from the bluest sky, and the wind came laden with the fresh tang of the sea and the pinewoods.

'I did not even feel guilty, then, when we stood together at the Reception Bureau. Ian, without flinching, asked for a suite, double-bedroom, bath, and sitting-room. It was a huge price, and made little Gail, who had been brought up economically, sit up a bit. Especially as I knew Ian was not well off. But the best was not good enough for me that day, in his estimation."

'He signed the book:

'*Mr. and Mrs. Dalmuir.*

'That made me feel a little sorry for myself. If only it had been true! If only I had, indeed, been married to him, my tall, gorgeous Ian with his black, black head, his splendid figure, that face at which most women looked twice. I hastily gave up my passport and felt glad it was France. They didn't think so much about such things over there, but it would have been most embarrassing in a strait-laced English hotel to call ourselves "Mr. and Mrs. Somebody" and then for the manager to see on my passport: *Miss Gail Partner.*

'Once upstairs in our suite, I refused to think about anything any more except Ian and the exciting, oh, so exciting thought that we were supposed to be married and that this was the first night of my honeymoon.

'I was glad I was young and pretty and had what Simone and the other girls in Lausanne called *'une taille ravissante.'* Glad Simone had made me go to Antoine's yesterday, and with great extravagance, have my hair done in lovely little sculptured curls, like a coronet round my head; my nails varnished the palest rose-pink; and even my toenails done like Simone's so that the red showed alluringly through my thin chiffon stockings and the open toes of my white sandals. New suit, in heavy blue linen with a short-sleeved silk shirt with a touch of white and a wide white leather belt. Ian said I looked about sixteen, and it gave him a guilt-complex; especially that absurd sailor hat on the back of my head. So I made a face at him and said I would change at once into sophisticated black and become a chic woman. Whereupon I was seized in his arms, the halo hat fell on the floor, and he kissed me with those slow, subtle kisses which drove me so crazy. And between the kisses, he said:

' "No, I don't want sophisticated women. I want just you, my little Gail. With your little-girl personality, and all your sweetness, and simplicity and humour. You're such fun, Gail. A man likes a woman to be 'fun' as well as seductive, and, my God, you're both. You can't blame me for losing my head." '

'Yes, I can remember every word he said. And what I told him. With hands locked round his throat, I let him kiss and kiss me, and told him what I felt about *him*. How different he was from any other man in the world, and what fun *he* was, and how divinely serious at times, too.

'I told him that I loved the soldier side of him and all his stories about life in the Army. He had adored Palestine. He had only been sent over there for a short time when the "flap" was on, but he had seen quite a lot of fighting against the Arabs. Palestine, in his idea, was a very beautiful country and he wanted to take me there one day.

40

' "But, most of all, I want you to see my beloved Scotland," he would always end all his stories.

'And, most of all, too, I longed to see his native land. Scotland and Ian, somehow, seemed integral parts of each other.

'A page came into the room with huge baskets of flowers. Ian must have ordered them by wire from Paris. Every spring bloom that could be picked, every hot-house flower from the extravagant shops in Le Touquet, was there to greet me. Masses of sweet-smelling jonquils, golden daffodils, great clusters of purple violets. Red roses beside the bed. Scent on my dressing-table. He discovered a new luscious perfume in Paris and he had brought a great bottle for me. Ian was always generous with his gifts. The most fascinating essence for my bath (oh, that marvellous green bathroom with the big hot fleecy towels, and the sort of luxuries that Gail Partner wasn't used to at home or at school! Ian was indeed teaching me how to live!).'

## FOUR

'We spent the afternoon by the sea. It was too cold to bathe, but we walked along the shore arm-in-arm, trying not to talk about tomorrow. Living only for today. Sometimes the pain

41

would break through the ecstasy and he would press my hand tightly and say: "Oh, my little one. If only this would never end. If only I could take you to India with me . . ."

'It was our mutual wish that we should not dine in public or dance despite the fact that there was a band and a Gala Night at the Casino. We avoided people. We wanted only our two selves. Ian had dinner sent up to our private suite. Just a few delicacies specially chosen by him. Our favourite wine. I put on my loveliest evening dress for him, alone. It was tucked chiffon of deep blue with a wide silver belt. He said that I looked pure Greek in it, with my curls piled high on my head. And he said that I had the most beautiful throat and shoulders that he had ever seen, and perfect arms. Young, defenceless arms, he called them. The extreme smallness of my wrists seemed to disturb him.

' "You look as though you could break at a touch, sweet. Sometimes I'm afraid of hurting you!"

'I remember putting my arms around his neck and my cheek against his. Ian had a tanned face, very smooth and warm to touch. And I whispered:

'I shan't break. I'm very strong really. It's my heart that's going to break, tomorrow, if anything.'

'Then he looked white and tense and drew away from me and looked as though I had

42

hurt him mortally. And when I asked him what was the matter he said he ought never to have taken me away because it wasn't fair, and he felt like packing up and taking me straight to Paris, to Simone.

' "It's so damnable," he said, and I'd never heard him speak in such a bitter voice, "when I love you more than I ever thought it possible to love a girl, and the Army and my people stand between us."

'I felt just as depressed and miserable as he did. But I didn't want the old arguments and difficulties to spoil our evening. So I laughed him out of his mood, and he became the old, gay Ian who could charm me with a look or a word. And I made him sit with me on a big sofa in front of the fire which had been lit, and tell me more stories about his soldiering, and his early life as a boy.

' "But one day I shall show you Edinburgh,' he said. 'One day I swear we shall be together there, my darling." '

'Heavenly intimate evening full of the enchantment of discovering so many new and exciting things about each other. Unforgettable night which made history for me, and, I think, for him.

'He was so gentle, so sweet, and yet the torch of our passion flamed between us until the sheer white-hot flame of it scorched away every other remembrance. He loved me then, I know, just as completely as I loved him. It was

43

real love, not just the infatuation of a moment. Real love given and taken. A miracle unfolded between us.

'I can still hear the soft sound of the wind through the pine trees outside our open window, the distant lilt of a waltz which was being played below; the occasional sound of a voice or a laugh drifting up from the gardens.

'And the moon coming into our room. Ian's proud, tender, darling face bending over mine. Ian's voice whispering:

' "You're as exquisite as a statue in the moonlight. Little heart of mine! Little moon-maiden. I shall adore you for ever!"

'But the passion, the excitement, the rapture of it all was bought at a heavy price. And when I started to think during that night, my heart sank and I was ice cold with the dread of leaving him and of being torn out of the enchanted circle in which we had placed ourselves.

'Once, during the night, he felt tears on my lashes, and kissed them away, and begged me not to be unhappy, but to remember only the beauty and the sweetness which we had found in each other.

' "I'd rather die than hurt you, Gail," he said, again and again, "and I'd have given my life for things to be otherwise between us than they are."

'Then it was my turn to dry my tears, and to comfort him. And until dawn we lay sleepless, whispering, kissing, not daring to dwell on the thought that time was slipping away and that the good-byes must soon be said . . ."

Gail, the wife of Bill Cardew, writhed at the memory of every word written in that diary, as she lay here in this room with her husband sleeping soundly at her side. Bill, who was so pleased with himself and his conquest of her, so unknowing of what lay in her heart. She could see the vast difference between the two men, the *incredible* difference, and she was wrung with suffering.

She had to clench her hands hard to keep herself from calling out:

'*Ian! Ian!*'

He had been torn by conscience as they drove to Boulogne to catch the boat. And when she had stood for the last time in his arms and his burning kisses drank in the cold bitter flow of her tears, he told her so.

But she never once reproached him. She said:

'It was worth it. You've taught me to love, and to love like that is to live . . .'

'It isn't good-bye,' were his final words, 'I'll see you in London. And I'll love you always, Gail. I'll *never* forget.'

But he *had* forgotten. At least, so far as Gail knew. For when she returned to England, that silent, changed Gail who had been such an anxiety to her mother, there had come no word from him. Only a letter from his mother.

45

Even now, three years later, Gail hated the memory of that letter with the Edinburgh postmark and the agony of anticipation with which she had opened it. It had been so awful without Ian . . . She felt so lost and alone, torn by conscience, torn by love, all the emotions rolled into one. But the letter was a cold grim little note spelling the death to any hopes Gail might have entertained of continued association with her lover.

And it told Gail that Mrs. Dalmuir knew all about the affair, that almost immediately after Gail had said good-bye to Ian, he had received urgent orders for India. The officer whose place he was taking in Bangalore had been killed in an accident at polo. There was no time for Ian to return to England and get his kit. It was being sent on to him and he was to join the trooper at Marseilles. He had telephoned from Paris to Edinburgh. What he said about Gail, the girl, herself, knew only from the letter which Mrs. Dalmuir wrote to her.

*'Ian has asked me to say good-bye to you and hopes you will not write to him. He realises that he has not the means to support a wife. His Colonel would not hear of it. Besides, at this juncture in his career, you must realise how fatal it would be for him.. It will only hurt him to hear from you, so please, for his sake, do not try to communicate with him.'*

Just that, and then a long, long silence.

From that day onwards Gail had neither seen nor heard of Ian again. And she had done as Mrs. Dalmuir had asked her. She had not written for *his* sake, and she could not blame him any more than she blamed herself for the anguish that she endured in secret for long months afterwards. Ian had warned her. And she had known within herself that those stolen hours with him must be paid for in full.

Nothing really mattered so long as *he* was all right. So long as that career which mattered so much to *him* was not spoiled.

Gail was young, and with the resilience of youth she was able to put grief aside and take up life again with apparent nonchalance. And she presumed that Ian would be leading the full busy life of an officer in India, with little time for brooding over a brief tempestuous love affair. Maybe he did not even remember the poignant sweetness of it all; the complete and utter love which they had shared in Paris that burning spring.

\*       \*       \*

When her honeymoon ended, Gail Cardew was a little relieved to find herself back again in her old room at home with the family. The dear family who were little changed by the vagaries of the war.

47

She missed Bill, of course. She had schooled herself to control her feelings, and to be lulled into some kind of passionate surrender to Bill. To enjoy her marriage when Bill was at his most charming. She had learned that marriage meant that one could never be really alone. But back at Kingston she was the old Gail again who belonged to herself. And it was rather good to have Mum to chat to while she knitted furiously for the Red Cross, and hear Dad's reminiscences of 1914, and listen to the light banter and chaff which went on all day between Chris and Scampie.

Scampie was full of curiosity about her big sister's marriage. She examined the narrow platinum band on Gail's finger and said in an awestruck voice:

'Is it *marvellous* being married, Gaily?'

'Of course,' Gail answered with a laugh.

'Do you feel like they do in books? That you'll never love anybody else till you *die?*'

'Of course,' repeated Gail.

But she did not encourage further questioning from Scampie. She did not want her innermost feelings dragged into the open and examined too ruthlessly. She was not too sure that they bore the strong merciless light of a child's criticism.

She was only a few days without Bill, then he was able to come back. She moved temporarily from her own home down the hill to *his* home. Mrs. Cardew was glad to have

48

her. Bill, in his old home, allowed himself to be waited on hand and foot. And Mrs. Cardew waited on him, and was barely thanked for it.

Gail could not quite accustom herself to that servile atmosphere which was in the Cardew home. Even the old servant who had been with Mrs. Cardew since her widowhood, was subordinate to 'Mr. Bill's' merest wish. He would ring for her frequently, ruthlessly, without thought for her old legs dragging up from the basement. He left his room in indescribable confusion, threw his things on the floor and expected them to be picked up, flung cigarette ends and ash into the fire-place and calmly watched both mother and maid stoop to clear them away.

To Gail it was a little frightening, this complete worship of Bill, and she instinctively and immediately revolted against it. She loved him, but she was not going to crawl to him. She compared it all unfavourably with the methods in her own home where her father and mother waited upon each other. Where service was mutual and neither was the slave to the other. That was what marriage should be. And as for Mum waiting on Chris, she wouldn't be allowed to do it. If Chris was thoughtless, his father—or Gail—soon pulled him up.

On the very first night in the Cardew home, Gail brought before Bill's notice the fact that his mother, who had retired early with an attack of neuritis to which she was a martyr, had asked Bill to go and say good night to her. Twice or three times Gail had reminded him, but he had stayed downstairs reading text-books (he was an ardent and able worker and a good officer), or talking to Gail. Now, of course, it was too late.

'Your mother will be disappointed,' Gail said.

'Oh, she won't care,' said Bill.

Gail was sitting up in bed, hands locked over her hunched knees. Bill, who had taken off collar and tie and thrown them on the floor, sat down on the bed, and buried his face against his wife's neck.

'Lord! You're a lovely thing,' he murmured huskily 'Don't talk about mother. Tell me you love me.'

But something in Gail tonight made her hang back. Gently she pushed him away and looked at him with grey, serious eyes.

'*Aren't* you an egotist! There you have a mother who worships you and you can't even bother to kiss her good night.'

He gave a careless laugh and ran his fingers through the red-brown curls.

'Oh, rot! Mother won't mind.'

'You just take love as your due, don't you?'

'Why not? Isn't it my due?'

'In a way. But it shouldn't be all one-sided.'

'It isn't with us. I give you all my love, don't I?'

'But I'm not sure you wouldn't let me pick

up that collar and tie,' she persisted, nodding toward the things which he had thrown on the carpet.

He laughed again.

'Oh, men are not supposed to tidy up, are they? That's a woman's job.'

Gail began to feel her fighting spirit arise.

'I don't agree that women are just put in the world to clear up after untidy men. But I suppose if you allow your mother to be a slave to you, you'll want me to be one, too.'

The smile left Bill's face. He was conscious suddenly that Gail was not being responsive to his caresses, and that she was criticising him. He hated being criticised. He said:

'Oh, don't let's pursue this stupid conversation.'

'But, Bill . . .' Her breath came unevenly . . . 'It isn't the right attitude, honestly, and if you choose to throw things on the floor, *I'm* not going to pick them up like your mother does. That's all.'

For a moment he stared at her. And for a moment Gail honestly thought that he would like to drag her out of bed and force her there and then to pick up that collar and tie in front of him. He looked furious. She knew all about Bill's temper. Even his mother admitted that he had one. But she wasn't afraid. Merely contemptuous. If he couldn't discuss these little things without losing his, temper . . . couldn't stand adverse criticism . . . what was

51

he worth?

Then it struck her that it was all absurd. To be thinking and feeling like this, within a week of her marriage.

'Oh, Bill, darling!' she said.

Those words were to him a sign of her surrender, even a plea for pardon. He caught her fiercely close and covered her face with kisses.

'Don't you dare tell me what I ought or ought not to do,' he murmured between the caresses. 'You belong to me, Gail, and nothing matters—except *this* . . .'

He reached over her head for the electric switch and plunged the room into darkness. She felt the violence of his passion like a relentless tide swamping her; her thoughts, convictions, everything. He was like that, she thought. A queer, cyclonic person. And she knew that she belonged to him. She was his wife. She was fond of him. He was an old friend, too. But one thing she also knew. That no matter what happened between them, she was not going to become his slave. To her own love a woman could be a slave, but not at a man's orders, only at her own.

The next day Bill went back to his unit. The little scene between them was forgotten. But there was a renewal of it under different circumstances about three days later. This time in the Partners' home.

Bill had been dining with the family.

Scampie was in bed, and Gail's father and mother had also retired. But Chris had stayed down to tinker with his beloved wireless. As usual, little conversation was exchanged between Bill and his young brother-in-law. Then Bill, on reaching for a cigarette, said:

'Damn! I've left my cigarettes in the pocket of my mac. Chris, would you like to run out and get them for me?'

Chris, who was sitting on the floor in front of the radio, looked over his shoulder with a scowl.

'Just a minute. I'm trying to get America.'

'America can wait,' said Bill indulgently.

'Well, so can you, if it comes to that.'

Gail bit her lip. The one thing she did not wish was for her young brother to be rude to Bill. They were so often on the verge of a quarrel.

'I'll get the cigarettes,' she said.

Bill stretched his legs in front of him.

'That's sweet of you, darling.'

Then Chris Partner gained his feet.

'Well, I'm hanged! Why the hell should Gail go to fetch your rotten cigarettes? You've got two feet. Why not use them and fetch them yourself?'

Bill froze up.

'I'll trouble you not to speak to me like that,' he said.

'Well, fetch your own cigarettes,' said the boy hotly. 'And don't chuck your orders at

53

me—or Gail—even if she is married to you. She's not used to be being ordered about in this house, anyhow.'

'Oh, Chris!' began Gail, her cheeks hot.

'Well, I think you'll be a fool to wait on him. He is a lazy swine, and I get sick of all this fawning you've got to do just because he's a young hero in uniform and all that rot.'

Bill Cardew sprang to his feet. Into those very blue eyes of his came the furious gleam that Gail recognised and dreaded. She said:

'Now, look here, this is a lot of nonsense, all over a packet of cigarettes.'

'You leave this to me, Gail,' said Bill, 'your young brother is too fond of being cheeky to me, and I'm not going to stand for it. If he continues, I'll give him the thrashing he deserves.'

The boy went white to the lips. For a moment he stood with hands clenched, staring at the older man, then he swung round and faced his sister.

'If it wasn't for you, Gail, I'd jolly well smack his face and find out who was going to be the one to do the thrashing,' he said. 'How you could have married such a rotten cad, I don't know. There are others who think the same, and . . .'

'Oh, Chris, be quiet, don't dare say such things!' interrupted Gail, shocked to the core. She found herself trembling from head to foot.

The next moment Chris had walked out of

54

the room and slammed the door. Bill said:

'And the next time he behaves like that I *will* thrash him. You're all too lenient with him. He's a spoiled young pup, and you've got to uphold me, Gail.'

Still trembling, she said:

'I'm quite willing to uphold you in what's right, Bill, and if he's cheeky to you. But you do rather throw your orders about and there was no real reason why you shouldn't have fetched your own cigarettes.'

'So you *are* upholding him.'

'Not in what he said. He lost his temper. But nothing that he did was so bad that you should threaten to thrash him.'

'I see!' Bill said with an icy drawl. 'Perhaps you'd have preferred it if I had got up and fetched something for your sixteen-year-old brother.'

'That's absurd. It's not in the argument. I just think Chris was not altogether to blame. You're always trying to put him in his place, at least the place you think he ought to be in. You have places you think we *all* ought to be in. You're wrong, Bill. You're not a dictator and surely you don't want to behave like one.'

He stood motionless, staring at her. His expression was one of horrified amazement. Then he said:

'So *you* are trying to put me in my place. You would rather criticise me than tell that young puppy of a brother of yours where he gets off.'

'Chris isn't a young pup. He's popular with everybody except you, Bill. You rub him up the wrong way.'

'And you, darling,' said Bill through his teeth, 'had better remember that you're my wife.'

She swallowed hard. It seemed to her absurd and awful that they should be reaching this pitch within a week of marriage. She must not, whatever happened, she told herself, regret that marriage. Bill was in the wrong about this. That side to his character which made him wish to be master wherever he went, was not an attractive one. But she must make the best of it or it would be fatal. If she started to be too censorious she would, never, never be happy. She *must* make the best of it.

Then Bill said:

'You'd better stay here tonight and stroke your little brother's hair and tell him what a dear boy he is. I'll go home alone.'

Her heart jerked.

'Bill, darling, don't be silly . . .'

He walked straight past her into the hall. A moment later she heard the front door close. She realised that Bill had really gone. He was angry and resentful, and he was not going to acknowledge that he was in any way to blame for tonight's incident.

Gail stared in front of her. Her eyes held

a frightened look. She realised that she *was* frightened, for how was she going to conduct a happily married life with Bill if he would persist in wanting everything his way and on his side. If 'take-all-and-give-nothing' was to be his motto, it meant a bad look-out for her. No marriage could survive it, unless a woman was weak, as weak as Bill's mother, for instance, allowing herself to be kept right under a man's thumb.

'I never will,' Gail said to herself. *'Never . . .'*

But she could not stay here tonight. Pride forbade that she should allow the family to think for a moment that anything was wrong between Bill and herself.

She felt already humiliated when she put on her coat, tied a scarf over her hair, and walked down the hill alone, following her husband.

Once she was with Bill, she found that he had got over his fit of temper. He was even ready to laugh about Chris and patronise him. He was just a young idiot, and would learn in time, he said, and she, Gail, was an idiot. They were all idiots—except Bill.

Eagerly he pulled her into his arms, anxious for her caresses. But the lips that he kissed that night were cold. And within Gail there was a coldness which, try as she would, she could not banish. A fear of the future that she could not eradicate.

That night she had one of her rare dreams

about Ian. They were in Paris, walking arm-in-arm through the Bois. The chestnuts were in blossom. And there were little tables under the trees. Coffee and drinks and the lilt of a band. And Ian said:

'*April in Paris!* Do you remember that old dance tune? It says something about *"what have you clone to my heart?"* '

And she answered:

'What have you done to *mine,* darling, darling. I didn't know life could be so sweet, yet at the same time hurt so much . . .'

He looked down at her with those dark Celtic eyes of his and whispered:

'Remember only the sweetness, Gail. Try not to remember the pain. .. .'

She burst into tears and he tried to comfort her, but his face, his voice, grew fainter and fainter. He vanished and she found herself alone standing there, in the middle of the Bois, looking blindly for him.

She woke herself up by crying, and sat up in bed with the tears pelting down her cheeks. Bill woke, too, and was aghast to find her crying. At once he drew her into his arms. She had had a nightmare, he said, 'poor little thing!' He kissed her. His kisses were, in his own opinion, the panacea for any woman's sorrow.

She turned to him, but found no comfort in his embrace. And she knew now that she ought never to have married Bill. For she might have known that the ghost of Ian was not to be laid aside. And that while she lived, it would haunt her, even without reproach for her disloyalty. Because he had told her to forget him. He had not demanded loyalty. And she had married Bill, believing that other love almost forgotten.

Now life seemed to have gone awry. She was doing just what Ian had told her not to do. Remembering not the pleasure but the pain. Unending pain.

She only hoped that she would never have to see Scotland, never have to stand alone and look at Edinburgh Castle. Up there, in the Lowlands, was *his* home, the home which he had so often described to her. And to Gail, all the romance of Scotland was bound up in Ian! He had, in those careless, early days of their friendship promised to show her Scotland himself.

Little was she to dream then that in the September of 1939, she would be married to Bill Cardew. And that she was to see Scotland, not with Ian, but with Bill.

For one afternoon, three weeks after his marriage, Bill came rushing back from Woolwich to Kingston to tell his wife he had immediate orders to go up North. There he was to train for a special anti-aircraft job which he had got because of his knowledge of electrical engineering.

Gail's heart knocked when she asked him:

'Up North! But *where*, where are we going?'

59

He said:

'Edinburgh. Are you pleased?'

And he was astonished because she did not answer: did not wait to hear all the plans that he wished to discuss. She just turned very white and walked away quietly upstairs to her own room.

## FIVE

Out of the square-paned window of a house in a little Georgian square, tucked away at the back of Princes Street, Edinburgh, Gail Cardew stood watching for her husband to come back.

Every evening like this for the last fortnight, she had waited for him. And every evening her conviction had grown stronger and stronger that far from looking forward to Bill's return, she dreaded it.

It had taken less than a month of marriage to show her the crazy mistake she had made in marrying him.

At moments he was still the charming Bill whom she knew so well and with whom she had so long been friends. But the charm was so often hidden behind the ugly side of his nature that it was difficult to find. She had learned, too, that to be Bill's wife was a very different thing from being Bill's next-door neighbour.

60

And to be pursued and wooed by Bill was not at all the same as being 'owned' by him. His possessiveness was suffocating. His arrogance seemed to have grown worse since they had come up here.

He was on a special course of instruction attached to an Anti-Aircraft Brigade. He was by profession an electrical engineer and he was quick to let Gail know how well he was doing and how much farther advanced he was than most of the other fellows. He boasted without ceasing. And she could see that he was good at his job. He was going to make a first-rate soldier. He enjoyed being an officer; liked flinging his orders about. But sometimes she wondered how much the men who were under him, cared about it.

She compared him hopelessly, perhaps foolishly, with Ian. She could imagine how Ian's men would adore him. He had always had a touch of sympathy, of great kindliness for those beneath him. But Bill was the superior officer, and, oh God, thought Gail, *how superior.* Just as he was with her. Delightful when she flattered him, gave in to his whims. Sulky and unbearable when he was thwarted.

And this was Edinburgh! She looked out this evening, as she so often looked, at the beauty of its buildings. The nameless charm that belonged to Scotland's capital, with its broad shopping street flanked by the rugged

61

magnificence of the Castle. Its grey spires and towers, its noble historic buildings, the cobbled roads and the steep winding hills.

She had grown to love Edinburgh and to realise why Ian had loved it. From the moment that she had arrived she had felt that the whole place was impregnated with Ian's personality. Little things kept coming back to her mind . . . details that he had described . . . places that he had told her she must see. She was so familiar with it all, it had been almost like coming home. Only *he* was not with her. Only Bill, who grumbled and called the city a 'dreary hole.' Bill missed London life and disliked the austere Northerners whom he could not too easily impress.

Most of the officers' wives were living in digs or hotels. Gail had met some of them. They exchanged visits. In the evenings they dined together and played bridge or discussed the international situation. And Bill was always in the limelight—he put himself there—broadcasting the fact that he knew a *little* bit more than anyone else.

Gail was not happy. This marriage had come back on her like a catapult which she had madly flung at herself. Coming up here, to Ian's native city where he had lived so much of his boyhood, had let loose in her all the old tearing love which she had tried to destroy, but which she knew now was deathless.

She had found out where the Dalmuirs

62

lived. Some miles out of Edinburgh. A big, grey, windswept house on a hill overlooking the city and the wild lonely countryside. But she only saw it from a distance.

She tried desperately to be faithful in thought, as well as in deed to the man she had married. She told herself that he might be soon sent to the Western Front. She must give him all the love and tenderness which she could muster up. She was patient with him, no matter how sorely he tried that patience. And perhaps the thing that was most difficult to bear these days was his insistent passion for her. For all feeling for him of that kind seemed to have died in Gail overnight . . . And she was submissive now to his kisses, but no longer wanting them.

This evening the sunset was particularly beautiful.

She had not yet grown accustomed to the poignant loveliness of these autumn evenings in Scotland. The northern sky was so clear and translucent, it was like a mirror reflecting the golden glow from the west. When she lifted the window a little, the air blew clear and crisp, straight across from the grey turbulent waters of the North Sea.

Down the street a company of men came marching by. A Scots regiment. Kilts, white spats, and glengarrys. Fine brave men in training. It gave Gail a tremendous feeling of patriotism and pride to watch those swinging kilts and to hear the measured tread of their feet. The officer at the head of their company was a very tall man, and as he passed the window, there was something in the turn of his head, the darkness of his eye, that reminded her of Ian. She had seen many Scotsmen up here who were his type, and it never failed to pull at her heartstrings.

She turned from the window, switched on a lamp and began to darn one of Bill's khaki socks. She liked to render him small services of this kind because he *was* a soldier, and she was his wife. But she wished to God that she had not married him and that she was back there in the old home at Kingston where she knew they missed her. Every letter she had from Mum told her that. And Chris said so, too. Chris who wrote regularly from Shrewsbury, but who never once mentioned his brother-in-law. She knew that Chris would never forgive Bill for threatening to thrash him that night.

It was very quiet in here. She rather liked the big, quaint, old-fashioned room, so Victorian in atmosphere. Bill called it 'lousy.' He preferred something very modern. They had this sitting-room and a bedroom, and Miss Dow, their old Scots landlady, 'did for them' and fed them well. Gail had never before eaten so many lovely scones and cakes. She would put on weight up here if she was not careful.

She felt a sudden draught, and rose to close the door.

64

As she did so, she heard the unmistakably Cockney accent of Hopkins who was Bill's batman, and who usually came in at this time of day to clean Bill's boots and belt before dinner.

His voice, raised louder than he intended, was lodging a complaint to Miss Dow:

'And I tell you straight, I'm not keen on being 'is bloomin' servant. I've bin batman more than once in my time, but always to the kind of gentleman like my Captain Martin dahn at Aldershot. Always 'ad a decent word for me, and says I was to take me proper time off. But Mr. Cardew, 'e wouldn't care whether you was breakin' your back to serve 'im. Chucks 'is boots at me this mornin' and talks to me as though he was the Commander-in-Chief 'isself. Right dahn snooty. But Mrs. Cardew, she knows 'ow to give 'er orders—a perfect little lidy she is. . . .'

Hurriedly Gail shut the door, her cheeks burning. When she returned to her darning, the hand holding the needle was not quite steady. She was miserable and ashamed. Ashamed of Bill. For she knew that Hopkins, who was a decent little fellow, was right. Bill was a bully. He would never, never be popular, no matter how far he rose to glory as an officer.

A few moments later and Bill had come home. She put down her darning and looked up at him whilst he unbuckled his belt, and threw it down on the sofa, and flung his gas-mask and stick on to the floor. He looked in a good temper tonight, she was thankful to see. And he was extremely attractive with that ruddy glow of health on his cheeks and the light shining on his golden hair. He *could* be so nice, she thought, regretfully, and there was time even now for him to regain her love, her admiration, if he would only try . . .

He said:

'Done a good day's work, and the Brigade Major is damn pleased with me. Told me today I'd come out on top with this exam. He's going, and we've got a new fellow, a Staff Captain, dealing with us now. Only arrived today. Can't say I care for him, but one's got to keep in with those in command. I believe he's related to the Brigadier.'

Gail gave a small rather derisive smile

'I see, Bill, then you must salute him nicely.'

'Salute be hanged, but I'll stand him a drink or two. Matter of fact, I asked him to come in and meet you this evening, and have a drink.'

Gail rose.

'Then I'd better go and tidy myself.'

She spoke without enthusiasm. She had no particular interest in Bill's brother-officers. He came up and pulled her roughly into his arms.

'What about a kiss?'

She raised her lips obediently.

'Darling,' he said, 'make yourself particularly attractive to this fellow, please. He

66

knows everyone up here. He's a bachelor. But I hear he's full of money and got influence and is worth cultivating.'

There was nothing that Gail disliked more than Bill's servility to those who 'mattered.' It upset her even more than his arrogance with those who did not. But she had learned not to argue or protest. It was best to keep Bill in a good humour.

She changed her tweeds for a black dress with a touch of white at the throat, brushed her red-brown hair into sleek curls, and put on her pearl ear-rings, and the brooch which Bill had given her for their wedding. His Army badge, designed in brilliants.

She heard Bill's guest arrive, hastily found a black bag, and her cigarettes, and walked into the sitting-room.

Bill was pouring out drinks. A very tall man with a dark smooth head stood with his back to Gail, his hands behind him. He was saying:

'I agree with you. One gets very sick of not hearing more news. I only landed back from India a couple of days ago and they've shoved me straight up here.'

He paused and turned around. He stared at the girl in the doorway, and she stared back at him like one in a dream.

Bill looked up from the drinks and said:

'Oh, look here, this is my wife . . . Gail, this is Captain Dalmuir . . .'

Gail did not speak. Dumbfounded she

67

stood there just staring blindly into the dark remembered eyes of Ian.

## SIX

It was as well that Bill was busy mixing the cocktails and had his back turned to Gail. She was so transfixed with astonishment, with shock, that she could not move, could not find voice with which to speak.

She went on staring, wide-eyed, scarlet-cheeked at Ian Dalmuir. And he stared back, obviously as dumbfounded as herself.

Bill turned round with that kind of smile which showed that he was pleased with himself.

And then Gail forced herself to move. Very slowly, like one in a dream she came forward, her gaze never leaving Ian.

Her lips moved:

'Why, hullo,' she said rather stupidly, 'I think . . . we already know each other . . . don't we?'

He took his cue from her and answered as remotely:

'Yes, of course. Years ago. How are you?'

But they did not touch hands. Gail made no gesture of that sort. She could not bring herself to place her fingers in his. Neither did she find it easy to tear away her gaze. Those dark eyes of Ian's mesmerised her. And her whole body was tingling, quivering. Her face was now drained of colour.

It could not be possible that Bill's superior officer was Ian. *Captain* Dalmuir! He hadn't been a captain when she had known him in Paris. No, only a lieutenant. They had often talked about his promotion. Once a man was a captain and thirty . . . and, of course, Ian must be thirty now . . . he could be married and have allowances for his wife. They had sighed because that day seemed so remote.

Now it had come. Ian was Captain Dalmuir. Changed and yet not changed. The same, yet not the same. What had happened to him inwardly, she could not know, but she could see the physical differences. He was a little broader in the shoulders, thinner in the face. He had that lean, hard brown look that men get out in the East. India had left its mark on him.

Bill advanced with two glasses in his hand.

'Gin and French for you, Dalmuir. Gail, will you have one?'

She did not care for cocktails as a rule, but she took this one, thankful for the stimulant. She had never needed a drink more badly in her life. And she watched Ian take his and lift it to his lips. The very way in which he did that smote her with a curious pain. A blinding pain of remembrance. The way his little finger curved in. The familiar signet ring with his crest; once he had taken it off . . . that night in Le Touquet . . . and he had slipped it on to her marriage finger and laughed because it was so much too big and had slipped straight off. Then he had put it back and turned it round so that only the plain gold band showed, and he had kissed her hand and said:

*'If only it was your wedding ring . . .!'*

'Did I hear you two say that you had already met? But where? How?' Bill Cardew was inquiring.

Ian Dalmuir looked to Gail as though uncertain of what she wished him to say. It was plain to him that she was intensely nervous and put out by this unexpected meeting. It had been an equal shock to him to find that Cardew's wife was the Gail Partner whom he had loved so passionately, so hopelessly, in Paris three years ago.

She said:

'Oh . . . we met long ago . . .'

Bill persisted.

'But *where?* Not in Kingston!'

Gail did not look at Ian. She kept her eyes on her glass. Her hand was shaking. She spilled some of the cocktail and wiped it mechanically away with her chiffon handkerchief.

'No, no. In France.'

'France!' echoed Bill. 'But when were you out in France, darling?'

She felt that she would scream and give herself away if he went on questioning her. She

70

answered:

'I was at school in Lausanne and once stayed in Paris with a French friend of mine. I met Mr. Dalmuir there. Or rather, Captain Dalmuir.'

'Ah, I see,' said Bill, and turned back to the table to pour out a drink for himself. He was a little surprised to find that Gail had already met Dalmuir, but it did not seem very significant. All he knew was that Dalmuir was important to him and therefore must 'be cultivated.'

Once her husband's back was to her again, Gail dared to raise her eyes to Ian. She had never before seen him in uniform and it gave her an extra pang to remember that there was a war on, and that he was a soldier, a regular, likely at any moment to be sent into action. How well the khaki tunic suited him, with the polished leather belt, the blue and green breeches, and black field boots. His glengarry was lying on a chair with his stick. His extreme tallness had always fascinated her. The poise and grace of him. He had lost none of it. She looked at the three gold 'pips,' as they called them in the Army, on his shoulders. Three for a captain. Bill had only one as a second-lieutenant. She looked at his well-cut khaki shirt and tie. Ian had always been carefully dressed. She remembered what well-fitting collars he used to wear. She looked at the smooth blackness of his head. (Oh God, that

71

attractive head of Ian's. How many times she had gathered it to her breast, threaded her fingers through his hair, and been reprimanded, then kissed for ruffling it.) She dared not let her thoughts carry her too far. She only knew that it was as though the three years since she had seen him had never been. That she had never lulled the old anguish of longing, never tried to uproot her adoration, never said good-bye. Just as though she was back in Paris with Ian, the Gail who was half-woman, half-schoolgirl, frantically in love.

And she thought:

'This is impossible. I mustn't allow myself to think like this. He doesn't mean anything to me any more. He's a stranger. And I'm married to Bill.'

Bill returned with his drink and they seated themselves in front of the fire and launched into general discussion of the war situation, of Edinburgh, of all the things that were of mutual interest. And Gail talked, too, quite loudly and quickly. She found refuge in the impersonal conversation.

Neither of them referred to their former friendship. Best, Gail thought, for Bill to imagine that she had only known Ian Dalmuir slightly and that this reunion meant nothing at all. But all the time she was talking, Gail was inwardly telling herself that she was a little fool to be shaken by this meeting. That Ian had never loved her as she had loved him. He had

72

walked out of her life coldly and heartlessly. It was up to her to show some pride and let him think that she was unmoved. Whatever he was feeling, he did not portray it. He talked easily and naturally. And for the most part with Bill. But when he turned to Gail and asked her how she liked Edinburgh, she shrank as though he had hit her. How could he ask her *that?* When he used to tell her that he, and he alone, would show her his home. But she answered with an indifference to match his:

'Oh I like it very much. It's a fascinating city. I adore the castle.'

'Gail's rather keen on history and gets all worked up about Mary, Queen of Scots, and that sort of stuff,' put in Bill in his hearty manner, 'not that it appeals to me.'

Ian Dalmuir made no answer. But he could have told Bill Cardew all about Gail's interest in history. She used to listen to his stories of Edinburgh absorbed and enraptured. Yes, he knew her mind so well. How much had she changed? Under his surface manner of nonchalance, he was intensely interested in every word she said and her every little movement. That she had forgotten their love seemed apparent, since she had married and had never written to him. It hurt him badly to see her as a married woman . . . belonging to this fellow Cardew. He had taken an intense dislike to Cardew from the moment they met. But he was quick to acknowledge a good

73

worker and a good soldier when he met one. Cardew had brains and application. Ian had come round here tonight not so much because he wished for any social connection with the fellow, but because there were difficulties in the job which they were on at the moment; Cardew knew his stuff and Ian intended to make use of the fact.

And then this . . . this staggering discovery that Cardew's wife was *Gail*.

Still so lovely. Little lovely Gail! Yet scarcely the rather gauche young Gail of Paris days. She had been so enchantingly fresh and eager for life—and for love! (Conscience smote Ian Dalmuir as he remembered many things. A conscience that had been sleeping for three years, but was by no means dead, where Gail was concerned. Dear God! There had been scarcely a day when he had not thought of her, suffered over her. But he had deliberately stifled that pain, that deep regret, believing that it was his duty never to seek to renew the affair which had been so fatally sweet.)

She still looked very young, he thought, but the three years had added a touch of maturity. She had a new gravity. A deep almost tragic expression in those big grey eyes, which had never been there in Paris. There, they had sparkled and laughed. They had been the radiant eyes of a young girl in love . . .

Bill was discussing the Forth Bridge.

74

They all talked about it. Then Bill cunningly manceuvred the conversation round to Ian's home.

'Very decent for you to have a home here and be able to live in it. Whereabouts is it, Dalmuir?'

Gail clenched her hands. She knew exactly where it was, and why Bill had put the question. Fishing for an invitation. Bill was like that. Ian said:

'It's just outside Edinburgh. On a hill overlooking the city. We get rather a fine view. Yes, it's extremely nice being able to live at home.'

Gail breathed a sigh of relief. Thank goodness Ian didn't suggest that she and Bill should call on him. Never, never could she bear to go inside Ian's home with *Bill*.

Ian was addressing her now:

'My mother died a year ago,' he said, 'and my father soon afterwards. And I had an uncle who you will remember me telling you about. He died a while back and left me his place, which is between Edinburgh and Galashiels. I think I once described it to you. It's one of the rather historic old places here. It is called the Loch Castle; built right on the edge of one of the loveliest lochs in the Lowlands.'

Gail braced herself to meet Ian's eyes, and took some more of her drink. Her pulses were fluttering wildly.

'I remember,' she said in a low voice.

75

And her mind teemed with thoughts. She longed to sympathise with him about his mother. He had loved the old lady and the death of both parents must have been a great loss to him; especially sad if it happened when he was so far away. And so the old Laird had died too, and Ian must be a rich man today. Her lips twisted a little at the memory of those talks they had about the fortune Ian would inherit from Uncle Alistair; the innumerable tales about the Loch Castle. It had a haunted room, and when he was a little boy and stayed with the Laird, Ian used to try to find that room, but never could.

She asked herself with a touch of hysteria what on earth Bill would say if she came out with all her store of knowledge about Ian Dalmuir.

But there was much she did not know, she told herself bitterly. Nothing about these last three years in India, for instance. Maybe he had found another love out there. Oh, there was little that she knew about the Ian of today.

Bill said:

'I'm a newly married man, you know, Dalmuir. Gail and I only took the plunge the other day. But it's damned nice being married to the right girl. I can recommend it.'

He laughed and held out a hand for Ian's empty glass.

Gail's cheeks went hot. Nothing would induce her to look at Ian now. She wished Bill

76

would not be quite so crude and wondered desperately what Ian felt about her marriage. What his thoughts must be . . . after all that there had been between them.

Ian's reply was brief:

'I imagine that there can be nothing better than a successful marriage.'

'Well, just take a look at my Gail,' said Bill with his boastful manner, 'and you couldn't doubt that mine's O.K.!'

Gail writhed. She wished the earth would open and swallow her up at that moment. She searched her bag, found a cigarette-case, and feverishly lit a cigarette. She kept wondering what Ian must be thinking. Her own thoughts were indescribable.

Suddenly Bill said:

'Blast it! We've run out of gin. I suppose that old hag, our landlady, won't do anything about it, so I'd better nip out to the pub and buy a bottle.'

Ian said:

'I shan't want any more drinks, thank you, Cardew.'

'Oh, but of course you must have another,' said Bill, 'never heard such nonsense. Must apologise for running out, but I told Gail to get in a bottle and she must have forgotten.'

Gail looked at the point of her cigarette. What Bill said wasn't strictly true. But she didn't mind. She knew Bill's character by now. Any white lie would do so that *he* need not accept the blame for anything.

She had a guilty sensation of relief when Bill insisted upon going out to buy that gin. She would be alone with Ian for a moment. Her heart was knocking, knocking . . .

Only when the door had shut behind Bill did she look in Ian's direction. He had risen and was standing in a characteristic attitude with his back to the fire, one hand in his pocket, the other lifting his cigarette to his lips. His expression was one that might almost be called baffled . . . remote . . . eyes puckered, lips drawn in. Then suddenly he swung round and looked straight down into her eyes.

'Well . . .' he said. 'Well, Gail?'

She tried to remain quite calm. Whatever happened, she told herself, she must not give away the agony of feeling that was tearing through her whole body. This man had walked out on her in the most heartless fashion and she must remember it. She must appear, like him, to have no heart.

'Well, Ian?' she said.

'This is a terrific surprise.'

'It certainly is.'

'The last thing on earth I expected when Cardew asked me round here.'

'The last thing I expected, too,' she echoed. 'He told me about you but didn't mention names.'

'The whole thing's an amazing coincidence. I was sent back from India at a moment's notice. Flew back. They wanted me up here on a Divisional staff job. I'm what they call a "G" man . . .' He laughed briefly and pointed to the red armlet which he was wearing, and which bore the initial 'G.' 'I'm in control of this course on which Cardew is working. It's all rather secret and important, and Cardew has engineering brains which we need. That was why I . . .'

He paused and Gail filled in the gap.

'Why you took the trouble to come round and talk to him outside the job.'

'Yes, I suppose so.'

Gail put a small clenched hand against her breast, wishing that her heart would not thump so painfully. But it was so very painful to sit here alone in this room with Ian. Ian who had for so long been a ghost which she had banished when she could. But this live, flesh-and-blood Ian, looking at her with the old magnetic eyes, talking to her in that remembered husky voice . . . could not be banished so easily. Nor could she deny the inner knowledge that he was the one love of her life, and that she had had no earthly right to marry Bill.

Ian spoke again:

'How long have you been married?'

'Just a few weeks.'

'I must wish you every happiness,' he said stiffly.

Her teeth bit hard into her lower lip.

79

'Thank you.'

A moment's silence. They both smoked. Ill at ease, glancing furtively at each other. Then Gail said:

'Are you . . . ?'

'No,' he broke in almost roughly. 'I'm neither married nor engaged.'

'Oh!' she said feebly.

He broke out:

'I suppose it would be tactless of me to refer to the past, but if you don't mind . . .'

'No, I don't mind . . .'

There was a perspiration breaking out on the palms of her hands and she was wondering how long it would take Bill to buy that gin and to get back here again.

'Then, Gail, I want to know just why you didn't write to me after . . . Le Touquet?'

The question staggered her, and she showed it. She looked up at him, her cheeks hot, her eyes widening. That name *Le Touquet* broke the silence of the sitting-room like the crack of a revolver shot, smashing all reserves, all attempts between them to pretend that the past had never existed.

She said:

'How can you ask that? Did you expect me to write after the message you sent me?'

'Yes, I think I did. But apparently I made a mistake. I imagined that it had all meant as much to you as it did to me, and that you would want to write to me occasionally even in a friendly manner. Yes, that's all I wanted. Just to keep up our friendship and feel that one day we might meet again. I couldn't tolerate the thought of a complete break between us.'

Still more astounded, she said:

'But you asked me *not* to write. That was the message your mother gave me. A particular request from you that I shouldn't write, and it would be easier for you if I let you go quietly out of my life. Those were her actual words. I respected that wish even though it half killed me. Believe me, I wrote a dozen letters . . . agonised letters, which I tore up again, *because* it was your wish.'

It was Ian Dalmuir's turn to look astonished. He stared down at her. How pale she was! What unspoken things lay in those great grey eyes under the black shadow of the lashes.

'My mother said that to you? But I can't believe it. It wasn't what I asked her to say.'

Her gaze was fixed, held by his. For an instant they drank in each other's gaze. Gail had turned a little paler and she felt faint, sick. She whispered:

'I don't understand. There must have been . . . a mistake.'

He began to pace up and down the room. Once before she had seen him walk like that, restively, with his long, graceful stride. In their room at Le Touquet when he had been debating as to whether or not to take her back

81

to Simone. Tortured by his conscience as now he was tortured by the revelation of facts. The real facts that neither of them had known.

He said:

'Listen, Gail. The moment you went back to England and I returned to Paris, I had a summons from the War Office. I was ordered to proceed to India immediately, picking up the trooper at Marseilles. I telephoned my mother here in Edinburgh. I realised that I couldn't get in touch with you. You had asked me not to write or telephone to your home, because your family knew nothing about me. You will remember, you said, it would only cause them needless anxiety and suspicion. So I told my mother . . . not everything . . . but some of the facts. I told her that I had met a girl in Paris and fallen in love with her, but that I knew I could do nothing about it for two or three years, so didn't think it fair to tie her down. But I asked Mother to communicate with this girl. I gave her your address, and told her to give you mine in India. I wanted her to ask you if you would continue our association, and write to me. Until then, I wished you to know I would not get in touch with you. And I wished it made clear that if I did not hear, I would know you thought it best to cut completely away. Then I would respect your silence.'

He paused and stood in front of Gail. Arms behind his back.

'Those are the facts, Gail. If my mother told you differently, God forgive her. She did me—and you—a great wrong.'

Gail was trembling now so violently that she could scarcely hold her cigarette.

'I was never given one word of that message, Ian. Mrs. Dalmuir's letter was cold and even cruel. She asked me particularly for your sake not to write.'

'Oh God,' said Ian Dalmuir. 'What made her do such a thing? Poor Mother! I can't speak ill of her, Gail, because she's dead. But if she were alive I'd reproach her bitterly. I see now what she did to both of us. Thinking, of course, that it was the best thing for me. Terrified that I had been caught by a pretty face or a casual affair in Paris. Her ambition was for me to marry some nice Scots girl in Edinburgh Society. What I told her must have terrified her and my father. Even though I was a grown man they always treated me as a boy who needed guidance. That was their way.'

Gail threw her cigarette into the fireplace and shaded her eyes with the back of one hand.

'It's so awful,' she said with uneven breath, 'because I would have written if I'd known you wanted me to. I'd never, *never* have lost touch with you, Ian.'

'And I thought you wanted to cut me right out.'

She looked up at him reproachfully.

'After all . . . that it had meant . . . to me?'

'It meant everything to me, too,' he said, visibly agitated, 'and I couldn't quite understand your attitude, but I presumed that you were taking the course which you felt to be best for yourself. After all, we had discussed it . . . and sometimes decided that a complete break was the only way, when two people were so much in love, and unable to get married.'

'I didn't want to lose touch with you. It broke my heart,' she said, without restraint, 'it nearly killed me, Ian. And all the time I was thinking it was *your* wish and that you hadn't really loved me. Oh, it doesn't bear thinking about!'

'No, and it doesn't really bear talking about. You're married, Gail, and when I first saw you here tonight and realised you were Cardew's wife, it just proved what I'd imagined all these years in India . . . that you were too young to know what love really was and you had just been infatuated with me, and easily found consolation.'

Now Gail stood up, unable to sit there quietly and listen to his words. She said:

'It doesn't begin to be true. I never for a moment forgot you. I tell you it half killed me, and for three years I never looked at another man. And then . . . then the war came . . . I think I went a little crazy. For all I knew, you might have had a dozen other affairs in India. And Bill was a friend of the family's and had proposed to me dozens of times. I just sort of *slid in* to this marriage and . . .'

She stopped, a hand to her lips, aghast with herself. It was such flagrant disloyalty to Bill to stand here, admitting in no uncertain terms that she was not really in love with her husband. Yet her heart was crying out the truth that this man, Ian, her first love, was the real person to whom she owed loyalty. Somehow she could not fit Bill into the picture at all. It was all so complicated, her mind refused to deal with it. Her thoughts seemed to be spinning in circles.

'God, what a mess,' said Ian Dalmuir.

'Then do you still . . .?' Gail could not finish the sentence, but he knew what she was asking, and answered her.

'Yes, God help me, I still love you, Gail. I went on with my job in India. There were plenty of distractions out there and I tried them all, but nothing really blotted out the memory of you . . . Paris . . . Le Touquet . . . the whole show.'

'Oh, Ian,' said Gail in a terrified voice, 'Ian don't let's say any more. I can't stand it.'

'No, neither can I,' he said harshly.

She turned and folded her arms on the mantelpiece and leaned her head upon them, seeking desperately for self-control.

Ian Dalmuir stood there, staring at her back with a baffled, hopeless look in his handsome eyes. His natural instinct was to go to her, put an arm about that slender young waist, draw her to him as he had done on countless occasions in the past, feel again the never-forgotten sweetness of her lips, revive all the perfect passion that had drawn them together long ago.

But he dared not. Dared not move toward her, or even touch her hair. It was an emotional crisis such as he had never imagined possible and certainly not anticipated when he came round here to drink with Bill Cardew tonight. He had imagined Cardew's wife would be just an ordinary girl . . . anyone, anything but Gail. He was half paralysed by the whole situation. It was so appalling to know that his own mother had let him down. He found that hard to forgive, even though she was no longer living, and had done it for the best. She had wrecked any hopes of happiness between Gail and himself. She had caused them both unnecessary and bitter pain. All these years when they might have been in touch, leading toward the promise of the future, they had been both of them endeavouring to forget . . . And perhaps Gail had felt as he did, that a little of the loveliness of their passion and friendship had been spoiled, because they each imagined the other heartless. Each believed each other's love to be less than it really was. He thought, bitterly, how 'utterly destructive the efforts of an over-anxious, virtuous mother could be.

86

Returning to England in war-time he had been far too busy to dwell much upon personal affairs, and if he had thought of Gail it was just with the old regret which was dimming with the years, and the faint hope that he might one day come across her. For there had never been anyone in his life like Gail. No other woman to take her place in his arms.

And now *this* . . . To find her married and discover not only that a terrible mistake had been made, but that she was not really in love with the man she had married.

He would not have been human if he had not been glad to know that she was still in her heart of hearts *his!* That this marriage was just the result of war-fever or, perhaps, a girl's natural desire to be married. Poor sweet! She had taken it for granted that he, Ian, had long since forgotten her, and that there was nothing to wait for or hope for where he was concerned.

But why Cardew?

The man was such an intolerable bounder. Good looking, yes. Ian could see that from the feminine point of view, Cardew might have a strong animal attraction. A hearty, vigorous sort of fellow who could carry a woman along on the crest of his ambition. But not really Gail's man. No, by God, *he,* Ian Dalmuir, was *that.*

Looking at her back, her drooped head with the red-brown curls which he had so often compared with the polished chestnuts in the Bois of Boulogne, Ian was smitten afresh by the sheer tragedy of it all.

For a moment his inclination to make closer contact with her half conquered sanity. He walked up to her, put out a hand, and laid it on her shoulder.

'Oh, my dear,' he said, 'my *dear!*'

She swung round, fencing him off, face milk-white and eyes enormous, dark with pain.

'For God's sake, don't . . . don't Ian. I implore you.'

There were footsteps outside. Ian Dalmuir braced himself. His hand fell away from her. He drew back a pace and said:

'You're right, of course. It's no use for us to do anything but face facts and make the best of them. You're married and that's that.'

She gave an hysterical laugh.

'And you're my husband's superior officer and he has to work with you.'

'But I needn't see you again if you don't want me to.'

'I don't want you to,' she said under her breath, her whole body shaking. 'I don't want to see you. I couldn't *stand* it.'

'But it may not always be possible for us to avoid it,' he said.

'We must. We *must,*' she said almost violently.

He, too, was shaking.

'I'll leave it to you, Gail. Everything will be

88

as you wish.'

She shook her head.

'Nothing, nothing is as I wish,' she said in a smothered voice.

'There's one thing I must know,' he said, 'are you comparatively happy, Gail? I suppose you wouldn't have married Cardew if you hadn't cared for him.'

She fought with herself for a moment before answering. It would have been so easy to tell Ian that she knew that she had made a frightful mistake and that Bill was not what she had thought him. Not what her family thought him. That he had shown himself to be a selfish, overbearing young man who was in love with her in his fashion but who could never begin to make her happy as she had hoped to be happy.

But she said nothing of these things. She dared not for both their sakes. She said:

'Yes. I'm—I'm all right. Don't worry about me.'

And then the door opened and Bill came back into the room.

## SEVEN

Ian had gone.

Gail sat at her dressing-table rubbing a little cream into her face. Her skin felt tired. She was altogether tired after the racking emotion of the evening. It had been too much for her nerves. And the thought that Bill was there in the bathroom, and would be coming in here in a few minutes, made her heart sink like lead. Of all nights, this was one when she would have wished to be alone. Just to close her eyes and sleep and try to forget that Ian had come back into her life. Forget the treachery which had parted them when they need never really have said a final good-bye.

Just now, they had shaken hands and wished each other good night so casually that it must have deceived Bill. But those deep dark eyes of Ian's had held a message of passionate regret. She knew what he must feel. She could not help thrilling to the knowledge that after all these years he was still in love with her. But it was so hopeless. So futile, from both their points of view. And knowing that he lived here in Edinburgh, and would be in daily contact with Bill, and that she must continually hear his name, if not see him, made things so much worse.

Her face looked back at her from the mirror, unlike the face of the familiar Gail. It was drawn and haggard, and she looked years older. She ran a comb through her curls, and glanced without enthusiasm at the reflection of her slenderness, her grace, in the violet-blue silky dressing-gown which was part of her trousseau. She thanked God that Mummy and Daddy and the rest at home in England could not know the tragedy which had befallen her.

90

They imagined her up here as a happy bride and they must never think otherwise, she told herself. She must make herself write cheerful letters to Kingston, otherwise it would only worry them all so dreadfully.

In came Bill in his Jaeger dressing-gown, smoking a last cigarette. He looked handsome enough with his fair glistening hair and that healthy glow on his face. And he was obviously pleased with life.

'Put in some good work tonight,' he said, 'that fellow Dalmuir is a bit "wet," but he's on the Staff, and it's a feather in my cap to know him socially.'

Gail picked up some stockings which lay on the ground and rolled them into a ball. She did not look at Bill. She said quietly:

'Why should you call him "wet"?'

'Oh, he's the artistic kind. Spouts a lot of boring stuff about history and architecture in Edinburgh and that sort of tripe.'

Gail bit her lip. She half smiled to herself in a cynical way. It seemed so utterly ironic for her to be sitting here listening to Bill running down Ian. Ian, who was in her opinion the finest man in the world. Ian who had an understanding, a sensitiveness, which Bill could never attain, no matter how long he lived.

'Funny you two having met before,' said Bill.

'Yes.'

He came over and gave her ear the customary tweak. 'What's wrong with you? You're very dumb all of a sudden. Didn't you like Dalmuir?'

'Yes.'

'Well, I hope you were nice to him while I was out getting that gin.'

She kept her face averted.

'Naturally.'

'And you've got to go on being nice to him,' added Bill, 'I tell you that chap can do a lot for me.'

Resentment welled up in her. She turned to him suddenly.

'Do you *always* think of yourself and your own progress? Would you want me to be nice to the man, for instance, whether I liked him or not?'

'Certainly,' said Bill, 'it's up to a wife to be diplomatic to her husband's friends, if they are of value to him.'

'Well I hate what Scampie would call "sucking up" to anybody,' said Gail coldly.

'Well, then, I think it's very selfish of you,' Bill accused her. 'Influence counts in the Army, and I tell you Dalmuir has got it, and a hell of a lot of money into the bargain. We'd be fools not to "suck up" as you like to put it. Besides, if I get on, it'll benefit you as well, won't it?'

'I suppose so,' said Gail wearily.

'Well, you might show a bit more

enthusiasm in my affairs. What's the matter with you?'

'Nothing,' she said.

She hoped to God that he was not going to hector her this evening. She couldn't stand it. She longed frantically for peace, for her own room, and to stop talking about Ian. But Bill went on:

'Now I come to think of it you weren't particularly cordial to Dalmuir. You didn't even ask him to come again. You know I want you to make a point of entertaining him.'

'He has his own friends, no doubt,' said Gail desperately.

'So have we,' said Bill in his haughty voice, 'but I keep repeating, it's a good thing for me to cultivate Dalmuir. When I saw him off, he suggested that I should have a drink with him at the 'Aperitif' tomorrow, and you can come too. When you see him I hope you'll show him that you're pleased to see him. After all, you say you were once friends, and why not make use of the fact.'

She felt goaded almost beyond endurance. She wanted to cry out: 'Leave me alone.' But all she could do was to sit on the edge of the bed holding the folded silk stockings in her hand, staring hopelessly at the carpet.

She was beginning to discover that Bill was a 'nagger.' He liked to worry the bone. And the less enthusiastic she was about seeing Ian, the worse Bill became. In the end, out of sheer desperation, she agreed to join the two men for drinks at the 'Aperitif' tomorrow. But she was reduced to a state of hysteria by the time she was in bed. If only Bill knew what he was doing! If only he was the sort of man in whom she could confide, and explain the whole situation. But she couldn't begin to give Bill her confidence. If he ever knew about Ian and Le Touquet, her life would be unbearable. And the irony of it all was that she wanted more than anything in the world to go on seeing Ian, but dared not. She had taken certain vows to Bill, and it was her innermost and sincere wish that she could keep them. With his ring on her finger, she disliked being unfaithful even in spirit.

When Bill's mood changed and he wanted to become lover-like, it was the last straw for her. She buried her face in the pillow and burst into tears. Then the better side of Bill asserted itself. He took it for granted that she was not feeling well, and offered to fetch her aspirin. He was much too conceited to dream for a moment that her tears, her attitude were due to any aversion to his caresses. She allowed him to bring her the aspirin and the water, and then he put out the light. He ceased talking, and at last she was able to be quiet. To lie supine, still her jumping nerves, and try to find some kind of mental tranquillity.

But it was difficult. She could think of nothing but Ian. Ian as she had seen him half an hour ago when he bade her good night, with that fascinating glengarry on the side of his dark head. Ian as he had said goodbye; saluting her, giving her that long eloquent look.

And one fact stood out in her mind beyond all others. That his return into her life had destroyed any hope that she might have entertained of settling down in peace and happiness to this marriage with Bill. But the longer she thought about it the more convinced she became that it was her duty to stand by Bill, whatever happened, and whatever she felt about Ian. She tried to argue with herself that it was not Bill's fault that this had happened . . . nor that the incident at Le Touquet had ever occurred. Bill loved her and it was up to her to be grateful for his love, and loyal to the name which she had taken.

At breakfast that next morning she felt ill, and as exhausted as though she had had no sleep. But she made a valiant effort to be cheerful. She was rewarded by knowing that Bill was cheerful in consequence.

'You were an old wet blanket last night,' he said. 'You must have had one of your imperial headaches. But you're chirpy enough this morning, darling. Now listen, I haven't given you anything lately. How about buying yourself a present. Go along Princes Street and see what you can find.'

She smiled and thanked him. She didn't

want presents. But she appreciated the offer. Bill was spasmodically generous in this fashion and there were moments when he laid aside his hectoring manner, and became the good sort, the amusing friend, whom she had always welcomed in the old days at Kingston.

When she walked down Princes Street that crisp autumn morning, it was with every intention of sitting tightly on her emotions, of doing her duty to the uttermost as Bill's wife. But so much conspired to make it difficult.

Every officer wearing tartan breeches, black boots and a glengarry, reminded her of *him*. The Castle standing there so proudly on the hill, its grey old walls wreathed in the delicate morning mist, recalled all the countless descriptions Ian had given her of the place when they were in Paris. The sound of a piper playing his bagpipes brought a lump to her throat at the thought of Ian marching with his men to the strains of that stirring, heart-breaking music. Marching into battle. He might at any moment be moved from Staff and sent with his regiment to the Western Front.

An air raid warning spoilt the morning shopping, and brought business to a temporary standstill. Gail would not go down into a shelter. She stood in a doorway looking up at the sky, wondering if a German raider would appear suddenly out of those clouds. The muffled boom of anti-aircraft guns from the Forth Bridge district broke the sudden silence which had descended upon the city once all the traffic was at a halt. She thought about Ian and wondered what he was doing. The defences up here were part of his job. And she wondered with a touch of home-sickness whether they were getting that same warning down in London, and if the darling family at Kingston would be gathering in the shelter which Daddy had built in the garden. Mum with her gas mask and her. knitting. Scampie, at school, lined up with the other girls. Chris at Shrewsbury. She could just hear him saying to the other boys:

'I say! What a thrill. Wish I were in the Air Force and could have a crack at those blighters . . .'

Then the 'All Clear!' And Edinburgh stirred again. And now the sun had come through the mists and the Castle stood proudly and clearly against the blue northern sky.

She could well imagine the pride of a Scot, like Ian, in his country, in this capital which they called 'Auld Reekie.' The glamour of the place was beginning to get into her own blood. And if only she had come here as Ian had intended, *with him* . . .

She trod ruthlessly on such reflections.

Her good intentions toward Bill continued through the day. At lunch-time he was in one of his best moods, full of amusing anecdotes about the morning's work, some racy stories that a brother officer had told him and no

97

mention of Captain Dalmuir to upset Gail's equilibrium. At two o'clock, just before Bill went back to work, he remembered to be solicitious about her headache of last night. When he was thoughtful and sweet to her like this, it gave her a guilt-complex which she could not easily banish. She was sincere as she lifted her face to be kissed and said:

'You're very nice to me. Thanks a lot. I'm all right, Bill.'

In the doorway he stopped to say:

'Lord, I've never mentioned one of the most important items of news for us. There's some talk about all of us on this Course being billeted together and taken out of the town. As time goes on we have to be nearer the gun positions.'

'What'll that mean?' asked Gail.

'Garrison life. The real Army stuff,' he grinned. It did not seem to trouble him.

'And do I stay here?'

Out came the hand to tweak the ear.

'Not likely. I'm not leaving my attractive wife alone in digs. I hope wives will be able to join us. It depends on what sort of chap the Brigadier is. He arranges it all.'

Then he was gone, and Gail thought no more about the proposed move. She was in a state of mind not to care particularly where she went or where she lived. Her main desire was not to allow herself to think too much about Ian.

But the evening had to come, and with it that six o'clock meeting at the 'Aperitif' which Bill had arranged.

Why hadn't Ian refused the invitation, she wondered, knowing what it would mean to both of them. Yet it was stupid to think he could cut away from an officer who was so closely connected with his work and naturally he would not want to offend Bill by refusing to drink with him.

And Gail didn't want to upset Bill by refusing to drink with *him*, so it was a vicious circle.

The 'Aperitif' did not seem to Gail to belong to the old, history-laden Edinburgh which she loved. It was just a piece of London, modern and attractive, with an oyster-bar, and little tables where one could sit and drink. It was crammed with people. A meeting-place for the Army, Navy and Air Force. Lovely girls perched on high stools with cocktails in their hands. Young men in uniform, snatching a few hours' gaiety from the great job of defending their country. Some of them looked so young that Gail remembered her brother Chris, and shivered, praying that the war would not go on long enough to include *him.*

And then Ian arrived and she saw no other man in the room. Her heart fluttered wildly as it must always do, at the sight of that tall, lithe body, that dark handsome head. He saluted her, then sat down at the table which Bill had found, removing his glengarry and belt.

'Rather warm in here,' he said.

'Yes, isn't it,' said Gail in a formal little voice.

'What'll you drink?' from Bill.

'A long one, I think,' said Ian, 'gin and lime. But you're having this with me.'

'That's all right, have the first with me.'

Bill moved off to the bar to get the drinks. For a moment Gail and Ian were alone. Through the gay chatter in the room she heard his husky voice:

'Gail, I'm afraid I've got news for you. It isn't going to please you very much. And I assure you it pleases me even less.'

Her heart raced a bit.

'What? You're not going to France . . .?'

He gave a half-smile. His eyes looked very tender . . . She had seen that same look in them years ago, and felt her whole soul rush to meet it.

'No, my dear, although perhaps it would be the best thing.'

'No, no, I couldn't bear you to go . . .'

'You're not supposed to care,' he said grimly.

'Well, tell me what *has* happened,' she said.

'Did your husband . . .' he used those words with difficulty . . . 'mention that there might be some change in billeting plans?'

'Yes.'

'Well, the Brigadier and the Brigade

100

Major have been in conference with me all day about this business. They don't want the officers in our lot scattered round the town. They're doing serious and important work in connection with anti-aircraft and it's essential they should be together, and if possible in the country. Most of the chaps like Cardew are not Regulars and are fresh from civilian life. The Brigadier, who is a very human sort of chap, doesn't want the married ones separated from their wives unless it is necessary.'

'Well?' said Gail impatiently, her grey eyes lifted with anxiety to his.

'Well, the fact is that he knew my uncle and all about the Loch Castle and he asked me if they could take it over. It has about thirty bedrooms and a skeleton staff there of old retainers who were in the service of my uncle, the Laird. I couldn't refuse. The Castle is empty and in a grand position for our men.'

Gail put a hand to her throat. A little pulse was beating there, fast.

'Why are you telling me all this, Ian?'

He gave a short hard laugh.

'Because, my dear, it's an ironic fact that you and your husband will be asked to accept billets in the Loch Castle . . . *my* castle, and that I, Captain Ian Dougal Dalmuir have been asked to take over the entire organisation of the officers there.'

For a moment there was silence. Gail stared at him blankly. She had absorbed every word he had said. Ironic, he had called it. To her it seemed fantastic. Another malicious jest on the part of fate. It had been bad enough to find Ian here in Edinburgh, Bill's superior officer. But to be billeted under Ian's own roof . . . to see him at all hours of the day and the evening, be in continual contact with him . . . that was *too* much.

The colour stained her face a vivid red. She said in a gasping voice:

'But I *couldn't* come. How could I? The complications would be endless. Neither of us could face it.'

Ian laughed again. It was a sound without humour.

'You don't know the Army yet, Gail. One isn't really asked whether one wants to do a thing or not. I've just got to take over the organisation, and your husband will have to accept his billet. And if the other wives are going to live there too, I don't quite see how you're going to get out of joining them—do you?'

# EIGHT

For a moment Gail sat silent, flung right off her balance again by the information which Ian had just given her. It did really seem monstrous that such a thing could happen. And just when she had made up her mind to do the right thing by Bill and avoid Ian as much as she possibly could.

She said:

'Well, *really* . . . *I* can't believe it possible.'

'I'm afraid it is,' said Ian. 'If you'd suggested it to me before I saw the Brigadier, I'd have said it was possible but not *probable*. Billets don't usually include wives, but this is an unusual case. The Castle is such a big place, and I think the Brigadier thought the wives would look after their husbands and keep 'em happy . . .' He gave a short ironic laugh . . . 'After all, the old boy doesn't inquire too deeply into the matrimonial lives of his officers and he presumes that they like being together.'

Speechlessly Gail turned from him. Her gaze rested on Bill. He had his back to her, and was struggling to get a place at the crowded bar. The electric light made the top of his hair shine like gold. His back was very straight. She thought mechanically how well groomed, how good looking Bill always was. Other women were looking at him, too. A pretty girl, sitting on a stool at the bar and who had just picked up an officer's glengarry and put it at a rakish angle on her curls, was giving Bill a very roguish look, making way for him to order his drinks. Oh, yes, the women liked Bill. And *she* had liked him enough to marry him. It didn't seem possible that she could sit here now with her heart so low, her spirit so bruised, and every instinct within her yearning toward this other man who sat at her side. This lover whom she had thought lost and dead to her, and who had come to life with such startling vividness.

She began to visualise life at the Loch Castle with Bill—and Ian. She gave a little gasp:

'Honestly, it can't be done, Ian.'

He bit his lip and leaned forward, tapping his boot with his stick.

'Well, what can you do? Go home?'

'I don't know,' she said helplessly, 'I can't very well walk out on Bill, and yet—'

'And I can't refuse to carry out the General's orders,' said Ian.

'Then,' said Gail. 'I suppose we'll have to make the best of it.'

Ian suddenly clenched his teeth.

'Oh, well, there's a war on. There might be worse to face. It won't be easy for us, but for God's sake let's cheer up a bit. We can't be perpetually miserable.'

Gail's slender fingers carrying her cigarette to her lips, shook slightly, but she managed to laugh and agree with him.

'You're quite right. Let's be happy . . . don't let's care about anything.'

That wasn't how either of them felt. They both cared passionately. But Ian was right, she told herself. Whatever fate had in store for them, there was a war on and things might be worse. She knew this mood of Ian's. He

104

never had liked being miserable. Even in Le Touquet, when he had dreaded the thought of losing her, he had laughed. They had laughed together. That was what one had to do. Be philosophical, and *laugh,* even when one's heart was sinking to the very depths of misery.

When Bill returned with the drinks, he found Captain Dalmuir and his wife apparently enjoying a joke. He gave them their drinks and said:

'Let me in on it . . .'

Gail did not meet his gaze. She just went on laughing, lifting her cocktail to her lips. It gave her a guilt-complex when Bill was cheerful like this and friendly, when she knew how ignorant he was of the real state of affairs between herself and Ian. And what it all did to Ian, she could not imagine. But she was sure that he must loathe the situation with his whole soul.

It was Bill who brought the conversation back to Loch Castle.

'I've been telling Gail about the billeting arrangements. But I didn't realise it was to be in your place, Dalmuir.'

'I didn't know it myself till I had the conference yesterday with the Brigadier and Cleghorn,' said Ian.

'The Castle sounds a hell of a place,' said Bill.

'It's big enough, and has plenty of historic value.'

'That'll suit my wife,' said Bill, and put out a

hand and took Gail's across the table. Gail saw the look in Ian's eyes . . . a sick, resentful look . . . but she could do nothing about it. She drew her fingers gently away from Bill's as soon as she could.

She asked:

'When is this billeting business likely to start?'

'As soon as the Castle is prepared,' said Ian.

'Will there be some sort of Mess?' inquired Bill.

'No, it'll be run like a hotel with separate tables in the dining-hall. Married couples will have their own sitting-rooms and there are plenty of other rooms—library and so forth—for bachelors. In fact, it's pretty well going to be just a private hotel for our particular fellows who are doing this job.'

'And you're going to be in charge of it, eh, Dalmuir?' said Bill.

'Yes,' said Ian, and added grimly. 'It'll be my place to see the wives don't get beaten too often.'

Bill gave his hearty laugh.

'Beaten, eh? That's a damned good idea. Think I'll start it on Gail. And how about not allowing us poor little husbands to be henpecked?'

'Quite so,' said Ian.

'God r thought Gail, 'what a fatuous conversation.'

A big burly Scot wearing tartan slacks and

with a major's crown on his shoulder, came into the 'Aperitif' with a small plump woman who wore tweeds, brogues, and a helmet-shaped hat. She carried a mackintosh and an umbrella. She was what might be called a very sensible woman. Gail, who recognised this couple as Major and Mrs. Naughton—Naughton was on the Course with Bill—tried to avoid being seen by them, but failed. Mrs. Naughton spotted Gail at once and made a beeline for her table.

'Ah!' she exclaimed, 'there's the little bride.'

Bill and Ian stood up. The men exchanged greetings. More chairs were found and they all sat down again. Gail was separated from Ian by the plump and solid form of Jean Naughton. In a way she was glad. Anything was better than that awful tension between herself and Ian. Yet to be separated from him even like this gave her a feeling of despair.

Jean Naughton was what Gail supposed was the perfect type of Army officer's wife. She exuded cheerfulness in adversity, unflinching patriotism and zeal both in hers and her husband's work, also a complete lack of interest in anything *but* the Army. She had neither belief in, nor use for, the artistic values of this life.

She was a ruthless scandalmonger and in confidential whispers tore to pieces the wives of the other officers. And she had an endless flow of hints about everything. There seemed

107

nothing that she did not know or had not experienced during her twenty years of life in the Army.

'My dear, it's so hot in here, one can't breathe. I think they ought to have more windows open. I suppose it's the black-out. No, I won't drink. I never do, not even a lemonade. And I don't advise you to drink too many cocktails if you want to keep that lovely complexion. How are you finding married life? Doing your bit, eh? I remember when I was first married to Harry and we were sent almost at once to India. If you ever go to India, I could give you a lot of advice . . . And have you heard about this billeting idea? We're all to go to a castle on a loch. Such a bore moving, but it sounds a good spot to me so long as it isn't damp. But I've got a wonderful anti-rheumatism cure . . .'

She rambled on almost without stopping and Gail was thankful that she had not to make many replies. Now and again she caught Ian's eyes. And she saw a glint of the old humour in them. She knew exactly what *he* thought about women like Jean Naughton. In Paris he used to make fun of the Armywives.

She thought:

'Shall I ever turn into a Mrs. Naughton? I sincerely hope not . . .'

The Naughtons could only stay a quarter of an hour. The Major was taking his 'mem-sahib,' as he called her, to see a show, and they had to dine early. They drifted out again, Mrs. Naughton adding a few last words of advice over her shoulder as she went:

'Now, Mrs. Cardew, mind you wrap up when you get out again. Edinburgh winds can be very dangerous after these hot places . . .'

Bill moved back to the bar to get more drinks. And once again Gail and Ian were alone. Ian drew a long breath and smoothed his dark head with a slightly nervous gesture.

'Phew! That woman gets me down.'

'Me, too,' said Gail, 'but I'm sure she means to be kind, and that's what I've got to live with for the next few months, according to you.'

'Poor little Gail. You weren't really cut out for a communal Army existence, were you?'

'I don't know what I was cut out for,' she said in a low voice.

'I think I told you once.'

She knew immediately to what he referred, and shrank from the memory as though from pain. The memory of the idyllic life he had once mapped out for both of them.

She could hear his voice . . . see his eager face, dark eyes, afire with imagination, in the forest at Fontainebleau . . . yes, that was where they had built up their dreams. She could hear his voice as clearly as though it were yesterday:

*'And we'll get married and I'll resign from the Army, and we'll just go up to the Hebrides and I'll show you what the charm, the tradition of the real old Scotland, can really be. We'll have*

*a house with many windows facing the purple mountains and a crystal river where the salmon leap. I'll teach you how to fish and we'll lead a glorious, free, healthy sort of life in the sun. And at night we'll go back to our house and sit by the peat-fire and have music and read the poems and books we love. And it'll be miles and miles from anyone else. Just you and I together...'*

That had been his dream—and hers. Poor dreamers! For *this* was reality ... sitting here knowing that she was married to another man, that there was a war on, and that they were all cogs in a vast machine from which there was no escape. The machine called Life. A life of reality, instead of dreams.

Just for a moment, however, they were back in Paris together and they were smiling into each other's eyes.

'I know what you were meant for, Gail,' he said, huskily.

'Oh, Ian, Ian,' she said.

'It's almost too much for me to realise what I've lost,' he added, 'to look at you and remember ...'

He broke off as though trying to harden himself against the unconscious attack made upon him by her beauty, her nearness, the perfume drifting from her hair ... all the sweetness that was hers, and which had once been *his*.

She tried to forget her own difficulties and to help him to surmount his.

'Don't worry too much about the Castle. I don't suppose we need meet too often. I'll hide myself behind Mrs. Naughton and take hints on how wives should behave.'

They both laughed.

A few minutes later when the third round of drinks had been consumed, Ian made an excuse to get away. He did not so much as touch Gail's finger-tips, but when he looked at her and said 'Good-bye' she felt as though he embraced her, secretly, desperately. She felt weak and stupid and ready only for sleep. Yes, these days the only time she was really, truly at peace with herself and the world was when she was asleep.

Bill was very cheerful as he walked home, guiding her through the pitch-dark streets. Gail was not good at seeing in the dark.

'You were in grand form, darling,' he said, 'glad to see you getting on so well with Dalmuir. He isn't bad fun when you can get him laughing, although he is usually a bit on the solemn side.'

'Bill,' she said, 'must we go to this Castle?'

'Good lord, yes. Why not?'

'I'm just wondering . . . ' She was glad that the darkness hid from him the fact that her cheeks were flaming . . . 'I don't know that I much care for a sort of garrison life, shut up all day with people like Mrs. Naughton. I mean, she's a good sort and all that, but you men will get away during the day on your job but the

111

wives will be terribly boxed up together. Not much chance even of getting into Edinburgh . . . the shops . . .'

'Oh, you must put up with that, darling. And as an officer's wife you might be in plenty worse places. Some of the married quarters abroad are rotten. Or you might find yourself in a hut with a corrugated iron roof in some garrison town in England. The Castle sounds pretty luxurious to me, especially with a war on.'

She was silent. It was so hopeless since she could not explain to Bill *why* she did not want to go to the Loch Castle. It was nothing to do with the other wives or the life itself, nothing at all. It was just the menace of being continually under the same roof as the man whom she had once worshipped, and with whom she was still secretly despairingly in love.

Bill continued to be in high spirits that evening. He was the Bill she had grown so fond of at Kingston. His boastful side, his bullying side, in the background. A Bill who had a sense of the ridiculous and could make her laugh at his imitations of the Major, of Jean Naughton, of a young subaltern who was called 'Pop-eyes,' at others. Bill could laugh at everybody—except himself.

She felt mean toward him, and guilty, when he ended the evening by asking her if he made her happy.

112

'I do want you to be happy, Gail. There have been moments when I've felt we weren't getting on, but you know I'm crazy about you, don't you? And you love me, don't you?'

She forced herself to answer in the affirmative.

'Dear old Bill!' she said when he took her in his arms and began to kiss her eagerly.

'I'm so damned proud of you. You're a damned sight better looking than any of the other women. I've seen Dalmuir looking at you . . . bet he envies me!'

She remained mute, closing her eyes, suffering his caresses. He went on:

'Queer chap, Dalmuir. What's his back history? Do you know? He seems a confirmed bachelor. Did some woman walk out on him when he was in India or something?'

'I don't know,' said Gail, and clenched her hands.

'Well, you'd better go on being decent to him. He's likely to be pretty useful, and if we're going to live in his place—'

'Oh don't talk about him or anything else except us,' Gail broke in desperately.

'You are a queer little hing,' he laughed, 'all right. We'll talk about "us" . . . and not so much talking . . . if it comes to that'

His lips were hard against hers. She tried with all her soul to be responsive because she felt that it was her duty and she had no right to let him suffer because Ian had come back into

113

her life. But his kisses left her ice-cold. It was as though she had frozen inwardly toward him, and that nothing could ever bring back that warmth which had deceived her into marriage with him. For unconsciously she had slipped back three years and become again that other Gail who had loved Ian Dalmuir. Yes, she was that Gail again, and it was as though the Gail who had married Bill Cardew had never existed.

## NINE

Within a week from that evening, her whole life seemed to change.

Her arrival at Ian's Castle was unspoilt by any jarring note with Bill. For that next night, Bill was sent down to London to inspect a batch of recruits who were wanted for the particular job on which he was working. He had to bring them up from Woolwich to Edinburgh. It meant him being away for forty-eight hours, and during those hours Gail was left to enjoy to the full all that the Loch Castle had to give to her of beauty and mental refreshment.

She described her arrival in her weekly letter to her brother Chris.

She had already covered four or five pages with a detailed account of the history of this

114

place. When Chris left Shrewsbury he was going to Oxford to read History. It was a subject which interested him as much as it had always done Gail herself.

Gail had only been here forty-eight hours, but already she had done a great deal of reading. Many books in the library had given her information about the Loch Castle dating back to 1100. And, of course, there was a room in which Mary, Queen of Scots, herself, was supposed to have slept when she made her escape from Edinburgh and began her last and ill-fated journey to England.

Gail's pen went on flowing:

'You would revel in this, Chris. I can't tell you what an effect it had on me when I first drove through the grounds and saw the Castle. Not a poetic sunset, but in the rain, a grey, weeping rain which seems somehow part of Scotland. We moved slowly up a steep incline through a kind of park. The trees have been glorious, scarlet and gold, but the wind has almost stripped the leaves from the branches. There are deer in the park which are so tame that they will almost come and feed out of your hand. Then suddenly through the mist of rain, I saw the Castle with its two round towers and battlements standing on the very edge of the Loch. Grey, like the water, silver-grey in the mist. And with a drawbridge and a moat to complete the effect. One could just imagine the Queen of Scots riding her palfrey across

115

that drawbridge and being taken by the Laird, who was an ancestor of Ian Dalmuir's, into the warmth and peace which she so sorely needed inside those grey old walls.

'You might think it is gloomy here from my description. And perhaps the first sight of that Castle, and the still silver Loch, is a little sombre. Plaintive like the cry of the heron which one hears in the dawn, and sometimes at night. And since I've got here it's never stopped raining But I'm told when the sun comes out, it's all sparkling and joyous and one can see from the battlements across the crags to the moors which are purple with heather. And in the distance on a clear day, I believe you can see Edinburgh Castle, itself. Otherwise, one might be in the most remote part of Scotland. A heavenly retreat.

'But the interior of the Castle is far from grim, and so filled with rare art treasures that I don't think I shall ever grow tired of wandering around. Ian Dalmuir is a lucky man to have such an inheritance and he is far from unappreciative. One day you must meet him. He, too, has a passion for history in spite of the fact that he is a soldier by profession. Everything has been arranged most perfectly for us. There are only twenty officers on this particular job, half of whom are bachelors. We all eat in the big hall which has gigantic windows looking out at the park, and is hung with superb tapestries. The smallest is very valuable indeed, and reputed to have been sewn by one of the famous Maries who were ladies-in-waiting to the Queen of Scots.

'The reception-room is more modern, and full of rare china, paintings, and lovely furniture, and has been given to the "wives" for their particular room when they wish to be communal. But in spite of the fact that Mrs. Naughton has tried to induce us to play a lot of bridge or get together for sewing, we most of us keep to our own little sitting-rooms which adjoin our bedrooms. The unmarried officers use the library and so none of us really tread on each other's corns . . .

Gail finished writing. She had said enough to Chris and it was time she wrote to little Scampie who was to be congratulated on having passed her music exam.

She got up and stretched her cramped limbs. She had been writing for over an hour. It was good to relax by the fire and have a cigarette, and look around her.

Ian Dalmuir was a very rich man—everyone knew it—and he was certainly seeing to it that those who occupied his Castle did not suffer for lack of comfort. There were huge fires all over the Castle. They burned peat and wood. Sometimes it made Gail's heart ache to smell the peat. It recalled their old dreams of life together in the Hebrides.

This sitting-room which she shared with Bill, was certainly an improvement on Miss

Dow's shabby, rather Victorian rooms in Edinburgh. It was a charming boudoir with dark oak panelling relieved by soft powder-blue carpets and silvery brocade curtains The bedroom adjoining was panelled, too, and most luxurious, with a modern bathroom leading out of it.

When they had come here three days ago, Ian had asked Gail to choose her room.

'I want you to have what you like,' he had said.

And this was the one she liked, because it was at the top and she could see for miles over the park to those heather-purple moors which spelt romance for her. The romance of Ian's own country.

She was only too pleased that Mrs. Naughton and some of the other wives should occupy the bigger suites downstairs. Mrs. Naughton was in the seventh heaven because she had been allotted the room in which the Queen of Scots was supposed to have slept. Gail had just given Chris a description of Jean, entering her room, in mackintosh and beret, firmly clasping her umbrella, and bouncing on the four-poster bed, looking utterly out of place.

It gave her extreme pleasure to live here and to see Ian day by day. But it was not an unmitigated pleasure. Until Bill joined her, she sat at a table in the big dining-hall with the Naughtons. And across the room at dinner

118

she could see Ian with the other officers who were single, and who had their own 'Mess' at the other end. They could exchange smiles and greetings. In the evenings she could talk to him for a while. But never for long, for she knew it would not do, and he generally retired to the library soon after dinner to play bridge with the Brigadier.

In a way she was happy. But when Bill came back, she wondered if she would know the same happiness. She rather doubted it. The very thought of her husband's return and the kisses which he would eagerly demand, made her heart sink. Nothing could bring back now the old glamour or even friendliness.

Bill Cardew, meanwhile, was taking very good care to mix business with pleasure during those forty-eight hours that he was in London.

At first he had been annoyed that he must leave Gail, not so much because she had all the work and packing up of the move alone from Edinburgh to the Castle, but because he liked being with her, and thought that the London trip might be a bore.

He discovered, however, that he could soon put Gail out of mind and take full advantage of being 'the gay bachelor' again. He did not take the trouble to go to Kingston and look up his old mother to whom such a visit would have been so much pleasure. Neither did he put himself out to get in touch with the Partners and give them the news which they would have liked of Gail. He had other fish to fry.

On the night journey down to King's Cross he met a man named Frank Pears, who used to be in business with him, and was now in the Army. This man had been asked out to a party in the West End. A supper dance at the 'Cafe de Paris'. His hostess, Lady Borley, one of the well-known Mayfair beauties, had told Frank to bring along another man.

'You're just the fellow,' Pears said, slapping Bill on the shoulder, 'Lady Borley said I was to choose a good looker, old boy.'

Bill's vanity was gratified. He only had work which would take him all day at Woolwich. He would be free in the evening, and he was only too glad to accept a good party at someone else's expense.

He was glad he had had his tunic cleaned the other day. With buckles, buttons, and belt polished up, and fair hair shining, he went forth to the party at the 'Café de Paris.'

And once there, there was everything to make him forget that he was a married man. A beautiful Society hostess who seemed to have money to burn, flower-decked tables, one or two lovely girls. A first-rate band and plenty of champagne, and the gay West End atmosphere which appealed to him so much more than Edinburgh. He hadn't time for all that nonsense that Gail talked about history and glamour up there.

And he was the 'lion' of the evening. The

khaki-clad hero boasting that he was 'on the Staff' and already talking glibly about his special billet in the Loch Castle.

The big surprise was when the prettiest girl at the table suddenly leaned forward, addressed him, and disclosed her name as June Naughton.

'You must know Daddy!' she said.

Bill, astonished, informed her that Major Naughton was on his own Course.

'Oh, what *fun!*' she exclaimed, and changed places with another girl who sat beside him. They talked a lot about her father and mother of whom he could give her first-hand news. Then she talked about herself. She had been training for the stage when war broke out, but her parents had asked her to give it up owing to the war, since when she had been living in the country with an aunt and uncle. She was once at school in Paris with Lady Borley's daughter. That was how she came to be at this party tonight which was Pam Borley's 'twenty-first', Later in the month, she hoped to go North to stay at the Castle with her parents, who had decided that there were not likely to be any air raids of importance, and that it would be safe for her.

Bill listened to June, who had a high flute-like voice, and decided that she was the most entrancing blonde whom he had met for a long time. He gave her a cigarette and when she put it between her carmined lips, he flicked his

121

little gold lighter into action and their fingers touched. A spark was ignited in Bill. She flickered her long lashes at him and smiled.

'A seductive young woman,' he told himself, and if *she* was coming up to the Castle, well, did it matter so much if Gail *was* stand-offish?

June had the tall, rather graceful willowy figure of a born mannequin. She looked as though she had been turned out of a Vogue pattern book. Her white tulle dress was sewn with glittering sequins and bunched out from her tiny waist, down to scarlet satin slippers. Her hair was of metallic fairness, and bunched in curls on top of her head, Nestling in the curls were two scarlet roses.

She looked at once *ingénue* and sophisticated. She wore a lot of bracelets which clinked whenever she moved her wrists and long fingers with their scarlet pointed nails.

A few minutes later, Bill and June were dancing together, and he was saying:

'What a break for me to come South, and be asked to a party and find *you.*'

'It's a break for me, too!' she said.

'You dance divinely.'

'So do you . . .'

He knew that, and he liked being told so, and June decided that although she had always had a penchant for dark men, Bill Cardew was *frightfully* attractive. His hair was so very golden and his eyes so very blue. She could see

122

that here was someone with whom she could flirt to her heart's content!

The party was an unqualified success. Bill literally commandeered his Major's daughter. They were tarred with the same brush.

'What *fun!*' June kept repeating all through the evening.

And Bill found it fun too. Especially as he managed to take June away from the party when it ended, on pretext of driving her home. He wrapped his British warm about the spangled, seductive young figure, and saw to it that their taxi meandered, rather than went any pace, along the dark Embankment.

Let the taxi-meter tick up. He didn't care. June, at nineteen, was a young woman of the world, *far* from averse to being kissed. She literally asked for it, he thought, lifting those red curving lips of hers. And he took them without scruple and without thought of honour. Quite aware that he had not yet told her that he was a married man.

The thought of Gail was receding well into the background. After all, he told himself, she was cold and reserved and it was boring for a fellow to have a frigid wife. All the love making seemed to come from his side. Now he came to think of it, Gail had never really welcomed his kisses since the earliest days of their honeymoon. He was beginning to feel that this marriage wasn't altogether a success. He liked to call a spade a spade. He told himself that in future he wouldn't bother with all this 'spiritual' stuff which Gail put over. He didn't understand her. But June he *could* understand. And why should he feel any compunction? It was *she* who set the pace.

She snuggled in his arms and sighed.

'Oh, Bill, what a wonderful night! I feel as though I'd known you all my life.'

'Well, I hope to know you for the rest of mine, gorgeous!'

'Then you *do* like June a teeny-weeny bit?'

He told her that he adored her. But adoration didn't really come into it. He was just thrilled by her sex appeal and her youth. Then he decided that he ought to say something about Gail, so reluctantly, he put over his story in the old, old way.

'We don't really get on . . . I'd rather not talk about it . . . Only, of course, I wish I were free . . . I oughtn't really to see you any more . . . you lovely little thing . . . you've bowled me right over . . .'

Many such things, spoken lightly and inconsequently, without much meaning. For Bill Cardew knew in his heart that it was Gail whom he loved and whom he respected. Only his passion for Gail was, as it had always been, half fanned by the fact that she was so aloof from him. He was not serious about June, but he thought it would be fun to have an affair with her.

Whether she believed all he had to say

about his marriage or not, he did not know. She played up to it. She stroked his hair, her bangles jingling prettily.

'You poor darling Bill. June wishes you were free too. June is fed up. She always finds *all* the nicest men are married! But can't she help to make Bill a teeny-weeny bit happier?'

Bill assured her that she could.

'I'm thrilled to the core,' he said, 'with the thought that you are going up to the North to stay in our billet.'

'Oh, what *fun* it will be,' she said, brushing his cheek with her lips.

He wondered how much lipstick he had on his face and whether it was the kind that came off easily. He also decided that the fare on the meter was enough and that now he'd better take June home. But not before he had arranged to meet her for lunch at the 'Berkeley' tomorrow.

'I've got some more work to do but I can meet you at the Buttery at one,' he said.

June was enchanted. She could go down to her aunt's place later in the afternoon, she said. And she would make quite sure that that visit to the Castle came off as soon as her parents could arrange it.

'June will be very, *very* discreet,' she cooed at him when he finally said good night.

He was intoxicated with triumph by the time he had left her. June was the sort of girl a fellow understood and, indeed, she gave kisses as passionately as they were given.

After leaving her, he lost his head a bit when he thought about her. But in his calmer moments, he decided that he must proceed with caution. He didn't wish to get into trouble either with the Major *or* his wife.

Their meeting took place at the Buttery as was arranged. And as he had also arranged, Bill had hired a car, and after lunch they were going to drive down to Richmond Park where they could have an exciting hour or two and more of those kisses and caresses which June offered eagerly enough.

While they were sitting on the stools at the Buttery, a party of three young men . . . they gave the impression of being schoolboys . . . came in for a meal and were turned away by the head waiter because there was not a spare table.

One of the young men stood a moment looking at the backs of those who sat up at the counter. He wore a black patch over the left eye. He was Gail's brother, Chris Partner. He had come up from Shrewsbury to see an eye specialist after an accident in a rugger scrum, and two cousins of his had asked him to lunch and a matinee. For a moment he stood staring, then, definitely, he recognised his brother-in-law's back. He was about to move forward when he caught sight of the girl beside Bill. Chris hesitated a moment. What the deuce was Bill doing in London? Wasn't he supposed

126

to be in Edinburgh with Gail? And who was the dizzy blonde who wore a little black sealskin coat and a sealskin toque on the top of her silver fair head, her silver curls falling with film-star effect down to her shoulders? Then suddenly Cardew and the girl raised their cocktail glasses toward each other and at that precise instant, Bill leaned forward and daringly dropped a kiss on the girl's hand.

Chris Partner's face went scarlet. He swung on his heel and said to his two friends:

'Let's get out of here. I've just seen a worm and I don't want to be recognised by him.'

Bill Cardew, without the least idea that he was noticed, went on drinking and making love with his eyes and his voice, to June Naughton.

## TEN

Within two days of Bill's return to the Loch Castle, he was on bad terms with his wife. At first he had been quite interested in his new billet and in spite of his secret penchant for June Naughton (he had only mentioned to her parents in the most casual way that he had met her), he paid a good deal of attention to his wife. She was still the most attractive woman in the world to him. June was merely a sideline. But Gail's lack of response at first irritated and then infuriated him. And then he began to grumble because the Castle was too quiet for his liking, and there were no bars and cinemas within reach, and no June Naughtons to fool around with. He became difficult and started bullying. Nothing that Gail could do was right.

It was impossible for Ian Dalmuir not to notice these things. Bill Cardew bickered with his wife in public! Seeing Gail again under such conditions had hit Ian harder than even he had anticipated. Keen though he was on his work, he found it difficult to put Gail out of his thoughts. Even when she was not in sight, he thought about her. The old passion which had overwhelmed him at Le Touquet burned even more fiercely today—and for another man's wife! That was what galled him. She was no longer his to love. She was the wife of a brother officer. And the awful truth was, that she never should have married Cardew. She should have waited for *him.*

He had braced himself to surmount the difficulties of living in the Loch Castle with her, but sometimes they seemed insurmountable. At meal-times he saw her ... must always see her sitting there alone with her husband, or flitting through the grounds of the Castle like the little ghost which was supposed to haunt the Loch. A pale, sad little Gail; not the laughing, radiant creature whom he had adored in Paris.

She tried to be that old Gail. He had seen her laughing and talking across the table to Bill. But he knew she wasn't happy. He knew

128

that from the furtive hungry glances which they exchanged from time to time. Tonight he knew it, when he looked down into her eyes. They held a baffled, almost childish look of sorrow as though she could not understand what was happening to her. And he realised that if this situation was unhappy for him, it was ten thousand times worse for her. After all, he was a man and had his job. But Gail was a woman and women were emotional, sensitive creatures to whom love and the happiness which comes with it, were all important. She was still so young, so tender . . . she, of all people, should have been happily married, he thought bitterly. It was a disaster that he, Ian, had come back into her life under such hopeless conditions.

Yet he could do nothing except suffer with her and for her. Pity himself, and more profoundly pity her. He, at least, had the satisfaction of being alone sometimes. But she was always with this man who was her husband.

At times it was more than Ian Dalmuir could endure, when his imagination ran riot on the subject of Gail and her husband.

There came one particular night when it was torture for him to look at her . . . that beauty of hers which made her shine like a star amongst all these other women in the room. Joyce Fenton was quite a pretty girl in her way; a fair, buxom, British type. Captain

Pitt's wife, Audrey, was considered a beauty, too. Marvellous red hair and fine figure. But there was something about Gail . . . a subtle something in the depths of those grey, black-lashed eyes; in the grace of that long slender throat; *(little swan neck,'* he used to call it) . . . in the transparency of her skin . . . he had never seen another like it. It had used to fascinate him to watch the burning colour leap to those soft cheeks in response to some word of passion or tenderness from him.

And now this was all for Bill Cardew.

'God!' thought Ian Dalmuir, and suddenly closed his eyes tightly as though to shut out the sight of her.

Before those eyes closed, Gail who was drinking her coffee near by, saw the look that leapt into them. She shivered from head to foot.

'He's remembering . . .' she thought, half-jubilant, yet wholly crushed by the futility of this passion which still so lucidly existed between them . . . 'oh, Ian, *Ian* . . .'

She came nearer him drawn as by a magnet.

'My . . . my husband says there's some big idea about getting up a dance for us next Saturday night.'

Ian opened his eyes again. He managed a grim smile.

'That would be quite unbearable,' he said, 'the idea must have come from our friend Mrs. Naughton.'

130

Gail took her cue from him and laughed back. That was what one must do, she told herself. Just laugh, and be casual and shut out these blinding memories of the past.

'Come, come, Ian, you know you adore dancing!'

'I did once,' he said.

Back came the past again. Memories of one wild unforgettable night in Paris. The *Quatre Arts* Ball. Carnival . . . confetti . . . paper caps . . . gay balloons . . . fantastic costumes. They had all gone to it. She, Ian, Simone and a young Frenchman who was an artist and who had got them the tickets.

Gail was a wood nymph in green chiffon draperies, with bronze leaves and violets clustering in her hair . . . 'The Spirit of Fontainebleau,' Ian had called her. And he was just a pierrot, but the black and white costume, the mask, had suited the dark-eyed, lithe young man. They had danced all night. Danced until dawn. Driving home exhausted and happy, she had lain in his arms while he had pointed out to her the beauty of the Arc de Triomphe against the opalescent sky.

Ian's voice cut in on her thoughts:

'Come back to Scotland, Gail. We're not in Paris tonight.' Her face and throat burned with colour.

'How did you know?'

'I saw the Spirit of Fontainebleau in your eyes.'

131

'You were a grand pierrot, Ian. So funny! Do you remember how you made me laugh?'

'Yes. And you were so sweet. The violets sewn to your dress were made of silk, but those in your hair were real, and the perfume of them was intoxicating.'

She bit her lip, conscious of the danger of such reminiscences, of such conversation.

'Come back to Scotland, Ian. We're not in Paris now,' she teased him with his own words.

'Damn it all,' he said under his breath, 'how right you are. I'd better think about a rubber of bridge with the Colonel.'

As she turned to leave him, he called her back:

'You *do* like being in my castle, don't you?'

'I love it. I love everything about it.'

'Be happy, dear,' he almost whispered the words.

'You, too,' she whispered back.

The smile they exchanged was an unspoken caress. The next moment Gail had left the big hall and was on her way upstairs to her sitting-room, thankful that Bill had decided to stay down and play bridge. She wanted to be alone, alone with her thoughts of *him*. But Mrs. Naughton and Joyce Fenton followed her.

She was not to be allowed the privilege of solitude this evening. Mrs. Naughton had just been told by Mr. Cardew that his wife was 'keen' to get up this dance. There was no escape for Gail now. She was dragged into

132

making the plans.

So eventually the dance took place. Some of the unmarried officers managed to arrange transport, despite petrol and blackout difficulties, for their girl friends from Edinburgh. The informal party grew into quite an extensive affair. Ian's housekeeper prepared one of the big reception rooms with a polished floor, for action. A big radio-gramophone supplied the music. The dance materialised.

Gail had the first three dances with her husband. He danced well. Bill always liked to show off when he did a thing well. He was conscious that they made a good-looking couple, and pleased that he had persuaded Gail to wear the most attractive dress in her trousseau, her long clinging dress of emerald green. Soft woolly material, with short sleeves and a little bow at the throat. A wide belt of sequins which glittered as she moved, and a little green sequin cape. She wore a sequin butterfly in her hair.

'There isn't a girl in the room to touch you,' Bill murmured ardently in her ear as they danced.

'Dear old Bill,' she murmured back and forced herself to add: 'And you're the best-looking man.'

He glanced over her shoulder as they revolved:

'Your friend Dalmuir looks as though he's

133

at a funeral. Doesn't he like dancing?'

Gail did not reply for a moment. She, too, looked in Ian's direction.

She had seen him do one or two courtesy dances, with the Colonel's wife and with Mrs. Naughton. Now he was standing by the fireplace, smoking. He seemed lost in contemplation of the big wood fire that leapt and crackled in the open grate. Poor Ian! She knew only too well how much he liked dancing. But she also knew what was passing through his mind now. Just those ruthless memories that would not leave either of them alone.

As far as the actual pleasure of dancing went, she enjoyed her fox-trots and one rumba with Bill. But not the way in which he would gloat over her. That was an awful habit of Bill's and it always made her spirit recoil.

He was indefatigable. As soon as he left Gail, he began dancing with Joyce Fenton who was looking particularly pretty tonight, her plump graces toned down somewhat by her black lace dress. Captain Fenton was a bad dancer and Joyce openly envied Gail.

'Aren't you lucky to have a husband who can move like Fred Astaire,' she called out, giggling as they passed.

Gail smiled and nodded.

'Very lucky!'

Then she saw Ian coming toward her. The moment he reached her side, she made a gesture of her hand almost as though to say:

134

'No.'

He knew that she was afraid to dance with him. But he was in a reckless mood. Bill Cardew was dancing with Joyce Fenton and Gail was alone. Little and lovely in her emerald dress with the little glittering cape, and the shining butterfly in her hair.

Wordlessly he put an arm around her and steered her on to the dance floor. Wordlessly she went with him whither he led her, and now it was as though the three years rolled completely back. This was not a stately Scottish castle in which they danced; not a dignified drawing-room with crystal chandeliers and floodlit water-colours by old Masters against satin panelled walls. This was the *Quatre Arts* Ball again and they were whirling together through time, through space, her curls barely reaching his heart, the pressure of his arm recalling a thousand poignant bitter sweet memories.

Somebody had put on an old favourite: 'Chloe.' It had been *their* favourite.

> '. . . no chains can bind you,
> If you live I'll find you.
> Love is calling me,
> I've got to go where you are. . .'

She had sung that to him in Paris with a provocative challenge which he had answered. But tonight she dared not sing it, dared not

135

provoke. She shut her eyes and wished that she might go on dancing with him into eternity, feeling the close beat of his strong heart under her cheek.

She heard his husky voice

'I used to call you "Chloe." Do you remember?'

'Yes.'

'We were happy then. Let's try to go on being happy.'

'Yes.'

He bent his face nearer to hers to catch her half-audible whisper.

'It is very hard . . . my dear, my dear . . . I know that we love each other still. That stands out a mile, but so much water has rolled under the bridge and we've got to make the best of it. It'll only wreck us both if we lack the courage to face it.'

'Yes,' again her lips formed rather than uttered the affirmative.

'Do you remember, we used to always say that the world was meant for happy people and that the miserable ones only contaminate those around them . . . infect others with their misery. We must never do that. We must never become miserable people.'

She put back her head and looked straight up into his eyes. She adored that little lecture from him because she knew perfectly well that he couldn't live up to it. She had never seen such naked pain in the eyes of any man. And

136

although she shared his pain, she also shared the ecstasy of what had been of what-might-have-been, between them.

'I love dancing with you again, Ian.'

'You haven't lost the art,' he smiled; the old swift brilliant smile which used to dispel his Celtic sadness suddenly and enchantingly.

In silence they went on dancing.

*'Chloe, Chloe! . . . I've got to go where you are! . . .'* said the music hauntingly, insistingly.

Through a kind of haze, Gail saw Bill executing nimble steps with Joyce Fenton. His white teeth were showing. He looked pleased with himself. He always looked pleased with himself. Gail envied him his self-confidence, the apparent pleasure which he extracted out of life, and particularly out of himself.

Dancing with Ian ceased to be a delight and became a torment; she said:

'I feel giddy . . . I think I must stop . . .'

Immediately he put a hand under her arm and drew her out of the room into the hall. Then she found herself in a room which she had not entered before. Ian's own private sitting-room which used to be his uncle's study. Very much a man's room. Tobacco-brown carpet, and brown walls hung with hunting scenes. Over the fireplace, a big oil-painting of a fierce-looking old gentleman wearing a kilt, carrying a staff, and with a balmoral on his head. Alister Ian Dalmuir, Ian's uncle and former Laird of Loch Castle.

Just for a moment Gail found peace in here. The door shut her away from the dance music, the crowd, Bill; transported her into another world in which there were only two people. Ian Dalmuir and herself.

He looked at her. His face was white and tense. He held out a hand and she knew then and there that if she placed hers in it, if she once allowed him to hold her, kiss her, she would be lost. As hopelessly lost as she had been in Le Touquet. Her own face was colourless. Only her rouged lips were red.

'Darling,' said Ian breathlessly, '*darling*, I think this is rather more than I can stand.'

## ELEVEN

But Gail did not take his hand, and although all that was most human in her hungered for his waiting embrace, she did not go into it. She knew that this was an occasion when *she* must be strong or there would be an end for ever of any possible peace of mind for either of them.

'Ian,' she said in a strangled voice, 'if there's one thing I want in this world, it's to let you kiss me. You know quite well what it would mean. So do I. Don't let's lose our heads completely, for God's sake.'

He had an instant's struggle with himself, then suddenly squared his shoulders and laughed. The light had gone out of his eyes

138

and the passion from his lips. He said:

'You're entirely right. A bit funny, the way I lectured you while we danced. And now you're returning the compliment.'

She made a gesture of despair. He found it very touching that she should have sensed the madness in him and beaten it off by her own strength. This slip of a thing with her large scared eyes. Yes, of course, she was scared of him and of herself. And he was a brute to put her to the test. Not that he had done it intentionally. It was dancing with her again that had sent him just a little bit crazy.

The glittering cape had come undone and was sliding off one of her shoulders. Somehow the sight of that bare defenceless shoulder roused extreme tenderness in him rather than passion. The tenderness that he had always felt for her. There was something so small and childlike about Gail. He found it impossible to think of her as a married woman.

He reached out a hand and gently put the cape back in its place.

'Sorry,' he said. 'It won't happen again.'

She drew in her breath. With the perversity of human nature she half wished now that she had not been so strong, so good. How she longed to feel those lips of his pressed against hers. Lips that had thrilled her beyond all reason three years ago. Lips which could so easily thrill her again to an even greater insanity. But there was a ring on her marriage

139

finger and there was Bill, her husband, dancing in that next room. (God help her!)

'It won't happen again,' repeated Ian.

Then she laughed.

'It may. I dare say it will. We're not made of stone, either of us, and once things between us were different; and if we go on living under the same roof for weeks and months, I shouldn't be at all surprised if I don't fling myself into your arms one day and *beg* you to kiss me.'

He took a cigarette from an ivory box on the desk, lit it, handed it to her, then lit one for himself

'You wouldn't have to beg, my dear.'

'Ian, I'm married !'

'Gail, my dear, I don't need reminding of that fact—no, that's wrong, perhaps I do. But you've reminded me very successfully.'

She seated herself on the edge of the desk. She felt that she could allow herself these few moments without fear now. They were both themselves again. She felt tired and hopeless.

'Why did this have to happen, Ian? Why should such hell have been detailed out to us '

'There's no answer to that question. My mother is responsible, but there you areóno good going over that old ground.'

'And I'm responsible,' she said in a hollow voice. 'I ought to have waited, oughtn't I ?' He shrugged his shoulders. 'You had no reason to. It looked as though I'd walked out on you, and

Cardew was on the spot.'

She bit hard into her lower lip.

'While we were dancing, you said that we must be happy and that we had always agreed that it was wrong to be miserable. So let's try. Let's go on trying.'

A short tussle with himself, then he evoked a smile, threw his cigarette into the fireplace, and held out his hand.

'That's a bargain. No, don't be afraid to take my hand. I want you to take it now.'

Her lips trembled and there were unshed tears in her eyes as she gave him that hand. He carried it very gently to his lips. She whispered:

'I need your friendship, Ian.'

'It's yours, Gail. That is, if friendship is possible between us.' 'It's got to be.'

'Then we'll have a shot at it. But Gail, don't let him bully you . . .'

She went scarlet and her head dropped. At once he was sorry he had said the words. He apologised.

'Forgive me, dear. 'Tisn't my business . . . but. . . .'

'I know,' she broke in, 'but he doesn't mean it. It's his way. He's devoted to me, really.'

Ian's dark eyes held a world of envy.

'He ought to *worship* you. If you were my wife . . . but what the hell? Let's go back to the others. I'm going to fade out of this party if you don't mind, Gail. The Brigadier and the

141

Brigade Major have drifted down to the library for bridge, and I think I'll join them.'

'I should if I were you,' she said, 'but I must go back and help the others make something of this dance.'

He gave her a long look . . . from the crown of the curly head to the tips of the small green slippered feet, he looked hungrily at her. He said:

'Give all the other fellows a dance, and the evening will be a success for them all right. You're an adorable person, Gail. Much too adorable. That's the trouble.'

He opened the door and she passed out in front of him, fighting her tears, longing to rush up to her room and cry, knowing that she must go back to the room and dance.

She stood an instant by the banisters and watched him walk down the wide circular staircase to the library. She knew herself to be still hopelessly and wildly in love with him as she watched him go. So tall, so handsome in those tartan trousers, and khaki tunic. Ian, the soldier, the matured man, so much more attractive even than he had been as the boy, in Paris.

Bill appeared, strolling out of the drawing-room with a glass in his hand.

'Hi! Where've you been, Gail? I've been looking for you.' The tears dried on her lashes and she smiled at her husband.

'Well, here I am.'

He glanced over the banisters and saw the top of Ian's black head.

'There's old Dalmuir going down below to play a rubber, I suppose. Thought you were dancing with him. Couldn't you make yourself sweet enough to keep him at it?'

Gail's smile was very set now.

'Apparently not, Bill.'

He grumbled at her.

'Have you been handing out the frozen mitt like you do to everyone else? I do wish you'd put yourself out to be nice to Dalmuir. You know—'

'Oh, don't nag, Bill,' she broke in, her nerves fraying.

He glowered at her. He was flushed after his success at dancing with Mrs. Fenton who had been flattering, him, and he didn't want his evening spoilt by his wife.

'I wasn't nagging! But good lord, you can be a bit more charming when you want to. Honestly, you're not the same girl that I knew in Kingston.'

She made no answer. But she thought drearily how right he was. She wasn't at all that same Gail. How could she be? That Gail had buried the past and faced life again as a normal, contented person. That Gail had learned to do without Ian, even though his memory haunted her. That Gail had managed to fall in love again . . . with Bill Cardew. But *this* Gail had had her whole emotional life

143

upset all over again by the re-entrance into it of her first lover. This Gail was a baffled and tormented creature continually torn between what she knew she ought to do, and what she wanted to do.

But she tried to remember what Ian had just said about miserable people contaminating others. She held out a hand to Bill with an enchanting little plea for pardon which would have softened any man's heart

'Come and dance with me, husband,' she said.

His brow cleared. He finished his drink, and with an arm about her, walked back into the drawing-room.

She did not see Ian again that night. She did everything she could to please Bill and make herself charming and amusing to the others. When they were up in their room Bill complimented her on being a big success.

'I must say you look a treat in that dress, darling. And I heard Jean Naughton tell the Major that you'd helped to make the whole evening go with a swing.'

'I'm glad,' she said.

She was sitting on the edge of the bed in her pink satin slip, peeling off her silk stockings. For a moment she held out her bare toes to the warmth of the wood fire. They were all spoilt in the Castle, even to fires in their bedrooms. She yawned, conscious of immense fatigue both of the mind and the body.

Bill, who was in bed before her, said:

'Hurry up. What are you mooning for?'

'Just thinking.'

'Well, how about kissing me instead?'

She shut her eyes. She thought:

'Not only tonight, but tomorrow and tomorrow *and tomorrow*. All the days and nights that I live . . . they must be lived with Bill . . . subservient to Bill. How am I going to bear it?'

In utter despair she looked back on that day on which war had been declared, when she had promised to marry Bill. If only she could get back to that moment, and be reincarnated in that Gail who had thrilled to Bill's kiss, Bill's touch. But it was all dead and gone within her. It had been an ephemeral passion without real substance. A passion born of war excitement, war fever, hero worship because Bill had joined up . . . and a loneliness within her which had wanted to be dispelled. A loneliness which she had felt ever since Ian went out of her life.

It had seemed such fun, being married, and to an old friend from home. And perhaps if Ian had never returned it would have gone on being fun, even although Bill could be horrid and disagreeable at times. There were plenty of other times when he was the reverse. But now, *now* she couldn't love him any more. And her marriage had only just begun.

She wondered what her mother would say to

all this. Poor Mummy! She would be horrified. Every letter she wrote from home, Mrs. Partner expressed the hope that her girl was happy. She would be heart-broken to learn the facts. She must never be told. Nobody must be told, thought Gail. She had made a ghastly mistake, but that was her fault . . . and the fault of that misguided woman, Ian's mother, who had thought it best to separate her son from his girl friend of Paris days. Separate them for ever.

'Do come on, Gail,' said Bill complainingly, and switched out the light over his head.

The room was plunged in darkness except for the flickering light from the fire which played upon Gail, shimmering against the pink satin of her slip. Her face looked pale, beautiful and intensely sad.

She would have liked to have gone on sitting there dreaming in the firelight. It was so peaceful. But Bill did not, could not, see things from her point of view. He suddenly sat up in bed and began a fresh onslaught against her.

'I do think you're a bit standoffish with Dalmuir. What's at the bottom of it? Didn't you like him when you knew him before?'

'Yes.'

'Well, you behave whenever you see him as if you want to avoid him like the plague. And he must notice it. Considering he owns this place and is my superior officer, I—'

'Yes, yes, I know, Bill, just how you feel

146

about it,' she said, and continued with her undressing.

'What's wrong with the man anyhow? Either he's got a perpetual liver or a broken heart. Was there some woman in his life?'

Her hands clenched so that the points of her nails dug into her palms.

'I . . . couldn't tell you.'

'Well, I should think he's been turned down by some girl,' said Bill as though it gave him some satisfaction.

In the firelight, Gail's face assumed a slightly cynical expression, but she made no answer.

'Anyhow, for God's sake,' added Bill, 'make yourself more pleasant to him. In fact, I'm going to ask him to come up to our sitting-room and have a drink with us tomorrow night.'

Her eyes shut. She prayed inwardly for patience.

'Don't do that,' she said before she could stop herself. Bill switched on the light again, his face aggrieved.

'Now there you go! The moment one mentions the fellow, you get all snotty. I tell you, Gail, it's worth our while to cultivate Dalmuir. I've no use for him as a personal friend, but he's damned important to me in my career. And it's up to you to support me. Please ask him, yourself, to come and have a cocktail with us.'

147

'We can all have one downstairs.'

'Yes, where he'll be got at by the rest of the crowd. I'm not the only one who thinks he's worth knowing. One can never get a word in. I want to talk to him about my future. If you don't ask him up, I will.'

'Very well,' said Gail hopelessly.

He looked at her, prepared to nag further. Then he chose to remember what a success she had scored at the dance this evening, and he felt more amiably disposed toward her, added to which she was looking lovely in that mist-blue négligée, with the little nine swansdown cape.

He held out a hand.

'Come here, my lovely.'

She went toward him, moving like clockwork. She had not the slightest desire to take that outstretched hand, nor respond to the kisses that would follow. She thought how dreadful it was to be married to a man and not want to kiss him any more. Dreadful to know that sleeping somewhere under this roof was another man whom she so adored that she dared not take his hand when it was held out to her.

In an agony of mind she wondered what could possibly be the end of it all. But one thing stood out clearly. She could not go on like this too long. She would have to make an excuse of some kind and get away from the Loch Castle. Go back home to the family.

Anything rather than face the continual strain of the present situation between Ian, Bill, and herself.

## TWELVE

Another week passed. A week of great emotional stress for Gail who swerved dangerously between the old flaming desire for Ian Dalmuir and her very genuine wish to remain loyal to the man she had married.

A week of trying to avoid Ian, gaining a little peace when he was absent, losing it again every time she caught sight of him, heard his voice, exchanged a smile or a word. A week of trying to do what Bill wanted, even going to the lengths of issuing special invitations to Ian to come up to their private sitting-room. A week of the 'other wives' . . . scandal, gossip, bridge playing, teas, cocktails, and the general boredom of this peculiar, stagnant war which never seemed to move a step farther.

Long hours of inner loneliness for Gail, the inner struggle which rarely ceased. Solitude in which to remember the past and wonder hopelessly what lay before her. Moments of extreme happiness in which feverish passion played no part, and instead there was a renewal of that heavenly comradeship which had existed between Ian and herself in France.

At the very end of October, one fine frosty afternoon when she was walking alone through the park, she met Ian in the company of a grey-haired old man wearing a kilt, and with a balmoral on his head. He had a couple of red setters on a leash. Ian introduced them. The old man was what they called in Scotland, the Grieve of the estate at the head of the many farms which belonged to the Dalmuirs. Gail shook hands with him, struck by his dignity and that rare charm which she was beginning to recognise in the people of this country. A kindliness which lies under a bluff exterior, an honest integrity of purpose which belongs, perhaps, to no other nation.

And though she found it difficult to understand some of the things which the old man said with his broad burr, she judged that to him, his master, Ian Dalmuir was a superman. A young god whom every man, woman, and child on the Castle estate adored.

For forty years the Grieve had served the old Laird, and he had known young Ian from the time he was first brought here by his mother, a tiny boy wearing his first kilt.

'A rare lad for mischief he was,' the old Grieve said. 'I can believe that,' said Gail.

She and Ian smiled into each other's eyes. And she thought how adorable he must have been, that little dark-eyed boy, with his bright roguish eyes, his thick dark curls, and the healthy red colour stung into his cheeks by the cold north winds. And here he was today, a tall grave soldier, but the devil was still there, lurking behind that gravity, and well she knew it.

Ian introduced her to the two dogs, Dougal and Morag. And there followed for her one of the most attractive hours that she had spent so far up in Scotland. For Ian was going a round of the farms with the old man, and Gail was invited to go with them.

The afternoon was perfect, with a golden glow in the west which would soon be changing to fiery red as the sun sank lower. There was that touch of frost in the air, keen and fresh, which sent a healthy glow through her whole body. The recent storms had swept nearly every leaf from the trees, but there lingered still the ardent tints of the copper beeches, the burnished bronze of the maple, and the everlasting green of the fir trees which, Ian told her, looked so lovely later on, when powdered with snow. They walked on a scarlet carpet of fallen leaves. The setters barked furiously and strained at the leash every time they startled a rabbit in the thicket or sent a bird winging up through the branches of the tall trees. The place was alive with pheasants. Plenty of shooting for those among the officers who cared for it.

And now beyond the Castle grounds, they came to the open fields, and Gail was introduced to the local farmers in their little grey stone houses which were built so sternly and strongly, fortified against the bitter winters which they had to face up here. The blue peat smoke curled softly from the chimney stacks. The women with their plaid shawls came out with their babies on their arms to greet their young Laird. They looked with shy curiosity at the young English lady in her smart tweeds, with the fashionable silk scarf tied over her curls.

It was obvious to Gail that they all worshipped Ian. And it gave her a poignant pleasure to see the way he talked with the women. The gentle fashion in which he would uncover the shawl from a baby's face, admire the infant, or joke with one of the small children who hung to its mother's skirts. Wherever he went, blessings were called down upon him. The old Grieve, watching him talk with one of the farmers, turned to Gail and said:

'Aye, there's no been a Dalmuir at the head of this Castle more popular than our young Captain. A rare one he is for doing a kindness whether it's putting a new roof on for a cowman, or giving money to them that need it.'

Gail nodded and felt a personal pride in the tall young officer beside whom she walked. And she felt that now she had gone these rounds with him, there was an even greater intimacy between them, a closer understanding of him and his kith and kin.

152

As they walked up the steps of the Castle together, he said:

'I'm glad you came with me, Gail. I like you to know my people. Somehow the Loch Castle is even more my home than the house in which I was born and bred. The people have always known me as my uncle's heir and their future Laird.'

'I understand,' she said. 'And somehow I feel you fit in here absolutely. I can imagine you leaving the Army one day and settling down in your Castle for ever.'

He gave her a quick look, then turned as though the sight of her hurt . . . He laughed.

'That was what I had planned to do, Gail, but I think I'm too restless now. Everything has changed.'

She understood what he meant and her heart was heavy within her. But nothing could take from her the mental uplift of this afternoon in his and the old Grieve's company.

Ian had said that at any time she wanted, she might go down to the kennels, find Dougal and Morag and take them for walks. That would be something to look forward to.

At the same time, she knew deep down in her heart, that the longer she stayed here, the closer she grew to Ian spiritually, the worse it would be for her in the long run—for them both, indeed. And at times like this, when all her soul seemed to rush out to meet his on a plane quite apart from their physical longing

153

for each other, she had a frantic wish to run away. Right away from Ian, from Bill, from the Castle.

She found her husband walking up and down their sitting-room with a look on his face which made her heart sink. He was obviously in a 'mood.' And the room was as untidy as only Bill could make it. Gas mask, cane, coat in a heap on the floor where he had flung them. Newspapers littered all over the sofa. A jumble of papers and maps connected with his work spread over the table. Not a chair that had not got some belonging of Bill's upon it. And, of course, he would not dream of tidying them. He would leave that to her just as he had always left things for his mother.

She took off her scarf and ran her hand through her curls. She felt flushed and healthy after the long walk through the fields and park with Ian and the Grieve.

Determined to be cheerful, she greeted her husband with a smile.

'Hullo, Billy Boy. What's up with you? You look as though something's annoyed, you.'

'So it damn well has,' he said.

'What?'

'Being mucked about by the Army,' he said. 'One's always mucked about. Just as I've settled down here, I'm being sent away.'

Her heart missed a beat and she stood still.

'Sent away?'

'Yes, temporarily, anyhow. Orders from

H.Q. The. Brigade Major had a word with me at tea-time. By the way, where were *you?*'

'Out for a walk. What did the Major say?'

'Well, of course, it's all due to the fact that I'm good at my job. They're sending me to Glasgow, Aberdeen and possibly Invergordon. Got to start some fellows there on this same course. It means being away a fortnight or even three weeks.'

'I see,' said Gail slowly, 'and do I go with you?'

'No, damn it . . .' he came and put an arm around her possessively, 'that's just what I'm annoyed about. I can't possibly take you. And I don't suppose you'll want to stay here in this god-forsaken place without me, so you'd better go home to Kingston until I'm sent back here, which is the present arrangement.'

And he did not mention the fact that part of his aggravation was caused by his knowledge that there would be a chance now of his missing June Naughton's visit to the Castle. He had looked forward to that.

Gail neither moved nor spoke. Her feelings were so mixed, she could scarcely analyse them. She was glad . . . sorry . . . relieved . . . disappointed.

Hadn't this been what she had wanted . . . a chance to get away from Ian and her turbulent feelings about him? Wasn't it just what they both needed . . . Complete separation again!

Yet it would be hard to say good-bye to him,

155

and to all this . . . this glorious home of his which Bill chose to call 'a god-forsaken spot.'

'I expect you're fed up about it too,' said Bill, giving her a little hug. 'I know you won't want to be away from me.'

Gail cleared her throat and moved uneasily under his arm.

'Of course not.'

'Well, you'd better write to Kingston and let Mother know as well as your people, won't you?'

'When do you go?'

'Tomorrow morning.'

'As soon as that?' she said with a sense of shock.

'Yes, the Major wants me to catch the first train in the morning to Glasgow. There seems some hurry about it all.'

'How can I possibly be ready by then?'

'You can't. You'll have to stay a day and pack up and get off the day after tomorrow. Dalmuir will probably arrange for you to be driven in to Edinburgh to get the ten o'clock.'

Gail moved away from him and walked through to her bedroom to change her things. She felt a little dazed. This was so unexpected. And she could think of nothing but Ian . . . Ian. Of course, the more she thought about it, the more thankful she was for this respite. It would be really rather marvellous getting back to her old home away from this secret torment which pursued her both inside the Castle and out of it, so long as Ian was here.

After dinner that night she spoke to Ian and mentioned her coming departure.

Whatever he felt about it, his face betrayed nothing.

'It'll be nice for you to get back to England,' he said. 'And the job they've given Cardew shows how well he's getting on.'

'Yes, he's very good at his work,' said Gail.

Silence between them.

Ian Dalmuir looked down at her with bitter regret. God, he couldn't tell her so, but he was going to miss her like hell. No matter what the strain was, he loved seeing her here in his home. It had given him a tremendous 'kick' taking her round the estate today. It was one of the things he had planned to do years ago, only he had meant that she should walk beside him as his wife.

Then, mentally, he pulled himself up. Much better that she should go away. Better for them both. They were only human and eventually the strain of it all might get them both down. For it wasn't as though he ever felt that he was committing the sin of loving another man's wife. On the contrary, he felt resentful that Cardew should be her husband. Because first of all, she had been *his*. *And in spirit she was still his, and he knew it.*

In the early morning, Bill Cardew left the Loch Castle. It was still dark when one of the Divisional cars came to fetch him into the station. He sat on the edge of Gail's bed and bade her good-bye with all the old charm which had first drawn her to him. Bill at his best. Thoughtful for her and obviously annoyed at having to leave her.

'Take care of yourself, darling. Don't get hit by a bomb or anything stupid like that.'

'The same to you, Bill,' she said.

He held her to him tightly.

'And remember that you belong to me,' he said with a sudden rough passion. 'I'll be crazy to get back to you.'

She shivered a little, but did not let him see that she could scarcely share that insatiable desire of his; neither would she let him know the relief it was going to be to her to have three weeks 'on her own.' His parting words made her feel half ironic, half ashamed.

'And for God's sake, be nice to Dalmuir. I want to get back here, not because I like the damned Castle, but because it puts me well in with H.Q.'

So typical of Bill! She smiled and promised that she would 'be nice' to Dalmuir. Then he was gone, and she was left alone. Yes, she thought, really alone for the first time since her marriage which was barely two months old. Two months too long. And only the beginning of what she must face for the rest of her life.

She spent the rest of that day writing letters and packing up. Ian was arranging for her to be driven into Edinburgh.

158

After tea, since another glorious sunset was indicated, she decided to go down to the kennels, find the setters and take them for a walk. On her way back she did not go straight in to join the others. They were dears, really, Mrs. Naughton, Joyce Fenton, and the others. And they were going to give her a special cocktail party tonight as a 'send-off,' but she wanted to savour the last shreds of glamour which could be extracted from Ian's home.

In the left wing of the Castle there was an old 'secret staircase' which Ian had once shown her. One of his favourite hiding places as a boy. The steep stone steps, centuries old, worn down with the imprint of mailed feet, wound upwards to the left tower. Here there was a kind of guardroom which had been used for prisoners in former days. The iron barred windows commanded an incredibly beautiful view. And at this hour the countryside had an unearthly glamour, when the western sky was streaked with orange and red from the setting sun. Through the blue mists across the forests and the moors, lay Edinburgh. It would not be discernible until those mists rolled away with the dawn.

Gail stood a moment in the little turret room, admiring the great wide oaken boards of the floor, the massive beams overhead, and the tattered remnants of banners which hung from the walls. They had been put here for safety when the Castle was threatened by

159

an enemy clan in the days of James I. There was a huge oak trestle table carved with the names of prisoners. Gail passed a small gloved hand over the table, wishing she might carve her own name there. For she, too, was a prisoner. A prisoner in her mind and in her heart, and she could never get out Eventually, she thought, she would die of her love, just as prisoners died serving lifelong sentences.

It was growing dark and cold. She supposed she had better leave this lonely historic spot and go down to the inhabited part of the Castle. She took a last fond look out at the gathering mists which were wreathing park and farmland. She murmured:

'Good-bye, my lovely Castle! Good-bye to Scotland! Goodbye to Ian, perhaps for always. Things change so in the Army. When I come back—if I come back—he may be gone!'

Sighing, she turned and walked down the staircase. Then (how it happened, she never quite knew), before she reached the end of the spiral, her foot suddenly slipped. She felt herself falling and made a violent effort to recover her balance, but failed. She went down; down only three or four steps, but enough to bruise every part of her body, and she felt a sickening pain shoot through an ankle as it bent under her. She landed at the bottom of the stairs, a humiliated bundle of pain and discomfort, and discovered that she could not get up. She must either have broken her leg or twisted her ankle, she told herself. And she knew that she could lie here and scream for hours and nobody would hear her. There was a long stone pas sage between her and the massive oaken door which led into the residential part of the Castle.

She could, of course, crawl. But when she tried to do so, it made her feel sick. She started to shiver from head to foot. It was ice-cold on the stone floor and growing rapidly dark.

She groaned to herself:

'You fool, Gail! You absolute idiot to do a thing like this . . .'

The effort at crawling to the door, however, was no longer necessary. And her fears of having to stay here half the night, frozen and famished, before being found, soon faded. For by the grace of God, Ian Dalmuir had taken it into his head to come here this evening. Not to look at the view from the old guardroom, but to find an antique weapon which lay in a cupboard up there and which he wished to show to the General, who was interested in such trophies.

The moment he opened the door and entered the passage, flashing his electric torch, the crestfallen little figure of Gail Cardew huddled on the ground was revealed to him. He hurried toward her with a cry.

'Good God What *has* happened? What in the name of heaven are you doing here, Gail?'

She was so relieved to see him that she burst

into tears. Half laughing, half crying, she made her explanation.

'I can't be more sorry, Ian. But I seem to have broken my leg or done in my ankle, or something. It hurts frightfully.'

Leaving the torch shining so that it illuminated her, he knelt down and put an arm under her shoulders.

'You poor little darling! You're ice-cold. How long have you been lying here?'

'Only a few minutes actually. I was just coming down the spiral staircase when I fell.'

'Well, thank God, I came along to fetch that pistol for the General. Look here, darling, you can't walk. You mustn't set foot to the ground until the doctor's seen what's gone wrong. And I'm not going to carry you. That might do more harm than good, if it's a fracture. I'll fetch a couple of the servants, and we'll put you on an Army stretcher. We've got one here.'

She controlled the desire to weep and laughed up at him.

'It's really too stupid.'

He bent down to her, anxiously searching her face.

'You might have been killed. You might have struck your head on those stone stairs.'

'I'm not dead yet. Just a mass of bruises . . .'

'Oh, Gail, my poor little sweet . . .'

'And I've got to get right. You know I'm leaving Edinburgh tomorrow.'

He shook his head.

'I don't think that's likely now. I should think you'll be spending the next week or so with your leg up. Right here in this very Castle.'

She did not answer. Her heart was beating too rapidly. Another jest on the part of Fate! A trick to keep them here together despite all their efforts to separate.

He knew what was passing in her mind. His own heart was pounding. Then he saw that one of her hands was grazed. She had struck it on the edge of the stair trying to save herself. He whipped out a silk handkerchief, bound up the little hand, and put his lips against it.

'I can't bear to see you in pain,' he said huskily. 'Lie still a moment, darling, and I'll fetch the men.'

'Thank you,' she whispered, her breath faint and sweet upon his cheek.

And she thought:

'I *mustn't* stay . . . I dare not . . . yet if I can't travel, what can I do? It means I *must* stay, and without Bill . . . quite alone. . . . Where Ian can see me, speak to me, be with me day after day.'

She dared think no farther. The thrill of her thoughts raced too feverishly alongside the pain of her injured leg. Intoxicating, dangerous thoughts, beyond her control.

## THIRTEEN

Gail's accident caused something of a sensation in the Castle. Two of the Army batmen carried her on a stretcher into the big hall and up the wide staircase where she was seen first by Mrs. Naughton and then by two of the other 'wives' who at once gathered round with words of consternation and sympathy.

Gail's face was white and her teeth were set, for she was feeling the pain of her ankle, badly, by this time. But she managed a smile.

'Isn't it silly? Anybody would think I'd been having a private war of my own with someone. Do I look like an air raid casualty?'

'You look as though you want a drop of brandy,' said Mrs. Naughton, 'and if it's just a sprain, I've got some wonderful stuff. My husband had a riding accident out in India—'

She was cut short by Ian who had been walking beside the stretcher, his anxious gaze resting on Gail's white young face.

'I think it's a bit more than a sprain, Mrs. Naughton. But if you would be kind enough to ask for some brandy I think it would do Mrs. Cardew a lot of good.'

Jean Naughton hastened to perform that service. She was never happier than when she was doing something of this kind. If there was any sort of a 'show,' as she called it, she liked

164

to be 'in it.'

The men reached the doorway of Gail's bedroom. She looked up at Ian and his eyes looked down at hers, warm and caressing, compassionate for her pain.

'Perhaps Mrs. Fenton and one of the maids will help you to get to bed. I'm going down to phone for the M.O. from Edinburgh.'

'Thank you,' she whispered.

Perforce he left her, although it was the last thing he wanted to do. Joyce Fenton, who had just dressed for dinner, came running from her room to help. Gail was lifted on to the bed by the two soldiers and left there. One of them respectfully and cheerfully saluted her and wished her luck, as he departed.

'We'll be painting a Red Cross over this place like they done at Edinburgh Castle, Mam,' he grinned at her.

Gail laughed and thanked him. Nice boys both of them . . . and they looked so young in their ill-fitting rough khaki uniforms. The one who had spoken, blue-eyed, curly-headed, made her think of Chris, her young brother.

She was ashamed to find tears of sheer weakness and shock coursing down her cheeks as she lay back on her pillows. Joyce Fenton started to help her take off her clothes.

'However did it happen, my dear?' Joyce asked sympathetically.

Gail explained how she had slipped and fallen down the stairs.

'Quite idiotic and I'm supposed to be going to London tomorrow.'

She grimaced with pain when Joyce took off one of the shoes and exposed a badly bruised and swelling ankle.

'That's hurts a lot,' she added.

Joyce touched the foot gingerly.

'Lord! It doesn't look to me as though you'll be able to walk on this for some time.'

Gail bit hard at her lip. There in a corner of the room stood two suit-cases which she had packed yesterday, all ready for the old home . . . well, now they'd have to be unpacked. It was all such a nuisance. And she would have to wire Mummy, and Bill's mother, and Bill himself who would be writing to Kingston. She began to feel depressed and disappointed because she would not now be seeing her family. She would just have to lie up here in this room, knowing that Ian was somewhere downstairs, and that she could not see him unless he paid her a casual and formal visit.

The first flush of intoxication which had been hers when she had realised that the accident had necessitated her staying at Loch Castle, had passed. What was the use of being ecstatic, of thinking emotionally about Ian? It was all so hopeless. Nothing really to look forward to but Bill's return which meant a return to the old bondage in which she had placed herself by her mistaken marriage.

Mrs. Naughton came back with the brandy.

And Ian announced from outside the door that he had got on to Major Willis, the M.O., and that he was coming straight out to see her.

The two women helped her into a nightgown and made her as comfortable as they could until the doctor's arrival.

Gail found herself shivering. The pain of her leg and the shock of the accident were beginning to tell on her nervous system. She found it hard to control her tears. She was glad when Jean and Joyce left her alone to go down to their dinner.

'We'll send her up some nice soup,' said Mrs. Naughton. 'That's the best thing for you this evening, my dear.'

Gail did not protest. Mrs. Naughton could 'boss' her to her heart's content. Gail hadn't the heart to argue, nor did she really want anything to eat.

She lay with closed eyes remembering only that moment when Ian had knelt beside her and kissed the hand which he had bandaged with his handkerchief. That handkerchief was still around her fingers. She lifted it and put it against her lips. A faint fragrance emanated from it. Tobacco, a masculine scent that was essentially *Ian.* And she loved him, she thought, oh God! so much too much! She hardly knew how she was going to endure it.

Within half an hour, Major Willis, the Medical Officer, had arrived at the Castle. Mrs. Naughton constituted herself as 'assistant nurse,' and helped him when he made his examination.

The injury was not as bad as Ian Dalmuir had imagined. There were no broken bones. Only a severe sprain which was painful enough, a mass of bruises on Gail's left side where she had fallen, and the cut on her hand.

She was soon bandaged and made more comfortable. The Major, a big genial man, grinned at her.

'First real casualty I've attended to since the war broke out except for a couple of influenza cases,' he said.

Gail smiled back.

'Awfully stupid of me, Major Willis.'

'Husband only went off this morning, I hear.'

'Yes.'

'That's what happens when a man leaves his wife behind him, eh?'

'Oh, he didn't expect me to go falling down secret staircases,' she said ruefully.

'Oh well, well, we'll soon have you right. Only you must keep that leg up and not attempt to use it, until I give the word.'

'How long must I stay in bed?'

'A few days,' he said, 'and then you can get up on a sofa.'

'I'm supposed to be going to London tomorrow.'

'Well, if you do, it'll be by ambulance.'

Another rueful laugh from Gail.

168

'Then I shan't go.'

Major Willis, washing his hands in the basin at the corner of the room, looked round and nodded.

'Charming room. The whole place is magnificent, of course. Lucky chaps to be billeted here. And I've never met a nicer fellow in my life than Dalmuir.'

Gail looked at Ian's handkerchief. It was lying on the bed. Her scraped fingers had now been properly bandaged.

'Yes, he's awfully nice,' she said in a low voice.

'Full of brains, too. There were brilliant reports of him in India. I got that from my brother, Colonel Willis, who was out in Delhi with him.'

It gave Gail a warm feeling to hear things like that said about Ian. She wished that Major Willis would say more. But he had switched on to another subject. And a few moments later he shook hands with her, thanked Mrs. Naughton for her assistance, and was gone. He would look in and see the ankle tomorrow, he said, and meanwhile she'd better get some rest. He left a sleeping powder with Mrs. Naughton. The fall had shaken little Mrs. Cardew up properly, he said. She might need a good night.

After he had gone, Mrs. Naughton fussed around, and with her, she brought a new arrival to the Castle. Her young daughter,

June.

'I've brought the child to see you, and hope you don't mind,' said Mrs. Naughton as she introduced Gail to the 'child' who was, as far as Gail could see, at the age of nineteen, a fully-fledged woman of the world.

Mrs. Naughton had been boosting her up for days before her arrival. She obviously adored the 'one and only' and wanted everybody else to know it, and there was no doubt that she was blissfully unaware of the true nature of her daughter. June was the appealing and innocent debutante to her parents and congratulated herself that she had them fooled.

It had been an extreme disappointment to her to arrive at the Castle and find that Mr. Cardew was away, further up North. Indeed, she had felt almost sick with disappointment. For, although she had not heard from Bill since their little 'flutter' in London, she had anticipated an amusing reopening of the affair. However, her heart was elastic and her spirits very volatile, and one look at the tall handsome poetic-looking young officer who owned the Loch Castle caused a readjustment of her feelings.

Besides, Bill was married, and Ian Dalmuir was single. There might be even more fun with Ian.

She shook hands languidly with the girl in the bed. She had no interest in Bill's wife,

170

merely regarded it as a bit of a bore that she existed. But June 'did her stuff.'

'Terribly tough for you, hurting your ankle like this,' she said, and added casually, 'you know I met your husband at the twenty-first birthday party of a friend of mine in town.'

'Yes, he told me,' said Gail with her charming, friendly smile.

'I'm just thrilled with this castle,' added June, 'it's too divine, and as for its owner...'

She paused, lifted starry blue eyes heavenwards and clicked her fingers, the bracelets jangling.

Mrs. Naughton laughed.

'Isn't she naughty! Such a one for picking the winners, you know. And the moment I introduced her to the boys she singled out dear Captain Dalmuir and said that he was her ideal.'

'I think he's *too* devastating,' said June, patting a curl into place.

Gail lay speechless, staring from mother to daughter. She was flummoxed. Nothing quite like June Naughton had come her way before. She had seen the prototype sitting on high stools at cocktail bars, seen photographs of them at 'Deb' dances, but at Kingston her own young friends had been a goad deal more homely and unaffected. She wondered how on earth Jean Naughton, who was definitely a homely sort herself, and the kind and unassuming Major, had managed to produce

171

this ultra-modern young woman with her theatrical effects.

'I can see there'll be competition amongst our subalterns,' said Mrs. Naughton with an arch smile as she bent over Gail to tuck in the bedclothes.

'I'm sure there will,' said Gail and wondered what 'dear Captain Dalmuir' thought of June. There could be no denying her physical attraction.

June bade her good night, murmured a few more suitable words of sympathy and departed.

Mrs. Naughton continued to fuss around and made Gail drink some Ovaltine which she did not really want.

'Of course, you'll think I'm a match-making mother,' she said, 'but I think it would be the most wonderful thing in the world if Ian Dalmuir fell for my little June. They'd make a wonderful pair. He's so tall and dark and she's so tall and fair. I wonder if he's heart-whole. You knew him before, didn't you? Has he ever been engaged?'

Gail had little to say on this subject of Ian. She dispensed with Mrs. Naughton and her rhapsodies about June as soon as possible. Mrs. Naughton gave her the sleeping-powder, then opened the window, taking all due precautions first of all, to turn out the lights.

'We have to be so careful of the black-out,' she said. Gail thanked her. She had been very

172

kind and helpful. And she could not but help wondering if Jean Naughton ever did anything incorrectly. She was the sort of woman who seemed to dot her 'i's' and cross her 't's' without failing.

After she had gone, Gail lay still, glad of some slight relief of pain in the ankle, hoping that the sleeping-draught would take effect.

Her thoughts were so confused, so wild tonight. She couldn't get her bearings. *Couldn't see straight.* Couldn't force herself to concentrate on the memory of the man to whom legally she belonged. Her thoughts were all downstairs with Ian Dalmuir, the man whom Major Willis had just said was 'the nicest fellow he had ever met.'

She tried to work out in her mind what other women might do in her circumstances. But she couldn't place anyone that she knew in her shoes. It was ridiculous, for instance, to imagine Mrs. Naughton in the grip of a *'grande passion'* for any man. She just wasn't built that way. And Joyce Fenton . . . never! She was too solid and unimaginative. She would accept marriage as a part of life to be played like any other. Strictly according to rules.

Perhaps that was the trouble, Gail argued with herself. *She* wasn't playing according to the rules. But then, what *were* the rules? It was right that a wife should forsake all others for her husband once she took a husband, and— if she carried out those vows in the marriage service to the letter—she must worship him, share everything with him, love, honour, and obey him, and be faithful to him until death.

Fine, gallant words . . . ambitious words . . .! And she had meant them all when she had said them, at Bill's side in the church at home. But if it had been Ian, her heart's love, whom she had married, she could have kept them. Yes, to the very letter. She would have worshipped him and been faithful to him till she died. The trouble was that she had married the wrong man in a mad moment, because she had thought Ian lost to her. And what about the rules of the game now that Ian had come back into her life? By rights, she supposed she should ignore the fact; ignore the voice of her heart and remain obstinately interested in Bill. But that wouldn't be human. And since Fate had flung Ian across her path so dangerously, how *could* she ignore him? How could she blind herself to the fact that he meant just as much to her now as he had meant in France, three years ago? How could anybody wipe out the past when it so materially affected the present? And now, remembering what Mrs. Naughton had said about Ian and June, the most blind and unreasoning jealousy possessed her. She knew that she had no right to feel it. No right at all. But it consumed her and left her in a state of blind panic. Just the idea that this pretty girl who was free and unattached *might* easily turn any man's head . . . and that man might be Ian. June was going to be here for a fortnight. She would see a lot of him, and it was obvious that both mother and daughter were going to make a dead set at Ian. And even although June was not his type, he might be flattered, and because he was miserable about *her* . . . he might just turn to June on the rebound! Well, and if he did, what right had she, Gail, to resent it, she asked herself wretchedly.

The sleeping-powder was long in taking effect. Her mind was so uneasy and her body felt hot and feverish.

Mrs. Naughton and Joyce Fenton both put their heads in last thing to see if she wanted anything, and to say good night.

'If you can't sleep, just bang on the floor. I'm right underneath you, and I'll come up,' said Jean.

Gail thanked her. She wouldn't want anything, she said. She had a drink by her bedside—and nothing much could go wrong with her now.

Very soon the whole Castle was wrapped in silence and darkness. Everybody had gone to bed. Through the windows from which the curtains had been drawn back, Gail could see the stars. They were very clear and bright. Millions of them in the heavens. A clear, frosty night, and a new moon. She thought how wonderful the old Castle must look in the still white splendour of the northern night.

She wished she could be detached from it, and look down upon it all. Indeed, she wished that she could be detached altogether from Gail Cardew, be taken right out of her tiresome body with all its emotions and feelings which were such a nuisance. They didn't leave one in peace for a moment. It might be very pleasant just to become a spirit and float in the vast spaces up amongst those stars. Freed from 'life's fitful fever.'

She lay there, drowsing, with Ian's silk handkerchief under one cheek. Her room was dark except for the smouldering glow of the dying embers in the grate. Through the open window blew the keen night wind from across the moors.

Later, she became conscious that her bedroom door was opening very gingerly. She turned her head on the pillow, wondering if this was Mrs. Naughton come back to make kind but unnecessary inquiries. Then her heart jumped, for she saw that it was not Mrs. Naughton's portly figure. It was the tall slender shape of a man wearing a dark silk dressing-gown. She could not see his face plainly, but she knew immediately who it was, just from the shape of that handsome head, from the tall remembered grace of him.

'Ian!' she whispered.

Her voice throbbed on the name, just as her heart was throbbing. It was as though with his coming, a great warmth and light suddenly flooded the dark and lonely recesses of her mind. She was no longer alone and fretful and hopeless. *He* was here with her. And now the door closed behind him and he was sitting on the edge of her bed, whispering to her.

'This is quite crazy of me. And utterly wrong. But I *had* to come and find out if you were all right, my dear. I've been so worried about you. I didn't like to come back while Mrs. Naughton and Co. were gathered around. It would look as though I took too much interest. But now everyone's asleep, and they're all on the floor below, so I can easily hear anybody coming up the stairs. They creak, those old stairs . . .'

He stopped and gave a little laugh under his breath.

She put out a hand and found his. Their fingers twined convulsively. She whispered:

'I'm glad you've come. Oh, Ian . . .'

He bent his head nearer her.

'Are you all right?'

'Yes. Only I can't sleep.'

'Willis told me there was only a sprain, thank God. No broken bones.'

'No, I'll soon be able to walk again.'

'You must. I want to take you round the farms again. It was so lovely walking with you yesterday.'

'Lovely for me, too.'

'If our friend Jean happens to come up and find me here, there will be a pretty scandal.'

Gail swallowed hard, excitement racing through her whole body.

'Of course. It would be absolutely frightful! We'd all be ruined.'

'I oughtn't to risk it. I'm going to go away immediately.'

'Oh, Ian . . .'

There were so many things that she wanted to say to him, to tell him, and that was all she could do. Just murmur his name. But he could sense the full, rich, feeling behind those two little murmured words . . . *'Oh, Ian.'*

He could not see her clearly, only catch the indefinable shape of her face lying there, against the pillow. But he knew every contour of it. He could remember threading his fingers through those silky red-brown waves of her hair . . . remember kissing every inch of that sweet upturned face on that wild and never-to-be-forgotten night in Le Touquet. He knew so well the soft hollow in her throat . . . every dear and lovely curve . . . knew them and had adored . . . yet all had been lost to him. The sweetness and the loveliness, everything but a bitter, burning memory. Now he knew her to be another man's wife, and there was nothing within him save burning resentment against Fate, and the bitter knowledge that he still adored, *vainly*.

He bent his head a little closer, till he could feel her soft breath against his cheek. How fast she was breathing!

'Poor sweet,' he whispered. 'This isn't very fair on you.'

'It isn't fair on either of us, Ian. It's just, well, *damnable.* There's no other word for it.'

'Why did you marry him, Gail. For God's sake, *why?*'

'Oh, don't ask me that,' she said brokenly. 'You know the answer.'

'Yes, I know. And I won't ask again. You had every right. And I am the one to blame. I should never have left you. I should never have let you go out of my life. I should have married you and said to hell with my people, my career, everything.'

'No, no, you mustn't say that. You must never regret what you did. It was right. You weren't to blame. And you did try to keep in touch with me. It was your mother who parted us. If she had given me your message, I would never have been so totally separated from you, and things might have been different.'

'Yes, they might have been very different,' he said with great bitterness.

Her fingers tightened passionately over his.

'But I'm glad you did the right thing, and stuck to your job. You would have regretted it terribly if you'd married me and perhaps had to resign your commission, disappoint your people, even have lost your uncle's inheritance. Think of that! The Loch Castle might never have belonged to you. Your whole life might have been wrecked, and just because of me.'

'Darling, darling,' he said, huskily. 'Sometimes I don't think that anything I possess is worth while. Even my beloved Castle. What does anything mean since I haven't got you!'

Her heart leapt to those words, but she argued with him.

'You're wrong, Ian. You would have regretted it. You'd have been happy with me, but you'd have lost too much to balance the happiness, and I'd have reproached myself for the rest of my life if I'd been responsible for it.'

He carried the little hand to his lips. She felt them burning, eloquent, against her palm.

'You're a brave, sweet thing, Gail. I've no right to be talking to you like this, but it's all got to come out. It's been half choking me for days. It's so hard to see you and be with you, and realise that you belong to Cardew.'

Torn by two loyalties, she struggled with herself for a moment before she spoke. Then she said:

'I *must* tell the truth. I must admit that I don't love Bill. I only thought I did, and then it all vanished. I must tell you the truth, Ian, for I've never loved anybody but you. Never, *never*. After Le Touquet I broke my heart. And I think it's been breaking ever since.'

'Oh, God,' said Ian Dalmuir. 'What a frightful mess!'

An instant's blistering silence between

180

them. Then Gail said:

'Ian, do you admire the Naughtons' daughter?'

'What on earth made you think of her?'

She bit her lip.

'I just wondered if you do admire her.'

'I haven't thought about it. Mother Jean has been whisking the offspring around the place, and she's caused a bit of a stir, I must say. She's decidedly a good-looker, and as full of sex as she can be, the little devil. But that doesn't particularly appeal to me. Sex without brains never did. You know that, Gail.'

Jealousy fell away from her like a cloak. She said:

'Oh, darling, I suppose I should be glad if you did fall in love with someone else.'

'My darling, I never could while you live. Oh, my *darling*.'

His lips were searching for hers again in the poignant darkness. But only for a moment did she allow that kiss and then she pushed him away.

'You must go, Ian. You'd better go, my darling. Please.'

'Yes. I suppose I'd better.'

'But I'm glad you came. It's been lovely, talking to you here in the darkness, feeling you close to me. I remember how you sat on my bed that night at the "Picardy." We talked together then. We were so terribly happy . . . Oh, my *darling* . . .' Her voice broke.

'You were mine then,' he whispered. 'You were all mine, Gail. I'll always have that to remember. I know you'll never belong to anybody as you did to me.'

She pulled his hand up to her face, and he could feel her lips quivering against it, and the wetness of her tears.

For one wild moment, he caught her into his arms. She did not resist. Her uninjured arm went round his neck, drawing him fiercely to her breast. In the darkness their lips met and clung in the delirium of a kiss that swept them back through the years to that other night . . . that other darkness . . . that other passionate perfection which they had shared.

During that kiss, Gail knew that she had lost the battle with herself. That whatever happened in the future, she must continue to love this man until she died.

Now, she thought, a little crazily, she was as she had wished to be, disembodied from Gail Cardew. She was a spirit, and the spirit of Ian was with her. They were whirling together through those starry spaces. And they had finished with the anguish of regrets, and of separation. They were eternally one in a sphere in which there could be no suffering. Only the most supreme ecstasy.

But that madness lasted with her only as long as the kiss which Ian laid upon her hungry lips. And when that kiss ended, she was hurtled down from the stars again, back to the grim reality, to life as it really was and as it must be lived.

He continued to hold her close against his heart, kissing every inch of her face, threading his fingers as he had so longed to do, through the remembered silk of her hair. He was begging her not to cry. Repeating words that he had said to her in Paris in those other days.

'Don't be unhappy, my darling, my sweet. Don't remember the pain. Only the happiness that we have known. Oh, my darling little Gail, don't cry, because I can't bear it.'

She clung to him, her slender body shaken with the tempest of her feeling, and he went on caressing her until finally, spent and exhausted, she begged him again to leave her.

'It isn't safe for you to stay, Ian. You really must go.'

Reluctantly he drew away from her, and laid her gently back against the pillows. There was a last fervent kiss for her wet eyelids, and one for her piteous mouth. He said:

'We must make the best of it, sweet. We must bury our dreams and do what is expected of us both. There's a war on, my darling. So many broken lives and broken hearts in the world. Our own tragedy seems small in comparison.'

'Yes, I know,' she whispered. 'Only it's big to us.'

'I love you,' he said abruptly. 'And I always will. If it's any comfort to you to know. There will never be another woman.'

She did not answer. Her heart was too full. She felt his fingers touch her cheek, her throat, then he was gone. He had left her, closing the door behind him as soundlessly as he had come. Choking, she put her face against the pillow, feeling utterly alone and defenceless without him. Wishing almost that she could have died while he was there with her, holding her as he had held her in Le Touquet, kissing her as he had kissed her then.

She knew beyond all doubt now that he loved her still. And when she thought how utterly hopeless it was, she was appalled.

She tried, as she had tried in the long ago, to do what he had asked her. To forget the pain and remember only the happiness.

*'We must bury our dreams, and do what is expected of us both,'* he had just said to her.

Brave words, typical of Ian.

She lay sleepless and feverish through the long hours, clinging desperately to the memory of those words.

And the thickness of the door prevented her from hearing the voices out in the passage. Prevented her from knowing that when Ian had tiptoed away from her room, a shock had awaited him, for at the top of the staircase he had come face to face with the girl whom he had just described to Gail as being 'full of sex.'

June Naughton, in pale-blue pyjamas and a tailored dressing-gown with very wide

184

shoulders and wide sash round the slender waist, stood before him, hands in her pockets, looking up at him with her blue languorous eyes.

'Why, Captain Dalmuir!' she whispered.

He went red to the roots of his hair.

'Do you want anything?' he asked and knew beyond a doubt that she had seen him come out of Gail Cardew's room. A little half-smile hovered round her lips. Her plucked eyebrows, like crescent moons, lifted. She said:

'Mummy suggested I might run up and see if Mrs. Cardew was all right. *Is she?*'

## FOURTEEN

If ever Ian Dalmuir felt angry in his life, it was then. Angry, not only with himself for having put Gail into this position by that ill-advised although perfectly innocent visit to her, but with this girl who was regarding him in such an insinuating way.

The little hussy! She was the type of modern girl whom Ian could hardly endure. He had met plenty of them in India. Shoved out there by match-making mothers. Hard-headed, scheming young creatures who could scarcely be called children although still in their teens. Able to put down more cocktails than the average man, and still keep sober.

Capable of dancing all night, and being ready the next morning for a day's amusement. Seemingly full of romantic notions, but the romance was merely a sugar-coating for a cool determination to get the best out of life and the most out of men, without paying the price for either.

Such was this daughter of Major and Mrs. Naughton. A not untypical young woman of the age, leaving the parents, who blindly adored, a bit dazed and baffled by the queer product so unlike themselves.

And, inevitably, Ian's mind flashed to Gail. And he knew why he had loved her so madly in France and why he loved her still. Because she wasn't a June. Because there was nothing of the schemer about her, nothing hard, brazen or heartless.

Because she was just sweet and honest and generous. Too generous, perhaps. She had given everything for love and had nothing in return, poor darling child!

June repeated her whispered query:

'Is Mrs. Cardew all right?'

He had no choice but to answer her.

'Quite, thanks . . .'

For he knew that if he had pretended that he had never been in the room, it would have made matters worse. June would have known at once that he was trying to hide something. Whatever happened, he must not allow a breath of scandal to touch Gail, because she did not deserve it. He must make the thing look as right as possible. So he said:

'You can tell your mother that I thought I heard Mrs. Cardew call, and as I was afraid she might be in some pain, I went along. But she's all right.'

June looked at him through her long lashes.

'I'll tell Mummy.'

But she made no effort to get out of his way. She was rather enjoying this nocturnal meeting with the young 'Laird' on the quiet deserted landing with nearly everybody else asleep.

She had seen from the first that Captain Dalmuir held himself rather aloof from women. She would like it to be said that June Naughton had pierced the armour and was the woman to conquer him.

It did not really matter to June with whom she flirted, so long as the man had some kind of attraction. Bill had been more than enough that night at Pam Borley's birthday party, and she had enjoyed every moment at the 'Cafe de Paris' and of the clandestine meeting with Bill the following day.

But Ian Dalmuir was a different proposition. Not only attractive and the owner of this fine castle and considerable wealth, but a man who was building up a fine military record for himself.

She had decided not to get married, but just to enjoy herself, flitting from flower to flower so far as the pleasures of life were concerned, until she was much older. But if Ian Dalmuir proposed . . . well . . . she saw herself as his wife and the chatelaine of this Castle. A June in marvellous creations . . . Molyneux, Lanvin, Hartnell . . . sweeping through these noble halls, a fair and lovely lady of the land, with this dark knight at her feet. A fine theatrical imagination had June and she liked what she visualised.

It had been a bit of a shock to her to see him coming out of Mrs. Cardew's bedroom. Possibly it was all quite above board. Why think otherwise? Mrs. Cardew had had an accident, and Captain Dalmuir slept somewhere nearby and it was not unnatural that he should choose to go to her aid if she called. But at the same time it must be remembered that Mrs. Cardew's husband was away and that she was young and beautiful. Not as beautiful as she could be in June's estimation. Gail could do with a lot more make-up and much more glamour about her clothes. But even June had been struck by the lovely burnished colour of her hair and those big grey eyes.

*Was* Captain Dalmuir attracted . . .?

'I think,' said Ian in a formal tone, 'that we had better turn in, don't you, Miss Naughton?'

'Oh, you must call me June,' she said reproachfully. 'Everybody does. I can't bear to be called Miss Naughton.'

He yearned to be rude to her and to tell her

188

that he didn't want to call her anything. His gaze kept wandering to Gail's door. His mind was in a turmoil. His heart was still racing from the memory of those few dizzy moments that he had spent holding her in his arms again. Damned awkward to have met the Naughton girl like this. But he realised that he couldn't be rude or too curt, or it might lead to trouble.

He forced himself to say:

'Well, I don't think you need worry any more about Mrs. Cardew . . . June.'

'I won't. I'll just worry about *you!*'

He began to walk away from Gail's door. June walked beside him.

'What on earth are you going to worry about me, for?' he asked uneasily.

She kept her languorous eye upon him.

'At dinner I thought you looked so tired and depressed. All the other men were laughing and joking, but not you. I did notice. Do you mind?'

Ian set his teeth and wished passionately he had a cigarette. The little devil was trying to 'put it across' and he knew it. He could have shaken her. Somehow he had to find a suitable reply.

'I may be tired, but I'm not depressed, thanks very much.'

'I'm glad. I think this war must be so awful for all of you. Never knowing from one minute to the next when you might get sent to the Western Front . . .' She stopped and sighed.

Ian gave a grim smile.

'I assure you, if I was sent to France tomorrow, I shouldn't regard it as a hardship.'

'Oh, but you can't want to leave your glorious home.'

He wanted very much to go to bed, to be alone, to think of Gail, to get away from the 'allure' that the Naughton girl was putting out. God, he was tired! In another moment he *would* be rude. He said:

'There's a war on, so in a war it's a man's job to fight, and not to hang round his home, no matter how beautiful.'

'And I suppose that includes women, no matter how beautiful,' June said with a meaning little laugh.

'Well, I'm going to say good night,' Ian announced firmly.

She paused and held out her hand.

'Good night. And I do want to thank you for letting me come here.'

'Not at all. I'm delighted.'

'Mummy says you have such glorious farms and dogs and things. Will you show them to me?'

'I shall be delighted,' he said, seeing no way out of it.

She smiled and, turning, moved away down the stairs.

In his own room Ian switched on the light, lit a cigarette, and walked up and down the room, smoking, feeling savage and restless. It

190

was some time before he could settle down for sleep.

His head ached violently. He could think of nothing but Gail. The sweetness, the all-too-familiar sweetness of her in his arms. All the old passion of Le Touquet . . . returning in full force to disturb his peace of mind and body. Of course, he had been a fool to go to her room and to make things worse for them. She was Cardew's wife, and the only hope of putting matters right was to avoid Gail like the plague and stamp ruthlessly on the memory of three years ago.

And the last thing he had wanted was to be seen emerging from her room tonight. What the devil would the Naughtons think when that confounded girl went down and told them? Perhaps he had a guilty conscience. Perhaps they wouldn't think anything. But he knew Mrs. Naughton. Under her kindly exterior she was an inquisitive, gossip-loving woman and she would be on the lookout for 'something' between himself and Gail. And he was well aware that she wanted to push her daughter before his notice. And the daughter left no doubt in a man's mind that *she* would like his attentions. But he wasn't going to give them. It was much too dangerous. Too much sex in June, as he had told Gail, and too few brains. Always the sort to get a man tied up before he knew where he was, and no matter how sensible he was.

Of course, the best thing of all would be for him to get away from Loch Castle and Edinburgh. Get a transfer to some other brigade. That was possible in peace-time, but almost impossible during a war. If he went to the Brigadier and said: 'Please, sir, I want to be sent South or to France . . ,' the Brigadier would open his eyes wide and remind him that the country was at war with Germany and any private wars of Captain Dalmuir's must be settled without annoyance to those under whom he was serving.

An ash-tray full of cigarette ends told the story of a sleepless night for Ian when dawn stole like a grey ghost through the dark castle and extinguished the last pale star in the misty sky.

He was thankful when he heard a faint bugle-call from a nearby camp and, exhausted though he felt, got up, shaved, and put on his uniform. Thankful that neither Mrs. Naughton nor June appeared downstairs to breakfast. Wondered if the Major did not look at him a trifle queerly, but that, again, he told himself, might be a guilty conscience. Then he went off to work feeling that, for a man, a life amongst men was the best thing, after all. The moment women came into it, there was trouble. Yet, at the thought of Gail lying up there in her room with her bad ankle, and her own unhappy thoughts, he could feel nothing but intense pity for her, and self-reproach because he was

192

primarily to blame for her difficulties.

He sent a note to her on her breakfast tray warning her of the contretemps between himself and June Naughton.

Gail, reading it, was dismayed. He only said a few words and ended with:

*'Don't worry. It was unlucky, but I think my explanation was believed. If Mrs. N. questions you, just bear out my statement that you called out, and I heard and came to you.*

*I.'*

A terse little note. Nothing like the wonderful exciting love letters which he had written to her in France. Every day in Paris he used to send a little note to Gail, even though they had met the night before. Burning, passionate outpourings of a man madly in love. In ashes, now, like that diary which had been the cry of her own heart's love.

Of course, she couldn't expect him to write like that today. It wouldn't be right, and it wouldn't be safe. But she was strangely depressed by the few curt words she received.

What a disaster it had been, June Naughton coming upstairs just when Ian had left her. Better if it had been anybody than that girl. She would undoubtedly be tactless and gossip about it.

A dozen times Gail cursed the accident to her ankle, and wished that she could have left

Edinburgh today as arranged.

She felt hot and embarrassed when Mrs. Naughton came in to see her and ask if there was anything that she could do.

'Major Willis says you mustn't set foot to the ground. So I think I'd better wash you, my dear,' she said.

Gail would have preferred it otherwise, but had no option. Mrs. Naughton rolled up her sleeves and started to run hot water into the basin. Inevitably last night's incident was mentioned.

'My June says that you called Captain Dalmuir in last night, You should have sent for me, my dear. What could he do? It must have been most embarrassing for him.'

Gail lay silent. Despite all her efforts at control, a burning blush spread across her face and throat. How she disliked this interfering, this prying into her private affairs. And Mrs. Naughton saw the blush and was at once distinctly uneasy. She had not really thought anything about June's report. Why shouldn't one of the officers, if he heard the injured girl call out, go to her aid? At the same time, June had said Mrs. Cardew's door was shut, and that Captain Dalmuir had crept out, and blushed scarlet when he saw her. And here was Mrs. Cardew also blushing. It really was a bit queer. *Surely there was nothing between these two?* But with Mr. Cardew away . . . and Gail was very pretty . . . (not, of course, in the same street as darling June, but she *had* looks!) and she and Captain Dalmuir used to know each other before the war . . .

Mrs. Naughton, whilst washing the patient, made it her business to ask a great many questions.

What had been wrong last night? Why had Gail called out? What had Captain Dalmuir done about it? Why hadn't he sent down for *her?* And so on, until Gail felt a nervous wreck and found it hard not to take the basin of water that she was holding and throw it at Mrs. Naughton's suspicious face.

Finally Jean Naughton said:

'We can't have you being night-nursed by our attractive Captain . . .' (Her playful voice!) 'My word! What would Mr. Cardew say? Perhaps it would be just as well if I move and sleep up here, while you are ill. That is, if there's a room anywhere on this floor.'

Gail, who was white and shadowy-eyed this morning, forced a smile.

'I don't think there's any need. I'm not really ill. I'll be quite all right tonight.'

Mrs. Naughton walked to the window.

'Such a bright morning! Cold but clear. Perfect for an air raid. Keep your gas mask nearby and I'll put some shoes and a warm coat on the end of your bed. Then if there is an air raid we can carry you down. And now I must find my little June. Bless her, she's got it *very* badly for Captain Dalmuir. I think she wishes *she* could twist *her* ankle and be carried through the Castle in his arms . . .'

A hearty laugh followed this jest, then Mrs. Naughton took her departure. She left Gail looking and feeling desperate. Really, as if things hadn't been bad enough before without *this* happening. Mrs. Naughton on the warpath . . . Out now to watch like a lynx for any hint of more than friendship between Ian and herself. And no doubt Ian wouldn't dare come up and see her today at all.

Gail turned her face to the pillow and groaned. She *must* try to stop thinking about Ian in connection with herself. She must write a letter to Bill . . . Bill who would expect a very loving one saying how much she missed him. How difficult it all was! And she wondered if Ian was feeling as depressed about it all this morning as she herself.

It did not add to her pleasure that same evening when Bill put through a long-distance call from Glasgow which she was able to answer from her private sitting-room in which there was a telephone. Jean Naughton, who had taken complete control of 'the invalid,' wrapped an eiderdown round her and helped her hop from the bedroom into the adjoining room in order to receive the call.

Gail had spent a boring and wretched day with nothing much to think about except her bad ankle and—Ian. Ian who had not even been up to see her; no doubt because he dare

196

not! She knew that she ought to receive her husband's call rapturously. She tried to do so; to infuse a warmth into her voice which she scarcely felt. He expressed sympathy about the accident, but spent most of a nine-minutes' call telling her how much he wished he were with her—and why.

Gail, married though she was to him, felt her cheeks grow hot as he enlarged on the various reasons why he wanted to be back in the Castle.

'My God, it's lonely in this dull hotel. I work all day, but I've got nothing to do at night but miss you. I can imagine you looking altogether luscious in that pink fleecy cape you wear . . . God, what wouldn't I give to get back. But *wait till I do . . .*' etc etc.

She finally protested:

'Bill, do be careful . . . someone may be listening.'

He laughed. He was not very sensitive about such things.

'I repeat,' he said significantly, *'just you wait till I get back!'*

Then he was forced to say good-bye because he did not want to spend any more money on the call. Mrs. Naughton, who had tactfully retired, returned to help Gail back to bed.

'There! What a lovely surprise for you, having a call from your nice husband. Aren't you a lucky girl? He's *so* good-looking. I always say to Harry, I've never seen such lovely

197

golden hair and blue eyes . . .'

She rattled on, and Gail listened, setting her teeth. And when she was alone again, with her supper tray, she tried to shut out the memory of every word Bill had said. That awful possessiveness of his! There was something so crude about it. His love for her seemed to lack any spirituality whatsoever. In his eyes, she was meant to be made love to, and just whensoever a hot gust of passion shook him. And she was supposed to like it, indeed to encourage and welcome it.

In a fit of despair, tonight, she asked herself how it was possible she had ever thought herself in love with him. But girls did these mad things. She wasn't the only one. The papers were crammed with news of war weddings. Oh, how crazy, she thought! How utterly crazy to allow the patriotic fervour or physical thrill of the moment to lure one into signing away the whole of one's freedom for ever.

She did not see Ian that evening. She did not even receive a message from him. Feeling thoroughly miserable, she cried herself to sleep. And Mrs. Naughton, arriving at breakfast-time in the morning, took great pleasure in telling her how 'well darling June was getting on with Captain Dalmuir.'

'You should have seen him yesterday afternoon,' she said, with her jolly laugh as she fussed around the room, 'when Captain

Dalmuir came back from work, he found that June had discovered where his lovely red setters are kennelled and she was taking them for a walk. They met in the grounds and went off together. I never saw a more perfect couple.'

Silence from the bed. Gail lay very still. Looking at Mrs. Naughton with brooding eyes which were hot with resentment. Like her heart. Wrong, all wrong, of course, to feel like this. She knew it. But she just couldn't bear the thought of June stepping into her shoes, taking out Dougal and Morag and walking with *him* where *she* had walked.

She tried to get herself into a better frame of mind The 'right' frame of mind And it would be right, of course, to hope that Ian would fall in love with June and marry her. Then everything would be *'right.'*

But would it? Gail wondered from the bottom of her heart whether Ian would ever find happiness with a girl like June Naughton.

Another lonely boring day which she spent reading one of the books from Ian's library—and writing long letters home. At tea-time, a knock came on the door. She said:

'Come in.'

And then the face of the world changed. It was Ian Dalmuir who walked into her room, carrying a huge bunch of apricot-coloured single chrysanthemums, and a great sheaf of autumn leaves.

She hardly saw the flowers. Only that tall figure in uniform, the finely-cut face, every feature of which she adored, those dark tender eyes which smiled so tenderly into hers.

'This is just to hope that the ankle is getting on,' Ian said, rather awkwardly. 'I can't stay . . .'

'Can't you?' she said helplessly.

He put the flowers on the end of her bed.

'They are perfectly glorious,' she added in a suffocated voice.

'Are you better, my dear?'

He hardly noticed the answer. He was drinking in the sight of her. She looked so unbelievably sweet, sitting up there in the little pink swansdown cape, tied with a satin bow at the throat. She had no make-up on. Yet she was lovely, with her soft pale cheeks and those big smoke-grey eyes.

'I'd like to stay for hours, as well you know,' he said in an undertone. 'But I daren't. Mother Jean is on the warpath. I've had that doll-like daughter of hers flung at my head until I could yell. Believe me; Gail, I can, quote the words of Queen Victoria: "We are not amused." '

Gail laughed. She felt almost happy for the first time in forty-eight hours. After all, it was only human that she should have been jealous of June, and it was good to know that Ian was unmoved by her pretty face and blandishments.

'It was awfully bad luck, her seeing you

come out of my room, Ian.'

'Infuriating. I know Mama is suspicious now. Every time she sees me, she asks some question about our past friendship.'

'She drives me almost frantic,' said Gail, gripping her teeth. 'She's terribly kind, but everything she does or says is calculated to annoy me.'

'Never mind, darling, stick it. You'll soon be up and able to escape her.'

The word 'darling' fell so naturally from his lips that it gave her a great feeling of warmth and happiness. He added: 'Have you heard from Bill?'

In an instant, happiness was destroyed. The name of her husband at once created a coldness and put an impassable barrier between Ian and herself.

'Yes. A phone call last night and a letter this morning. He goes to Aberdeen tomorrow.'

'What does Willis say about your foot?'

'Oh, it's much better. I'm to dress tomorrow and sit up. I can't lie in bed as though I'm ill.'

'Well, you look very lovely, anyhow,' he said impulsively.

Her great grey eyes were fixed on him, but she could not speak because there was a little lump in her throat. Between them flamed the thought of the night before last. Of their wild and desperate embrace here in this very room, in the poignant darkness. Ian's teeth clenched. He took a swift step toward her, picked up her hand, and crushed it to his lips.

'I love you, Gail. I wish to God I didn't.'

And those were exactly the words which Mrs. Naughton heard as she stood outside Gail's bedroom door, holding a large crystal vase full of water.

Mrs. Naughton had not been asked to bring up that vase. But she had seen the Laird of the Castle going upstairs with a bunch of chrysanthemums. At once she had taken it for granted that he was on his way to visit little Mrs. Cardew. She disapproved of him going into the bedroom. She also disapproved of him taking her flowers. She decided that the sooner she followed the better, and she could say she had noticed the flowers, and knew Gail would want a vase.

When she heard those words, '*I love you,*' uttered in Ian Dalmuir's familiar husky voice, she went hot, then cold. Her round blue eyes looked startled. Her mouth tightened into a button of shocked disapproval.

'We-ell!' she said to herself. '*We-ell!*'

Just for an instant she stood irresolute. She could hear no more being said inside the bedroom, and that seemed to her *most* suspicious. No room for doubt was left in her mind that there was an 'affair going on' between Captain Dalmuir and Mrs. Cardew. *Disgraceful.* And the husband away; a brother officer, too! What a little hussy, that Gail Cardew. Not content with her own husband, indulging in a violent flirtation behind her husband's back with the Staff Captain! No excuse whatsoever. And grossly unfair on poor June. Poor innocent child! What chance did she stand against a wicked, scheming married woman.

Mrs. Naughton decided, then and there, what she was going to do.

She marched straight into Gail's room.


## FIFTEEN

'I thought this would be wanted,' she said, with a freezing smile. She set the vase down on the table beside Gail's bed, and took her departure again. It couldn't be said that she had interrupted a love scene, for when she entered the room, Captain Dalmuir was standing some distance from Gail, lighting a cigarette for himself But she had heard quite enough, and she made up her mind to act secretly and decisively. Without saying anything to 'the guilty pair,' she walked down into her own private sitting-room. Major Naughton was sitting at his desk looking at a map. June was reading.

'June, darling,' said Mrs. Naughton. 'Run downstairs, pet, I want to talk to your father?'

June was only too ready to obey. It was more amusing downstairs, where there was likely to be one or two officers to talk to her. She was violently in love with Captain Dalmuir, but there was a young subaltern whom they called 'Pop-eyes' who amused her, and he had a definite 'crush' on her.

The moment the girl had gone, Mrs. Naughton excitedly confided her story to her husband.

'Did you *ever*, Harry?' she finished, flushed in the face. 'And who would have thought it of that nice Ian Dalmuir?'

The Major pulled the lobe of his ear and looked embarrassed, if slightly incredulous.

'But are you sure, my dear?'

'Of course I'm sure. I heard it with my own ears.'

'Well, I don't suppose you heard it with anybody else's,' said the Major and laughed at his own little joke.

'Don't be tiresome, Harry. You can see this is very serious.'

Major Naughton cleared his throat.

'Mustn't make too much out of it, my dear. You may be exaggerating.'

'*Exaggerating!* When he said that he loved her, *and* June saw him coming out of her room that night?'

'Oh, come, come, Jeannie. That's going too far. Dalmuir's a very decent chap, and if he went into—er—Mrs. Cardew's—er—room, it was to see if she was all right. He said so himself. I'm quite sure there was no real harm in it. As for being in love with her—well, perhaps he is. She's a very attractive young woman.'

He paused and coughed, avoiding his wife's stony stare.

There followed a good twenty minutes of abuse from Mrs. Naughton who accused him of being lax in his own morals because he was not critical enough of Ian's conduct. Finally, Major Naughton, who was a much-managed man, gave in, and said that he thought that even if there was no harm in it now, it should be stopped.

But it wasn't up to him to speak to Ian Dalmuir, he said. He was a senior officer, but had control of Ian only as far as work was concerned. As for telling the Brigadier, that was unthinkable. One didn't spy on a brother officer and report his conduct. What Dalmuir chose to do in private was surely his own business. Major Naughton wished to wash his hands of it.

'Well, *I* am not going to let it go on,' said Mrs. Naughton, assuming in her own righteous mind the wrath of a female judge whose duty it was to pronounce judgment on everybody in the Castle whom she thought deserving of chastisement.

She made a decision to say nothing to Gail. If Gail was keen about Ian Dalmuir, she wouldn't listen to good advice from a friend. And she wouldn't speak to Ian, because that too would do no good, and of course they would both deny it. So she would speak to the husband.

The Major protested. 'My dear Jean, you really must not interfere in people's business like this.'

'I consider it as my duty,' said Mrs. Naughton, 'my duty to the community not to allow such things to go on. Besides which, you know I have great hopes of Captain Dalmuir and June. I'm not going to allow that chit of a Cardew girl to come between them.'

The Major gave it up. He never had been able to control his wife, and considered women impossible creatures anyhow. He couldn't be bothered with it. There was a war on, and he was much more interested in that. He uttered a feeble word of warning to his wife about getting herself tied up in the affair and making herself very unpopular, then declined to make further comment.

Mrs. Naughton, still bristling with righteous horror, knew exactly what she was going to do.

Every night Bill Cardew telephoned his wife. Tonight Mrs. Naughton would give orders that the orderly should switch that call through to this room before it went upstairs to Gail.

The call usually came at dinner-time, so Mrs. Naughton had her sitting-room to herself. The orderly at the switchboard carried out his instructions. Mrs. Naughton was summoned to the telephone just as the soup was being served. She left her husband and daughter, and marched firmly to her own private 'battle.'

'Mr. Cardew,' she said, her heart beating a trifle fast with some agitation. 'This is Mrs. Naughton speaking.'

'Oh, hullo!' came Bill's drawl. 'I hear you've been most frightfully kind to my little wife. Terribly decent of you, Mrs. Naughton.'

'I was delighted to do anything I could for her, Mr. Cardew, but I would like to say this before you talk to Gail. I think you should do your utmost to get back here *as soon* as you can.'

'Good lord, why? Is she worse?'

'No, her health is very good and the ankle improving. But there are *other* reasons why you ought to be with her. Or if it is impossible, insist upon her leaving the Castle and going down South for a bit.'

'But why?' came Bill's voice sharply.

'It's very hard for me to explain,' said Mrs. Naughton, red in the face. She was half wishing she had not taken this upon herself, but continued with it mainly for June's sake. 'It's just that everything is not as you would wish it, Mr. Cardew. Reluctant though I am to say so.'

'Mrs. Naughton, what on earth are you insinuating?'

'Well, your little wife, whom we all know is a *very* pretty girl and most attractive to men, ought not to be left here alone,' said Mrs. Naughton significantly.

A second's pause, then Bill said a trifle thickly:

'Look here, you *are* insinuating something. I insist on knowing at once, what you mean!'

'I intend, to mention no names,' said Mrs. Naughton wildly, 'but I suggest that you ask your wife if her conscience is quite clear. That's all. And just take my advice, Mr. Cardew, and I'm sure you'll accept what I say in the friendly spirit in which it's meant. Either come back, yourself, or send her away, even with her bad ankle. We can easily put her in the train.'

'Look here, this is too much!' burst out Bill.

But Mrs. Naughton had said enough and was aware of the fact. Gail could tackle it now, she thought spitefully. She bade Bill good night, went downstairs, and told the orderly to switch the call through to Mrs. Cardew's room.

Gail could now hop, without assistance, into the sitting-room. She answered that telephone call in good spirits. Ian had said good night to her almost immediately after Mrs. Naughton had brought up the vase. But the look in his eye and the single kiss he had imprinted on her hand had left her with a feeling of warmth and security in his love. And she had his flowers to look at. Such lovely chrysanthemums with their curled apricot petals, pale and exotic against the dark autumn tints of the leaves.

208

Flowers from his own greenhouses, specially chosen by him.

She aimed at getting herself into a better state of mind to answer Bill's call tonight. To be dutiful, no matter what it cost her. She and Ian could never belong to each other again. They must be friends—never lovers. No matter what it cost them both, they must try to face that fact. For honour's sake alone.

And it was with these high sentiments that she spoke to Bill tonight, only to receive a greeting from him which shook her to the depths of her being. It staggered her.

'What the *hell* have you been up to while I've been away? What does Mrs. Naughton mean by telling me just now that the sooner I get back to you the better? Which of the fellows have you been fooling around with? My God, what a pretty piece of news for a hard-working husband to receive, when he's away on a job . . .'

This, and plenty more, before Gail could draw breath. She was shaking from head to foot when he had finished the tirade. She said:

'I don't know what you're talking about. I simply don't know.'

'You must know. Mrs. Naughton wouldn't have dared say what she did unless she had foundation.'

Gail's fingers trembled so that she could scarcely hold the receiver to her ear. Of course, she knew at once what had happened.

That *cat*. She had dared insinuate things to Bill because of the other night . . . because of her general suspicions . . .

At least Gail was thankful that Mrs. Naughton had mentioned no man's name. Whatever happened, no slur of scandal must touch Ian Dalmuir. That would be too awful.

Gail pulled herself together and managed somehow to calm Bill down.

'This is all ludicrous. Don't for heaven's sake start being the jealous husband. There's no need. No, I have *not* been fooling round, you can take my word for that. A lot of the officers have come up to my room to see me . . . Mrs. Naughton doesn't approve and she has her daughter here and she wants them all to pay attention to *her* . . . It's all stupid and a lot of fuss about nothing. You must believe me, Bill.'

'Well, it's a damned awful thing for her to have said if there's no truth in it.'

'Well, there isn't,' said Gail and shut her eyes, feeling sick.

'Anyhow, she's right. You're too damned attractive to be left there among all those fellows. You'd better let them drive you to the train and go back at once to Kingston, whether you can walk or not. Your father can meet you at King's Cross and drive you home.'

Gail agreed feverishly. Anything, she thought, to soothe Bill and avoid further suspicion falling upon Ian and herself. 'I'll go

210

tomorrow,' she said. 'By the night train. If they just put me on to a sleeper, I won't have to walk. I'd rather be at home than here, I *assure* you.'

It was a long and expensive call for Bill Cardew that night. But he waived expense. Mrs. Naughton's few words had roused a devil of suspicion and jealousy in him. He would not let Gail go until he was reassured, and by the time she had finished, he was sure that Mrs. Naughton was just a gossiping old fool and took it for granted that Gail had been the object of attention amongst the officers, and that had annoyed the woman.

'I dare say she's annoyed because nobody would look at her twice,' Bill announced. 'But she's right. If I can't get back, you'll darn well have to quit, yourself. You're mine, do you hear? *My wife!* And you're not to forget it. You can come back to the Castle when I come back, and then you can show me just how much you *do* love me, my too-attractive wife!'

A moment later Gail was back in her bedroom, sitting on the edge of her bed, shivering, her eyes full of a sick despair.

For Bill to add jealousy to his possessiveness would make things a thousand times worse for her in the future. She could foresee what a ghastly time she would have in trying to prove her love for him when they met again. She knew what that would mean! As for leaving the Castle, yes, the sooner she left the better.

Now that Mrs. Naughton had declared open warfare, it would be insupportable to stay.

She covered her face with her hands and sat there for a long while in acute and silent misery. With all her soul, she longed to see Ian, to talk to him, to tell him of this fresh ordeal. But she must not. Much better spare him from further worry.

When she had sufficiently recovered from the shock of Bill's telephone call, she took pen and paper and wrote a brief note to Ian.

*'I would be grateful if you would arrange to have me taken into Edinburgh to catch the night train tomorrow. Maybe you'd book me a sleeper. I've decided that I must go home at once, for every reason.*

*Thank you for everything. Good-bye.*

*G.'*

In that one word, 'good-bye,' she knew that she was bidding him more than an ordinary farewell. She knew that he would guess it. It was good-bye to their love and the memory of Le Touquet. If, and when, she returned to the Castle, those memories must never be allowed to flame into life. They must die, just as her personal happiness had died . . . and his.

Then she rang the bell and told the maid that she would like to see Mrs. Naughton.

The Major's wife entered the room with some trepidation. Her first righteous

212

indignation having cooled down, she was feeling a little awkward about her interference in the case. Somewhat nervously, she bade Gail 'good evening' and without her usual smile.

Gail, with heightened colour, looked Jean Naughton straight in the eyes, and said:

'I believe you thought fit to insinuate all kind of things about me to my husband on the telephone tonight.'

The older woman tossed her head.

'Yes, I admit I did think fit. I mentioned no names to Mr. Cardew, but I think *you* know exactly what I meant.'

'No,' said Gail, clearly and distinctly, 'I haven't the slightest idea of what you mean.'

Mrs. Naughton cleared her throat and avoided Gail's direct gaze.

'Oh, yes, you do know, but I don't intend to discuss it with you. I leave it to your own conscience. And I don't think that can be so completely clear.'

'You've taken a great deal upon yourself, haven't you?'

'As the wife of a senior officer, I've done what I considered the right thing. There must be no scandal in the Regiment.'

Gail clenched her hands.

'I admit no evidences of scandal. But I do not intend to stay here a day longer until my husband returns. I'm leaving Scotland by the night train tomorrow.'

Mrs. Naughton's face cleared. That was good news. And she had a wild, if fleeting, vision of Captain Dalmuir getting over what was possibly a silly infatuation very rapidly once Gail had gone, and falling back on the pure, idealistic love of her sweet June.

'Well, that being so, I'll say no more about anything,' she announced, and deigned to smile at Gail.

But Gail did not smile back.

'I know, you're older than I am, Mrs. Naughton, and that Major Naughton is Bill's second-in-command, but I do not admit that you had, nor ever can have, the right to interfere in my private affairs. Neither should you concern yourself with matters about which you really know *nothing*. If that's discourteous, I'm sorry, but you've asked for it.'

Mrs. Naughton's smile froze.

'You're very young, my dear,' she said. 'And you haven't been in the Army long. In time, no doubt, you'll learn how an officer's wife should conduct herself.'

With this parting insult, she turned and left the room.

Gail, trembling, put the back of her hand against her lips and felt herself on the verge of hysteria. She had really too much to cope with today. And there would be more to cope with in the future. She fully realised that. How *dared* Mrs. Naughton? If Ian knew, he would tell her what he thought of her. And she knew, too, that Mrs. Naughton's match-making instincts were largely responsible for her incredible interference.

*How dared she?* When she knew nothing about the facts. Nobody knew them! Nobody in the world knew that she and Ian had belonged to each other long, long before Bill ever came on the scene.

Gail left her supper uneaten. She began to write out a telegram asking her father to meet her train, and knowing that a fresh ordeal awaited her in Kingston. The ordeal of having to pretend that she was happy with Bill in order to spare them unnecessary suffering.

## SIXTEEN

Gail was lifted out of the car by her father. She hopped into the old home with one arm round his neck and the other round her mother, and everybody was much too excited and happy to notice at first that anything was wrong with her.

It was a glorious welcome home which brought emotional tears to Gail's eyes. And there was a surprise for her. Her young brother was home, and also there to welcome her. It was a curious coincidence that both Gail and Chris had met with an accident about the same time, and so Mrs. Partner had both

215

beloved children home together. Gail with her ankle, Chris still with a black patch over one eye. He had almost recovered from his eye injury, and was now enjoying an extended leave at home.

Gail had arrived on the Night Scot from Edinburgh. She had slept badly. She could never sleep in trains, and in any case her thoughts were worried and unhappy ones, and would not allow her much rest. She was afraid that she looked a wreck and that the family would comment upon it as soon as they had taken a closer look at her.

They did so at the breakfast table. It was a happy meal for them as they sat eating heartily, exchanging their news, all of them wishing the youngest member of the family had been there to complete the reunion. But Scampie wouldn't get back from school till Christmas

Then Mrs. Partner took a long look at her eldest daughter, and received a sudden shock. Heavens, but the child had grown thin! She was all eyes. Her cheekbones were standing out, and there was a harassed, troubled air about her which did not escape the mother. With a painful throb in her heart, she remembered only once before having seen Gail look a little like this. That had been when she had returned from Paris, three years ago, after her holiday with her French friend, Simone.

216

But what had happened to change Gail so completely since her marriage? She had looked radiant enough when she left Kingston with Bill. And her letters had seemed bright and cheerful. Perhaps, thought Mrs. Partner, it was imagination on her part. The children always said she worried about them unnecessarily.

Then Mr. Partner spoke the very words for her.

'Can't say Scotland is agreeing with you, my dear,' he addressed Gail. 'You don't look at all well.'

'That is exactly what I think,' said Mrs. Partner.

'We'd better both go into a hospital and die together, Mum,' said Chris, winking at his sister with his one visible eye.

Gail sat there, the object of attention and discussion, trying to laugh things off but aware that her face was flushing painfully.

In a way, it was a distinct relief to have left the Loch Castle . . . to be back in the old home with these dear people who were her own flesh and blood. A relief to be so far from Bill. Yet she was conscious of an aching void within her. An anguish of longing for Ian which threatened to consume her. A longing ten thousand times fiercer than that which she had known when she had left him in France after their first parting.

Both 'good-byes' had seemed final and

irrevocable. But it was worse now, because she was a married woman and had a husband to whom she must answer.

Ian, she knew, had wanted to see her off from the Waverley Station last night, but had not dared, because of Mrs. Naughton and public opinion in general. But in her sleeper she had found a note from him. Brief, non-committal:

*'Take care of yourself and be happy. I shall miss you.*

*I'*

He would miss her! And God knew, she would miss him. But what was the use of continuing with the awful emotional strain and suspense which they had endured since they met again?

After breakfast, up in her old room, Gail lay on the bed and watched her mother unpack for her and chat about all the little things which she thought would interest her. Annie, their cook, had a brother who was a seaman on one of the big ships which lately had gone down, and he had been drowned, poor fellow. Later on, Gail must go down and sympathise with her. Parker, their gardener, had gone. Joined up, and they had an old man in his place. Barbara College, one of Gail's many girl friends at Kingston, had got married, but her husband had had to leave her forty-eight hours

218

later, and go out to Egypt.

'The whole world's upside down,' sighed Mrs. Partner, and added: 'Of course, we see Bill's mother regularly. I drop in on the old lady. I'm rather sorry for her as she says Bill never seems to write to her. But she says that you do.'

'Bill doesn't like letter-writing,' said Gail.

'Bill's a bit of a spoiled boy, I'm afraid,' said Mrs. Partner a trifle tartly. Then with a long searching gaze at Gail: 'Look here, darling, you know I never ask questions, but I'm very distressed at your looks. Something's wrong. Aren't you happy, Gail? Isn't this marriage turning out right for you?'

An instant's silence. Gail held herself rigid. Her heart-beats were shaking her thin body. She longed passionately to throw herself into her mother's arms and tell her everything. Tell her about Ian. Tell her that she had found out what a ghastly mistake she had made in marrying Bill. It would be a relief to confide in somebody. And yet wouldn't that relief be selfish? It would only hurt her mother deeply to learn about the affair in Le Touquet, and without knowing that, how could she ever understand the present position? It seemed to Gail much best to keep up some sort of appearances, and spare her parents the truth. So she laughed. It was a very gallant laugh.

'Oh, my marriage is all right, Mummy, dear. Bill and I are very happy. Falling down the

219

Castle steps shook me up a bit and I haven't felt the same since. That's all.'

The mother went on unpacking.

She did not really believe the girl. But she forbore to question her further.

'I must go down the hill to see my mother-in-law this afternoon,' added Gail.

Mrs. Partner went downstairs to do her ordering. Then Chris came in. He sat on the edge of the bed, and looked affectionately with his one comic eye at the sister he adored.

'Damned decent to see you again, Fish-face,' he said.

Her heart warmed to him. 'Fish-face' was not a pretty name, but it meant a wealth of affection from Chris. And although he was only sixteen, there had always been an understanding between them. And suddenly Gail reached the conclusion that although she could not worry her parents with her personal troubles, she *could* talk to Chris. He would be sympathetic, but he wouldn't be hurt in the same way as the old ones. And she knew that he would keep her secret. So presently she began to talk to him about Bill.

'Don't marry too young, Chris,' she said with a bitterness he had never before heard from her. 'And make quite sure of your choice, first of all.'

Chris kicked his heels together and shoved his hands into his coat pockets.

'You're not so keen on Bill as you were, are

you, Fish-face?'

She bit hard at her lip.

'I suppose it's frightfully disloyal of me to say a word, but I'm not happy, Chris. *I'm not.*'

'I knew that! And I knew you wouldn't be. You were an idiot to have married him. You know I always loathed him. What the hell made you do it?'

She dissolved into tears. Putting both her hands before her eyes, she felt ashamed to let herself go like this in front of her brother. Yet she could not control it now.

'Oh, I don't know, I don't know, Chris! I think I was carried away. You know he never let me alone. He kept proposing and he seemed so devoted, and when war broke out I thought of him in khaki, going out to die, and . . .'

'And instead, he's mucking about London spending money and kissing the hands of dizzy blondes in West End restaurants,' said Chris through set teeth. *'Damn him!'*

The tears dried on Gail's lashes. She opened her eyes wide and stared at her young brother. He did not look back. He was glowering at the tip of his toes.

'Chris, what on earth do you mean?'

'Oh, I wasn't going to tell you. But I've had it on my mind and it's upset me no end .'

'But what, Chris? What do you know about Bill?'

'More than he thinks. I haven't told anyone,

221

especially the parents. And if I thought you were happy with him, I'd have kept it from you. But now I know you aren't, I don't see why you shouldn't know what sort of chap he is. I don't doubt he's a good officer, but he's a rotten cad for all that.'

'Chris, tell me at once.'

The boy blurted out the story.

How, on his second day up in town, he'd been asked by his cousins, Tommy and Dick Carruthers, to lunch at the Berkeley Buttery and see *The Little Dog Laughed*.. They couldn't get a table at the Buttery, but he had suddenly spotted his brother-in-law's back and would have gone up and spoken to him, only at that moment Bill had kissed the girl's hand!

'Just making love to her blatantly,' Chris added in a voice of disgust.

Gail sat very silent, chilled. When Chris had finished she said quietly:

'Will you please describe the girl as accurately as you can.'

In his boyish fashion Chris did so.

'Good-looker and all that. I only saw her profile. Sort of deb type and film-star combined. You know, Sis, golden curls flopping down to her shoulders. Goo-goo eyes and all that. Sort of makes me sick.'

Gail gave a set little smile. The description left no room for doubt in her mind that the girl with whom her husband had lunched that day was the Naughtons' daughter, June, and she,

222

too, felt thoroughly disgusted. Perhaps there was no harm in it, but Bill had taken great pains not to mention the fact that he had taken the young girl out to lunch. And he had talked as little about his meeting with June as though it hadn't counted, in his life.

She reflected on the story.

So that was how Bill had spent his spare time when he went down to Woolwich to fetch those recruits. Indulging in a clandestine meeting with the daughter of one of his senior officers! As for that little hussy . . . Gail could well imagine June being up to any tricks. She had started them on Ian at the Castle.

Much as she disliked Jean Naughton, Gail was sorry for the woman. And sorrier still for the nice old Major. How heart-broken he would be if he knew how that girl of his behaved.

It was not that she was jealous of June. There was no room left in her heart for jealousy of Bill. It just seemed to her rotten that he should pretend to be still so much in love with her, his wife, to be so possessive and exacting, and at the same time to spend time and money on another girl.

Apart from loving him, she could not even respect him now. What right had he, at his age, and married, to have an affair with a girl like June?

'It's a pity you can't get out of this marriage,' said Chris. 'He isn't good enough for you, Sis.'

223

Gail did not answer. But she buried her face in her hands and thought:

'And I might have belonged to Ian. I might have been *his wife*. God! if I only *could* get out of my marriage. If I only *could!*'

## SEVENTEEN

Chris Partner, his boyish face scowling, turned in the direction of his sister. Young though he was, he could understand something of what she was feeling. This business about his brother-in-law had seemed pretty ugly to him. To Gail it must appear even uglier. He wished intensely, for her sake, that she had never married Bill. He, alone, of the family had cordially disliked their neighbouring friend from the very first moment he had become acquainted with him, and Bill had started to patronise Chris. Of course, Bill had always made himself very charming to the parents, and occasionally brought Scampie sweets and that sort of thing. He could be very ingratiating when he wanted. Chris knew that. And he supposed that girls who were impressionable would be attracted by Bill's good looks and that air of superiority which he affected. But beneath it, Chris had always been sure that Bill was an inferior person, and now he knew it.

Gail gave a deep sigh and lifted her face

from her hands. She wondered if she looked as worn and weary as she felt.

'Oh, well, Chris,' she said dully, 'it's no-good crying over spilt milk. I thought I liked him a lot when I married him, but there's no getting out of the marriage. No question of divorce, anyhow. I don't think Bill would be . . . unfaithful . . .' Her cheeks coloured as she turned to her brother's gaze. 'June Naughton is a decent girl—'

'Supposed to be,' said Chris bluntly, 'but I don't think much of a girl who fools round with other women's husbands—'

'You're quite right, darling, and I like you to have high standards,' said Gail.

But she sighed deeply, and her thoughts were painful ones. For what would her young brother have said had he known about Ian and herself? Only all that was so long ago, and now they were both fighting against their love. It was no use feeling guilty about it.

'Serve that bounder Bill right, if you walk out on him,' said Chris.

Gail laughed a little.

'Darling, I have no real proof of anything awful, and even if I had . . . even if I walked into a room and found June Naughton in my husband's arms, I couldn't walk out on him. I'm not trying to make myself out to be a plaster saint, but I appreciate the fact that Bill is serving his country and that he's a good soldier. It's up to me to help him keep his reputation instead of help to ruin it.'

'Are you going to tell him that you know about him carrying on with that girl?'

Another sigh from Gail. 'Maybe. I'll see, but whatever happens, I don't want Mummy and Daddy to know about it—nor that poor old lady down the hill who thinks he's an angel.'

Chris burst out:

'You're a sport, Fish-face. A damned, decent sport, and much too good for that—'

'Don't, darling,' interrupted Gail, 'it's no good cursing him. He's my husband,, and I've just *got* to make the best of it.'

'Well, let's talk about something more pleasant,' said Chris, and began to tell his sister stories of the O.T.C. at school.

Gail only half listened. Her thoughts were whirling—up to Edinburgh and Ian. Up to Aberdeen, where Bill would be tonight. Back here to herself. A dozen varying emotions were contained in those thoughts. Longing for Ian. Contempt for Bill and his affair with a young girl—Major Naughton's own daughter. And it was for a man like *that,* she had flung away her chances with Ian.

Inevitably, Gail's mind turned to the memory of a stern old Scottish lady who had failed to carry out her son's request before he left for India, three years ago. Mrs. Dalmuir, now dead. Bitterly, oh! *bitterly* Gail thought of her. She, who was responsible for all the suffering. For had Gail only known that Ian

226

wanted to go on writing to her—wanted to keep up their association, she would have never looked at another man, even although it meant waiting for Ian for twice three years or more.

Before Chris left her bedroom, she warned him against letting their parents guess that there was a rift between Bill and herself. Neither must they know about how she, Gail, felt about her marriage.

The rest of that day passed uneventfully. Gail gave herself up to the pleasure of being back in her old home. Many of her Kingston friends dropped in to see her. The family doctor also looked in to examine the ankle, and assured Gail that it was getting along splendidly. It wouldn't be long before she would be able to get on a shoe and walk about again.

The one unpleasant hour was a visit from old Mrs. Cardew who came up the hill to the Partners' house to save Gail from the effort.

The old lady was pathetically interested in every detail of her son's life up in Edinburgh. His work, all that he was doing.

She was delighted to hear that he had been sent off on a special job.

'I knew Bill would be picked out for something special,' she said with a pleased smile, 'you must be very proud of him, my dear.'

'Of course I am,' said Gail.'

But she thought what a farce it all was and what a lot Bill would have to answer for by his betrayal of his mother's immense faith in him. His perpetual neglect of her. The poor old lady had had one letter from him in six weeks, and that merely a scrappy note. But she wrote faithfully every other day. Letters which, Gail knew, Bill merely crumpled up and said:

'The usual weekly mail from Mother. Too boring to read . . .'

It was said that as a son treated his mother, so would he treat his wife. She had been a fool, Gail told herself, not to think about all these things before she had rushed headlong into marriage. But she gave Mrs. Cardew a brilliant report of Bill and sent the old lady away bursting with renewed pride and happiness. And that same evening, she managed to bring herself to the point of writing to Bill, and writing normally, as though nothing had happened.

She knew that she could have told him outright that she knew he had met June Naughton, and made such obvious love to the girl at the 'Berkeley.' She could use that as a lever for her own ends if he adopted his bullying or unduly possessive manner. At the same time, she did not want to employ any such methods against her husband. It would only create the most unpleasant atmosphere between them. Besides which, she was in a delicate position. There had already been a mild scandal about Ian and herself up at the Castle. And for Ian's sake alone, Bill must be placated. If he was sufficiently thwarted by his wife, or annoyed, he might look more closely into Jean Naughton's report. And that would involve Ian. She must tread warily. She was fiercely determined that Bill should never be given a chance to sling mud at *him.*

Not a pleasant position for a newly-married bride to find herself in, and Gail loathed it. But the whole of the circumstances of the last month or two had forced it upon her.

On her second evening at home she received a long-distance call from Aberdeen.

Bill, after a few preliminaries, informed her that he was returning at once to the Castle.

'As usual, the Army has changed its mind without warning,' he grumbled. 'Orders from H.Q. have just come through. This thing I am working on is still in its experimental stage, and the brigades I've been visiting are not ready for it. I'm going back to Edinburgh tomorrow. You'd better come back, too.'

Gail's heart gave a lurch. For an instant she did not reply. She only knew that the last thing she wanted on earth was to go back to Bill—and to the Loch Castle. She had told her mother the truth when she had said that the accident had shaken her up. Her nerves were bad and she did not feel fit to take that long journey again immediately. It didn't seem worth while having come all the way home if she couldn't stay at least a week. Besides which, it would be so disappointing for Mummy. They had planned to do a lot of things this week-end. Daddy had saved up his petrol, and they were going to go down to Bexhill to see Scampie.

But her greatest reason of all for not wanting to go back to Edinburgh was—Ian. To go through all that tension again . . . that agony of being under the same roof with him, knowing that she belonged to another man! And since the Mrs. Naughton scandal, it would be all the worse. And June was still there. How would Bill behave with June?

'Hullo! Hullo!' came Bill's voice.

'Are you there?' 'Yes, I'm still here.'

'Then come up tomorrow, precious. I'm crazy to see you.'

She set her teeth. She knew what *that* meant. She thought of June, and felt slightly sick. She said

'If you don't mind, Bill, I won't come back until Monday. I don't feel awfully well, and I need the rest with Mummy to look after me.'

Bill took another three minutes in which to express his disappointment, mainly on his own behalf. He was not so worried about her health as his own annoyance, because he wouldn't have her there at the Castle to welcome him and make a big fuss of him. He had no intimation that June was still there to amuse him. But Gail was stubborn and he could not, in all conscience, insist upon her immediate return.

Then he let drop a piece of news which was of considerable interest to Gail.

'I've just this minute been speaking to the Brigade Major at the Castle. There seems to be a "flap" on. Our noble host, Dalmuir, has gone down to London to the War Office.'

She felt her whole body grow hot, then cold. Ian *here* in London . . . so near . . . and she had been imagining him up there four hundred miles from her.

She tried to make her voice appear casual as she said: 'You mean for some time?'

'Oh, I don't think so, only on some temporary job. He'll probably be recalled as speedily as I was.'

Then the three 'pips' went, and Bill decided that he couldn't afford any more, but would write to Gail from the Castle tomorrow.

Gail put up the usual pretence with the parents, that evening, that all was well. They played rummy, which was always a family favourite, and then Gail was helped up the stairs to bed. Chris followed, slightly depressed because the oculist had pronounced his eye fit enough for him to return to school tomorrow. He besought Gail to write often and tell him all the news, which she promised to do.

She half wished that she could confide in her young brother about Ian. But that story was something that she could not, must not,

231

tell *anybody*. Yet what a pity! How Chris, would like and admire Ian!

When she was alone Gail gave herself up to the thought of the man she loved. She realised that she was tremendously stirred by the knowledge that he was in this very city. So near and yet so far. She did not even know where he was staying. Possibly at some club. It might be better, perhaps, if his Staff duties kept him at the War Office for a time. It would be easier for her to go back to Scotland without the presence of what Bill had called their 'noble host' in the Castle.

London seemed a more thrilling place now that she knew Ian was in it. She shut her eyes tight and pictured him walking down Whitehall; a conspicious figure in London, with his tartan trousers and glengarry, and that 'air' about him which was essentially Ian Dalmuir.

She found herself praying:

'God bless you, my darling Ian. May no harm befall you, whatever happens to anybody else in the world!'

## EIGHTEEN

The first thing that Mr. William Cardew did upon his return to the Loch Castle was to approach his major's wife.

In spite of Gail's attempts to lull his

suspicions, he had not forgotten one word that Mrs. Naughton had said to him on the telephone that night. Just before the evening meal he knocked on the door of her private sitting-room and asked if he might have a few words with her.

She was embarrassed to say the least of it. She was a woman who had spurts of intense feeling about this thing and that, but never managed to keep up the intensity for long. She had regretted her interference between husband and wife, especially now that Gail had left the Castle and, incidentally, Captain Dalmuir had taken his departure. Darling June's hopes were practically at an end, and she herself would be going back to England in a week's time, anyhow.

So when Bill spoke to her Mrs. Naughton was in no way anxious to further his suspicions.

'Perhaps I did wrong to suggest that your pretty little wife shouldn't be left here alone,' she said in her most friendly voice. 'But you quite understand, don't you, things get a little awkward sometimes when an attractive young woman is alone in the midst of gay bachelors . . .' she ended on her heartiest laugh.

Bill would have liked to have been rude and told her that she was an interfering old cat, but remembering that she was the wife of his superior officer, and June's mother, he did no such thing. Why worry about Gail's affair, anyhow? If he could find out anything at all,

233

well and good. It would give him an excuse for thinking twice of June. He had been excited by the thought of returning to the Castle and finding June here.

When the door of the adjoining room opened, and the girl came into the room, he completely forgot Gail. He was struck, as he had been struck on that night at the Cafe de Paris, by the girl's glamour. She was wearing that dress in which he had last seen her on that afternoon when they had driven to Richmond Park. It was at once simple and sophisticated, some soft, black, woollen material with two little diamond clips at the neck. A wide belt accentuated the slenderness of her waist, and when she lifted her arm to shake hands with him, the familiar sound of her jangling bangles thrilled him. How demure she appeared, looking at him through her long lashes. She was doing the 'little girl' stunt in front of her mother.

'So nice to meet you again, Mr. Cardew.'

He replied with equal formality, but the moment that Mrs. Naughton was out of the room she came closer to him, put both hands on his shoulders, and invited a kiss.

'I thought you weren't coming back in time to see me. I was just heart-broken when they said you were away for three weeks,' she murmured.

He put his hands over hers, but looked furtively round. He was aching for her embrace

234

. . . one of those long, exciting ones that they had experienced in the car at Richmond. She was not ice like Gail. She was all fire, the little witch! But he was alive to the fact that he must be damned careful in the Castle. He knew from the way Mrs. Naughton had behaved about Gail, that she wouldn't spare him if she found him fooling around with her daughter. And that job of his was important. June *must* be careful.

'Aren't you going to kiss me?' she whispered.

She was all out for pursuing the affair with Bill. She had lost hope of Ian Dalmuir. He was much too standoffish. And the other subalterns were a bore. Bill had a quality that excited her.

'Of course,' he whispered back. 'But for God's sake let's be careful, sweet. Where's your father?'

'Downstairs. I'll hear him coming.'

He snatched a kiss. She was disappointed. She would have liked it to be longer. But Bill, pulling his khaki handkerchief from his sleeve, carefully wiped his lips and looked in the glass to make sure there was no trace of red on his face.

She said: 'You are a "meanie"!'

He gripped her wrist, smiling

'Little devil, you know what effect you have on me, but we mustn't lose our heads. We'll find ways and means of meeting outside the Castle.'

With a jingling of bracelets, June lifted her hands above her head, and drew a deep breath.

'You've said it.'

'We'll have every chance,' he said rapidly, 'because Gail's away with this foot and I think I can keep her down at Kingston a good bit longer.'

'Sure you love me best?' she asked.

He was spared from having to lie because at that moment there were footsteps and he drew himself smartly to attention. June, with a secret smile, busied herself pouring out some sherry. When Major Naughton came into the room Bill was full of talk for him about his trip up north, and only cast an occasional eye at the girl. He told himself that even June would never be able to seduce him away from his work, nor must she be allowed to spoil his popularity with his senior officers. But tactfully managed there could be a very good time for them both up here, and perhaps there would be some means of suggesting that old Gail might like another week or two down South with her parents!

When he telephoned to his wife that next evening, Gail was astonished by the subtle change in Bill. She was also perplexed. He seemed, somehow, different. Much more thoughtful about her health and her happiness than usual. Thoroughly unselfish, for Bill.

'I've been thinking, darling, and you're not to dream of coming back until that foot's right. Besides which, I know the family would like to have you for a few more days.'

Gail tried not to feel relieved.

'If you're sure you're not too lonely without me, darling,' she said dutifully.

He assured her that although he was lonely he understood, and that he wanted her to be quite fit before she undertook the return journey.

At the end of the call Gail joined the others in the drawing-room, feeling slightly ashamed of herself. She'd been harbouring unkind thoughts about Bill and had labelled him a self-centred cad.

It was not for an hour after his call that she suddenly woke up to the realisation of *why* he had been so considerate. Then her feelings changed again and her thoughts became very cynical.

'I'm just too "green" and simple for words,' she told herself bitterly. 'I might have known ... *of course* ... June Naughton is up there.'

That was why he did not want her to hurry back to the Castle! Chris had not: exaggerated about the girl at the Berkeley Buttery. Bill was having an affair with her.

For a while Gail wrestled with herself, wondering what she ought to do in the circumstances. All her inclinations leaned toward staying down here with her parents where she could find some peace and happiness. She had not the slightest wish to return to the Castle. She would feel a hypocrite if she accepted Bill's kisses, knowing that he would not hesitate to make love to another girl.

It would mean that eventually she would have to tell him what she knew. Then there could be nothing but wretchedness between them.

For the next few days the struggle within Gail continued. Bill continued to telephone because he had no time to write letters, he said, and each time he spoke it was with sympathy and to the effect that she need not hurry back. She had all she could do to control the desire to sneer at him and mention June's name. But she forbore to do so. Who was she to judge, she asked herself hopelessly, feeling as she did about Ian! Yet how could she compare the two things? Bill's was just a senseless, selfish intrigue *pour passer le temps,* and hers was the result of a great and enduring love which had lasted through the years.

Finally she came to the conclusion that it was her duty to go back to the Castle and save Bill from his own folly. The ankle was almost healed and she could put on a shoe again and limp around. She must get back to Edinburgh, no matter how she dreaded it.

The Partners went to King's Cross to see their daughter off. She was travelling on the night train. It was so much less boring than sitting for ten solid hours during the day-time, especially now that the black-out came so early, which meant that one had hours in a carriage so dimly lighted that one could not see to read.

Mrs. Partner, although maintaining her usual motherly cheerfulness, was a little anxious about her daughter. She embraced her tenderly.

'Take care of yourself, darling. Write often and be happy,' she said.

'Oh, I'm very happy,' said Gail, also on a cheerful note.

Once the good-byes had been said and the train moved out, Gail sat on the narrow bed in her sleeper, and started to pull off her gloves. She sighed a little.

Back to Scotland! Back to Bill! And at the thought of the reunion awaiting her, she winced a little. But she had made up her mind to make a good show of it now. For everybody's sake she must not allow this marriage of hers to be an obvious disaster.

Just over a week ago she had said good-bye to Ian and left him four hundred miles behind her. Now she was doing exactly the same thing. She was leaving him in London. Her beloved Ian! Well, he would have plenty to do at the War Office. That would keep him busy. It was good to be busy when one didn't want too much time for thought. Men weren't like women, anyhow, Gail told herself. Work was so important to them. They rarely allowed their personal griefs or desires to affect them so that their work suffered.

She must try to get a good night's sleep, and be at the top of her form when she reached Edinburgh tomorrow morning. She had wired her husband to meet her train, and drive her out to the Castle. It seemed to her a long time since she had seen them all there. She wondered how they were. Whether that Naughton girl was still there. (She grimaced at the memory of Mrs. Naughton and her scandal-mongering.) But it would be much better without the presence of Ian.

'I'll take the setters for walks again,' she thought. 'In a way it will be lovely to be back in *his* home.'

The door of her little sleeping compartment was open. The conductor put in his head and asked if madam had everything she wanted. He would bring her a cup of tea early tomorrow morning half an hour before they were due in at the Waverley Station.

Gail remained seated on her bed. Taking off her hat, she glanced at her reflection in her handbag mirror, and ran a comb through the red-brown waves of her hair.

'I mustn't get any thinner,' she told herself, 'or I shall soon look like a hag!'

She got up to close her door. Several people were moving up and down the corridor before settling down for the night. Elderly men in civilian clothes, officers in uniform, women in fur coats, a small boy with his nurse; the train was now well out of King's Cross, winding through the suburbs.

Then, as Gail was about to close her door, a tall man wearing a British warm and glengarry came down the corridor. Came face to face with her. Her heart gave a tremendous jolt and brought the colour surging into her cheeks.

'*Ian!*' she said breathlessly.

Captain Dalmuir saluted her. His own face had flushed a deep red.

'Why, *Gail,*' he exclaimed, 'you're the last person in the world I expected to find on this train!'

## NINETEEN

He collapsed weakly on to the edge of her narrow little bed again.

'Oh, Lord!' she said in a voice of dismay, and with a helpless laugh. 'This *would* happen! Fate just won't allow us to escape each other, will it, Ian? I, thought you were safe and sound in Whitehall, my dear.'

The train jolted. Ian put a hand up on either side of the narrow door, swaying a little as they rounded a curve.

'So I was. But only on a very temporary job.

I have to be back in Scotland tomorrow.'

'And so we both chose the same night for the journey north,' she said with another laugh.

But there was not much humour in her heart. She was considerably shaken by this unexpected meeting. And nothing could stem the tide of wild happiness that surged across her at the sight and sound of him. He could change the face of her world in a few seconds, and she knew it. There was no room in her mind for thoughts of Bill at this moment. She just looked up at Ian with big, luminous eyes, which betrayed all her feelings.

He looked back, conscious of his own intense pleasure at the meeting. Yet that pleasure was sharply allied with grief. Grief for Gail because he knew how she suffered. He knew her so well. She had always been ultra-sensitive, poor little Gail. More emotional perhaps than the average girl. It was much harder for her to take a grip of her feelings than for some. And she had been so brave. She had struggled so gallantly not to betray what he already knew. The fact that she regretted her marriage to Cardew and that she was still as much in love with him, Ian, as she had been three years ago.

He could pity her because he pitied himself. The whole thing had caused him an anguish which he had not bargained for when he returned from India. It was the very devil to be madly in love with another man's wife—especially when that woman was, by every right, *his* and should never have married Cardew at all.

He sought refuge in flippancy.

'What a gorgeous slice of scandal for Mrs. Naughton! Captain Dalmuir and Mrs. Cardew travel together on the night train. Not by accident. Oh, no! By evil intent, having arranged the whole thing. A dastardly assignation, what?'

He laughed and Gail joined in, then protested.

'Don't! It makes my blood run cold to think what Mrs. Naughton will say when she finds out.'

Ian moved right into the sleeping compartment to allow a ticket collector to pass down the corridor.

'Oh, yes, you might as well come in,' said Gail drily, 'leave the door open and then it'll look above-board.'

He sat on the edge of the narrow bed, beside her, feeling in his coat pocket for a packet of cigarettes which he had bought at King's Cross.

'Here's one,' said Gail and handed him her case.

He took off his glengarry. Holding the cigarette case, he smoothed the enamel with his thumb.

'You didn't have this in Paris, did you?'

'No, I didn't smoke then.'

'What a child you were, really.'

'A little idiot, Ian.'

He winced.

'Don't say that as though you regret it all.'

'I don't regret *us*. I never will. It was too beautiful and too wonderful. I only regret all that's happened since.'

Silence, while he lit his cigarette. Then he said abruptly:

'Jesting apart, you realise, don't you, that this will land us in for a spot more scandal, Gail?'

'Yes, and it's absolutely unfair.'

'I was a madman ever to be seen coming out of your room that night,' he said in a low voice. 'I started the whole trouble. I ought to be shot.'

Gail looked at the stern fine profile of the man.

'The one thing I am most determined about is that you shouldn't be made the subject for gossip, Ian.'

'My dear, what the hell do I matter? It's your reputation that I'm worried about.'

'Well I'm worried about yours, so there we are,' she said.

'Is Cardew meeting you?'

'I wired him to.'

'Hell!' said Ian under his breath.

Gail shrugged her shoulders.

'It's hopeless. Whatever our good intentions

are and however much we try to do the right thing, we seem to get cornered. And yet they couldn't be so stupid as to imagine we *arranged* this. It would be too silly, too flagrant.'

He smoked hard at the cigarette for a moment.

'I wish I could say that I don't care a damn what they think. I know it matters in our circumstances. But why *should* one be dictated to by people like Mrs. Naughton?'

'Of course,' said Gail, 'you don't know what she did just before I left the Castle, do you? I didn't see you alone again so I didn't tell you about her conversation on the phone with Bill.'

'No. What was it?'

Gail related the story. Ian's face was white with fury when she had finished.

'Confound the woman's impudence for interfering in our private affairs. It was a damned dangerous thing to do, too. She'd better be careful of the laws of libel. My God! I'll never forgive her for it.'

'At least she didn't mention your name,' said Gail.

'She would have had to answer to me if she had done so,' said Ian between his teeth, 'and if she does any more interfering when we get back to the Castle, I'll soon fix it. I'll tell the Brigadier that I'm disposing of the Castle and that the whole billet must be moved.' He added hotly: 'I told him when we first made the plans that it wouldn't be a good thing to have wives in the billet. But he's a silly old fool. A bachelor who has never had anything much to do with women, so he thinks them all angels.'

'That's a nasty one,' Gail laughed.

He gave her a quick passionate look.

'Well, you know what I think of *you,* darling. But you see I've met Army wives before. You've only got to live in a garrison in India to see what incalculable harm such women as Mrs. Naughton can do by jealousy and gossip.'

'Well, what are we going to do?' asked Gail.

'Nothing. You say your . . . that Cardew is meeting you. Well, we'll just behave as though it was pure coincidence (which it is) that we're on this train, and we'll all three drive back to the Castle together. And any more trouble from Mrs. Naughton, and I swear I'll carry out my threat and close down the Castle.'

Gail sighed.

'Oh, Ian, it must have been so lovely and peaceful there before the Army took it over!'

'It was. It still is—in patches.'

He looked down at her feet and added:

'How's the poor little ankle?'

'Almost well again. I just limp a bit.'

Impulsively his hand went out to take one of hers.

'Poor darling! Life hasn't been very good to you just lately.'

She trembled at his touch and in answer to that throbbing note of tenderness in his

246

deep voice.

'No, it hasn't been too good,' she whispered.

'I wish we could see some way out of the tangle.'

'I wish so, too.'

'We must just put up a good show, my sweet.'

She nodded dumbly.

With some difficulty, Ian added:

'Cardew's a good fellow.'

She remained silent. She could not, would not, tell him about June. What good would it do to let Ian have an insight into Bill's real character, and prove that he wasn't such a 'good fellow' after all. It would only make matters worse, and further Ian's anxiety about her. He had important work to do for his country and the less personal anxieties he had at a moment like this, the better.

Their eyes met. Neither of them spoke. But volumes were said in the long look they exchanged. His fingers crushed hers so hard that they hurt her. She knew exactly what he must be thinking. She was thinking it too, longing for him to stay here with her, talk to her; wishing they could spend the long precious hours of this journey together. There was a war on. Air raids! Neither of them knew how long they had to live. And they loved each other desperately. Why waste the hours? Why miss golden opportunities?

The tension between them became

unbearable. Gail felt her head spin. And she turned so white that he said:

'Darling, *darling,* are you all right?'

She nodded, smiling.

'Yes. Hadn't you better go?'

'Yes?'

He stood up. She looked at him dumbly. That tall, khaki-clad presence seemed to dominate the little compartment. She adored him. She couldn't bear him to leave her; to know that when they reached their journey's end it would only be to face fresh separation, fresh pain.

He saw what lay in those lovely smoke-grey eyes. Eyes that had haunted his dreams for nights past. And with all the will, the strength in the world, he could not totally resist the sweet temptation of her. With a swift movement he shut the little door behind him. They were closed in then out of sight of the world.

With a slow deliberate gesture he pulled her up into his arms and held her crushed against him.

'Darling,' he said, 'darling, I'm going to kiss you good night.'

She made no effort to restrain him. Her powers of resistance had for the moment deserted her. Like a creature dying of thirst, she lifted her lips for his kiss and drank it in deeply, deliriously.

The moments sped by. The train gathered

248

speed and whistled sharply once, twice, as it sped northwards. Outside there was the darkness, the desolation of the great blackout. All the accoutrements of war. The camouflaged aerodromes. The military huts and tents. The munition factories. The air, raid shelters and first aid posts. The incredible trappings of the incredible war against Germany. And in the little sleeper on this train, two desperate young people clung together in a desperate embrace, forgetful of world problems, steeped in their own insoluble one.

Again and again they kissed. In each single caress, the sweetness was edged with despair. Gail's arms were inside the big military overcoat clasping Ian's waist. His brass buttons hurt her soft breast, but she did not care. She sought to hold him closer, as though she could never let him go again. His fingers threaded through her hair, caressed her neck, her soft cheeks, while his lips travelled from her lips upwards to both her eyes in which the big tears were gathering.

'Don't cry, my sweet, don't. You know how it breaks my heart.'

'I won't,' she whispered, and blinked back the tears.

'You know I'd give my life to save you suffering and be able to put this right. But I don't see any honourable way out.'

She reached up on tiptoe and pressed

his warm, tanned cheek against hers. In a suffocated voice, she said:

'I know! I know! Ies a frightful muddle. There *is* no way out.'

'Yet I still feel you're mine, Gail. I can never feel you're *his*.'

'I want you to feel that. It's how I feel myself.'

'Darling sweet! If only it could be different.'

'It's awfully cruel, Ian.'

'Life seems rather cruel one way and another, darling. Crueller than death sometimes.'

'I wouldn't mind dying here now, like this,' she said passionately, straining nearer him. 'I wouldn't mind if we were bombed and put right out of it . . . except that it would be an awful waste of you.'

'And what about you?'

'I don't matter.'

'My adorable Gail, that's sheer nonsense. And the whole conversation is nonsense. We neither of us want to be bombed really. We mightn't be so conveniently put out of our misery. We might just lose an arm or a leg— and what then?'

She shuddered in his arms.

'*Don't.*'

He laughed, trying to calm her down. The slim young body was trembling so violently. Poor little darling! He thought what a lot he would give to be able to stay with her . . . to know once more the ecstasy that had been his in Le Touquet. God! .How little they had both thought that life would lead them to *this!*

'Don't be depressed or think gloomy thoughts, once I leave you, sweet,' he implored, 'just shut those marvellous eyes of yours and go straight to sleep and be happy.'

With a long, long sigh, she disengaged herself from his warm embrace.

'I'll try. And when we both get back to the Castle we must be terribly careful and terribly formal—mustn't we?'

He picked up his glengarry which had dropped to the floor.

'I suppose so.'

'Good night, Ian,' she said, 'go now, darling, please.'

He did not trust himself to touch her again. Turning, he opened the door and let himself out of the compartment. As the door closed, she sat down rather heavily on the bed. Heavens! How weak she felt. Bodily and mentally weak and stupid, and quite without hope.

But she tried to do what he had asked. She undressed, crept into bed and lay there, making an effort to sleep. But her whole body throbbed with the memory of him and of those wild kisses which they had exchanged. The movement of the express jolted her. Every time they stopped at a station, if she was half dozing, she woke up again with a start at the sound of voices and shouts from the platform, and all the usual clamour and paraphernalia of a night journey.

It was not until they were long past Newcastle that she drifted into unconsciousness

## TWENTY

Bill Cardew, muffled in his great coat, hands in pockets, marched up and down the platform at Waverley Station awaiting his wife's arrival.

It was one of those piercingly cold mornings in Edinburgh when the wind from the North Sea sweeps across the city and cuts like a knife At seven-thirty it was still quite dark. The Castle was obscured by the grey mists of night. Not for another half an hour would it be light.

It was not the best time for a man to feel in high spirits and Bill's face was sullen and his sense of humour completely missing as he waited for the night-mail.

Damned decent of him to have got up and come out with the car at such an ungodly hour, he told himself. And it wasn't as if he was really anxious for Gail's return.

Something had happened about Gail, in Bill's mind. He wasn't quite sure yet what. Just a sudden queer reaction from the old adoration of Kingston days. He had been crazy about her then, he thought as he walked

252

moodily up and down, tapping his cane against his legs. Quite crazy, and held her almost in awe. Proposed a dozen times or more, and was always refused, thwarted. He wasn't used to being turned down. It had piqued his inordinate vanity, and he had finally worked himself up into a fever of desire for her. And then . . . she had suddenly caved in. She had married him. He had gained possession of that cool fragile, beauty which had so tantalised him in the past.

For the first month or two he had been anxious to please her. (Although he had told himself that nothing would ever make Bill Cardew a slave to any woman. His wife was his wife and had got to remember it! He would always be master in his home. He would 'train' her, as he had trained his mother.)

Lately he had felt that all the warmth was coming from his side, and none from hers. It wasn't good enough. He had returned to the Loch Castle from Aberdeen with resentment burning in him. A desire stronger than ever to bend and break Gail to his will.

But now there was June. During this week their 'friendship' had waxed fast and furious. He was quite aware that the young girl was now madly in love with him. In the way that *she* understood love. A mixture of blatant schoolgirl passion and sophistication that described June Naughton. They had had many of those secret little 'walks and talks' outside the Castle together already.

Well, now when Gail was back, things would be more difficult. He had judged from one or two talks with June that she did not like his wife. And on one occasion when she had hinted that her mother's inferences about Gail had been well founded, he had had a flash of loyalty and defended Gail. Called the whole thing nonsense but he did not forget what she said. And now he was determined to keep an eye open. If Gail *had* been indiscreet in his absence, he'd soon find it out and then, by God, he'd have the upper hand. She wouldn't be able to do that 'poor angel' business with him. Oh, no!

This, therefore, was the mental attitude of the Bill who met his wife that grey winter's morning.

Gail was quite unaware of it when she stepped out of the train and waved at him. She only knew that she was wretched in the extreme—that a little way down the corridor the tall figure of Ian Dalmuir was standing apart from her. Just as he must always stand apart, figuratively speaking, through the rest of her life. But she had made her mind up to go through with the thing properly, and so she greeted Bill with her sweetest smile, inwardly hopeful for a little real affection and tenderness from him.

'Hullo, Billy Boy!' she exclaimed, and held up her face to meet his kiss.

He brushed her cheek with his moustache, his blue eyes dark, sulky-looking.

'Oh! Hullo! My God, what a ghastly hour to meet anyone. I'm half frozen. Give me your suit-case.'

She felt rebuffed. The smile left her lips. She knew at once that Bill was in a bad mood.

'I hope he's going to be nice,' she thought unhappily. 'It'll make things much more difficult if we plunge straight into a scene.'

One of Dalmuir's own cars from the Castle was there to meet her. The driver, who was in khaki, came forward to take her bag. Then suddenly Bill looked over Gail's shoulder, and said:

'Good lord, there's Dalmuir.'

'Yes,' said Gail. 'We came up on the same train.'

'Oh!' said Bill shortly.

Now, he supposed, he must appear more pleasant. Dalmuir *was* Dalmuir, and no good forgetting it.

He saluted Ian smartly.

'How are you, sir?'

'Fine, thanks,' was Ian's brief reply. He did not, dared not look at Gail. 'You've got the car here? Good! Well, the sooner we get back to the Castle, the better. I need some breakfast. And I expect Mrs. Cardew could do with a hot drink.'

They drove out of Edinburgh station into the dark morning, Ian beside the driver, Gail

255

and her husband at the back.

In silence Gail stared before her as they moved up the hill into Princes Street. She could not even thrill this morning at the sight of the Castle standing up so splendidly silhouetted against an ever lightening sky. The age-old battlements looked stark and grim. Overhead there were storm clouds. The streets were glistening and wet, looked as though it had been raining all night. Wild, northern weather!

The car moved rapidly down the tram-lines out of Edinburgh and into the country. Not a word was spoken by any of them in the car during that journey. Gail wondered desolately what Ian must be thinking. She could only see the back of his collar which was turned up and the dark head with the glengarry. He did not turn to converse.

And Bill seemed in no mood to ask her anything about her holiday, or even her ankle. So she, too, said nothing.

It was not a very happy drive, nor an encouraging welcome back to Scotland. Gail felt both chilled and depressed by the time they reached the Castle. But here at least her spirits rose a little. It was so beautiful, Ian's Castle. And now the morning was light and the grey old pile rose proudly against a magnificent stormy sky of red and orange. The lawns were soaked in the heavy rain. There seemed not a single leaf left on the trees in the park. But inside the Castle there was warmth and light. Gail was glad to go up to her sitting-room, where a log fire would be burning. Just before she went upstairs, Ian Dalmuir broke the silence by saying:

'See you at, breakfast, Cardew. Hope you're not too cold, Mrs. Cardew . . .'

So formal . . . so distant . . . it made Gail's heart ache. But she answered with equal formality:

'I shall soon get warm now, thanks very much.'

And then she found herself in the sitting-room alone with her husband. Bill flung off coat, hat, stick, and gloves. The coat on a chair, the rest rolled on the floor. He spread his hands to the blaze of the fire and cast a sullen look at his wife.

'So you're back at last!'

She, drawing off her gloves, tried to smile.

'Yes. Sorry I was away so long, darling. But Mummy's doctor . . . you know, old Thomson . . . did think I ought to rest the ankle a bit longer. And you said on the phone it didn't matter.'

'Oh, no,' said Bill, 'it didn't matter at all. Believe me, my dear girl, I'm in no hurry for a wife who isn't in a hurry to come back to *me*.'

She pulled off her hat, and walking to the mirror over the mantelpiece, began to tidy her hair. Her heart was like a stone but she was not going to show it. She could see now that this was going to be no pleasant homecoming. Bill was such a changeable, difficult person. On the telephone he had been friendly and thoughtful for her. Now he was like a bear with a sore head. Resentful because she had not hurried home. She supposed she would have to try to 'do her stuff.'

'My dear old Billy,' she said lightly, 'there's no need for you to feel that way. You know perfectly well I wanted to come back. But my foot—'

'Oh, the foot was a good excuse,' he cut in, 'but it wouldn't have stopped you dashing back to one of your admirers. I'm not sure, of course, who he is. Mrs. Naughton seems to think there were one or two! But, of course, as I'm back too, it spoils your game.'

Gail went scarlet, then pale. She looked her husband straight in the eyes.

'Do you want to start all that over again? I thought we had it out over the phone?'

'We didn't have it out at all. Mrs. Naughton made very serious insinuations which I don't think a woman like that would have done without cause. You denied them.'

'You accepted my denials.'

'Yes, but I'm not so sure now that I was right. I've been putting two and two together. You've been damned chilly to me for weeks. Always on the high horse, too tired to be kissed or some rot. Who are you interested in? What's the counter-attraction?'

She felt herself beginning to tremble. The last thing in the world she had wanted was this sort of return. She tried to make her voice quite casual, as she replied:

'I'm not going to talk to you, Bill, if you're out to be nasty to me.'

Suddenly he caught her with both her arms, hurting her, pressing his fingers into the soft flesh.

'Well, neither will I put up with all this spiritual stuff and nonsense from you. If there isn't a man who attracts you more than I do, then you can make me feel that I'm a bit more wanted—*by you.*'

She felt as though she was in a trap the jaws of which were about to snap at any moment. She saw no escape. With all her heart crying out for Ian Dalmuir, she must needs surrender to this kind of intolerance and bullying from Bill. And yet . . . why should she? She asked herself passionately. She had a weapon which Chris had put into her hands. Why not use it? Why not tell Bill that she knew about his secret meeting with June in London. Wasn't that sufficient excuse on her part for not wanting to surrender body and soul to him? It proved that he was ready to go straight from her arms to a flirtation with a young débutante. It was so degrading. Yet she forbore to throw it at him because she felt a certain sense of guilt about her love for Ian. She stood helpless and hesitant in Bill's arms. Then suddenly his passion cooled.

The flash of desire for Gail passed. He wasn't going to worry about her. There was June in the Castle. Pretty, eager June who showed that she liked a fellow and was such fun.

'Oh, to hell!' he said violently, 'I'm not going to demean myself begging for kisses from you. But what I *am* going to do is find out who the hell you've been playing around with while I was away.'

## TWENTY-ONE

A moment's silence, and then Gail turned and began to walk, limping very slightly on the ankle which was still weak, into the adjoining bedroom. She was too sick at heart and disappointed by her reception from Bill to make any answer to his threat. Not that the shaft failed to find its mark.

For Bill to find out about Ian was the very last thing that she wanted; for Ian's sake so much more than her own.

She had reached the stage when, if she had only had herself to consider, she would gladly have told Bill the whole story. She disliked all this enforced deceit, this dissimulation. It was foreign to her nature. Just as in the same way she had hated keeping the truth about Ian and

Paris from her mother three years ago. But it was not her story to tell. It never had been her story alone. It was Ian's, and Ian's reputation as a soldier now, more than ever, was her first and foremost thought.

If Bill had been different he, too, would have been uppermost in her mind. She would have wanted to spare him from disillusionment in her. When she had married him, she had meant to bury the past, and make Bill a generous and complete gift both present and in the future. But all her resolutions were scattered and her good intentions baulked. For Ian had come back and Bill had proved unworthy and she felt that she had built this marriage on such shifting sand that the whole structure of her life was in danger of collapse. She felt isolated and afraid.

Bill followed her into the bedroom. For a moment she pretended not to notice his presence. She unlocked her suit-case and began to unpack. He watched her, standing by the door, smoking, his eyebrows drawn together in a scowl. She was looking tired and washed out after the all-night journey. He did not find her particularly attractive to him this morning. The vision of June, so pretty and warm and seductive, was far more enticing. And yet there was something deep down in him which was doggedly determined to break this young wife of his completely to his will. Her continued aloofness maddened him, some quality in her, perhaps, which made him ashamed of himself. That would madden any man. He was of coarser fibre than Gail, and he knew it, and he knew that *she* knew it, which was like a red rag to a bull.

She was very quiet and almost disdainful, he thought, keeping her head turned from him, bringing out the clothes which she had carefully packed. Always so damned tidy, he thought. So damnably correct. What was she made of? Ice, or flesh and blood? Ice to him, perhaps. Fire to some other man. *Who was the man?* Why had June hinted several times that she knew what her mother had meant about Gail's indiscretions?

Rage suddenly seized Bill Cardew by the throat. He walked up to Gail who was shaking a blue velvet bed-jacket and about to put it on a hanger. Childishly he knocked it out of her hand on to the floor.

'Damn it,' he said in a thick voice, 'why don't you say something? You can't practise this injured-innocence-and-dignity stunt on me. You've got something on your conscience? Well, let's hear it, and be done with the thing. Come on! Who *is* the man? *Who is it?*'

Her cheeks had burnt fiery red at his rough gesture. Now she was white and trembling. She said:

'Don't treat me like this, Bill. You'll be sorry if you do. I haven't the slightest intention of standing for it. The next time you knock something out of my hand, I'll pack up and go home to my family, and stay there.'

He controlled himself with an effort. She could see that he was in one of his towering rages and that it was not easy for him to master himself She was sick to the depths of her soul, but she was not going to let Bill get the upper hand of her in *this* fashion.

'You're quite mistaken if you think you can try this rough stuff on me,' she added, 'I tell you I won't stand for it.'

'And neither will I stand for the way you treat me.'

She spread out a hand with a gesture of hopelessness.

'How do I treat you? What are you complaining of, Bill?' He said through his teeth.

'This damned coldness. You shrink away when I touch you. Anybody'd think you loathed me. We've only been married a few months and you were supposed to be in love with me when you married me. *Supposed.*'

She put a small clenched hand against her breast. She could feel her own heart thumping. *Supposed.* Oh, but it was true! She, herself, had supposed that she was in love with Bill before she married him

In a suffocated voice, she said:

'Don't let's talk to each other like this, Bill. We are dramatising ourselves rather absurdly. Let's stop it, and . . . and be friends.'

'I don't want to be friends with you. I'm your husband.'

She gave him a bitter look.

'You've never said a truer word. That's the whole trouble . . . you *don't* want to be friends with me. You think a husband should only make love to his wife, or turn her into a domestic servant. You don't think there should be real companionship between us, do you? My dear Bill, you're out of date! You should have been one of those autocratic husbands of the Victorian era, when a wife was not supposed to have any intelligence, only—'

'Oh, shut up!' he broke in violently and rudely, 'I'm not going to waste my time arguing with you. I've heard enough from Mrs. Naughton . . . and others,' he added significantly. 'And I don't think you're the plaster saint you make yourself out to be. Don't forget, either, when you're practising this frigid business, that I've seen the fire behind it. You were crazy about me down at Kingston when we got engaged. You didn't mind being kissed then, and I don't think you mind being kissed now. Only not by me. But I'll find out who it is you're keeping yourself for, my dear little angel!'

His face was red, suffused, ugly. All good looks were wiped from it. And Gail; watching him, felt the last shred of respect, of affection, die within her as she looked upon him. But because of what she knew about Ian . . .

264

because of her own hopeless position she had nothing to say. She could not even bring herself to throw in his face what Chris had told her about Bill's clandestine affair with June Naughton.

Bill turned and walked out of the room. She heard the sitting-room door slam and knew that he had gone downstairs. Mechanically she went on with her unpacking, but her fingers trembled so that she could hardly hang up her clothes. She wondered why she had left the peaceful happy home at Kingston where her nice normal family had made her feel so welcome, and where there had been none of this ugly, threatening atmosphere. She saw herself and Bill and Ian all together in a tangle . . . a ghastly muddle from which there seemed no escape.

Downstairs, Bill Cardew seated himself at the breakfast table. He was still in a towering rage. He did not even bother to tell one of the servants to take a breakfast tray up to his wife. Let her order it for herself, he thought. He wasn't going to wait on her, or even consider her.

Then as he ate a hearty meal and one or two of the other officers drifted in and discussed the morning's news with him, he regained his good humour. He wondered why he had bothered to flare up and make that scene. He'd be seeing June at lunch-time, and he had arranged to have half an hour with her in those woods fringing the Castle grounds, just before tea. At dusk, when it wasn't easy for them to be seen. It would be a pleasant change, he thought, to hold a flesh and blood creature in his arms who enjoyed his caresses. He wasn't going to waste his time any more over Gail. But he'd pay her back for her attitude toward him. He'd damn well find out what all these rumours were, which emanated from the Naughtons concerning Gail.

The first inkling of the truth that lightened his rather dull imagination was later in the day, during that half-hour with June.

They were strolling down a beaten track in the woods. It was dark and bitterly cold, but June did not seem to mind. She wore a fur coat and cap and high suede boots with fur round the ankles.

'I don't feel cold when I'm with you, anyhow,' she had said to Bill when they had first met, and clasped each other in a hotly passionate kiss.

Now she was asking him about Gail.

'I must say I'd like to know what my position is, Billy, darling,' she said in her cooing voice, and pressed his arm against her side. 'Do you really love me, or are you just one of these married men who want both wife—and girl friend?'

The darkness hid his scowl. He laughed.

'I did love my wife, but the affection is rapidly diminishing through her own fault.'

'She's rather stupid,' said June, 'you're so marvellous.'

That soothed his vanity. He paused and caught her close, burying his face against her warm neck.

'Little witch! You're the marvellous one! But June, my sweet, you and I are going to have to be extremely careful with the whole of the Castle watching us.'

'Poof!' said June, 'nobody has the slightest suspicion. You're the blue-eyed boy with Daddy. He thinks you're one of the best junior officers he's ever had under him. And Mummy adores your blue eyes and golden hair. And she's got her knife into your wife, I tell you.'

Bill drew back from the girl. His old flaming jealousy of Gail returned, despite the seductive presence of June who chose to brave the darkness and the cold of the northern twilight in order to give him her kisses.

'Look here, June,' he said, 'hasn't there been a lot of nonsense talked about Gail? I mean . . . you're always hinting . . . and so is your mother . . . and to be quite honest, I haven't noticed Gail casting an eye at any of the fellows here.'

June twisted her lips.

'Haven't you?'

He walked on with her. Their feet crunched on the frosty leaves.

'No.'

She gave a little tinkling laugh.

'Aren't men blind. I saw from the first moment, and so did Mummy.'

'Saw what? Why don't you tell me?'

'I would if I thought you didn't care. But I don't understand you sometimes. You pretend to be in love with me, and at the same time you're jealous of your wife. It's so inconsistent.'

He laughed.

'Not really. A man may himself be in love, outside his own home, but dislikes the idea of his wife looking at another fellow.'

'Well, if you care who Gail looks at, I shan't tell you,' June said with a pout. 'And anyhow, Mummy is anxious we shouldn't make any mischief.'

Bill burned with curiosity. For many reasons he wanted to know what June was driving at, and if she had any definite information, he meant to get it out of her . . . he wanted a weapon to use against Gail. Out of pure spite, because her very aloofness had defeated him.

But June was not entirely to be drawn. She was a little uneasy about giving Bill the full facts as she knew them. But an opportunity to drop a still broader hint came when Bill mentioned that Gail had come up to Scotland by the night-mail last night with the Laird of the Castle.

'Good lord!' June exclaimed. 'She came up on the night train with *him?* Well that's pretty brazen, I must say, and you *still* maintain you don't know . . .'

Bill stopped dead. Through the purple gloom he tried to see June's face, but it was a white blur. He gripped her slim wrists, making the bracelets jingle. He said:

'God! Do you mean to say that *Dalmuir and my wife—*'

'I'm not saying anything,' June broke in hurriedly, 'it isn't my business, Bill, and Mummy would be very cross if I said any more.'

For an instant he was silent. He alternated between the desire to kiss her and shake her. Tantalising young devil. At the same time, a torrent of dark suspicions were let loose in his brain. June had opened the flood-gates. Gail and Ian Dalmuir. God! That was something he hadn't thought of, but of course, it might be true. They had known each other in France years ago. Gail had never spoken much about it, but she had always been rather secretive on the subject. Perhaps there was a good reason for her secrecy. Perhaps Dalmuir was an old flame of hers, and now the flame was being rekindled.

'Darling,' said June, 'if you're going to get all het up about your wife instead of telling June how much you love her, June's going to toddle home. She's getting a bit bored!'

Cardew controlled himself and his thoughts. Whatever he thought about Gail . . . whatever he meant to do . . . he was at the same time

269

anxious to maintain his popularity with this lovely girl. He caught her close to him again, loosened her furs, and put his hands on either side of her slender, supple waist.

'To hell with everybody else,' he said, 'I'm crazy about you . . . *and* you know it.'

She laughed softly, reached up her arms and pulled his lips down to her mouth.

## TWENTY-TWO

That first evening back at the Castle could hardly be called a pleasant one for Gail.

Bill had been out at work most of the day and when she had been alone with him, he'd ignored her. When she spoke to him he did not answer, so she gave up trying. If he was going to behave in this childish fashion, she could do nothing about it. At dinner-time downstairs he had a change of demeanour, however. Perhaps it was for the public eye. She knew that Bill liked to shine in the eyes of others. So when he chatted to her and joked and made himself conspicuously attentive during the meal in the big dining-hall, she presumed that he was just playing to the gallery. Nothing that he said seemed sincere, and the expression in his eyes when he looked at her was certainly not friendly. It was almost malevolent.

She could not feel that anything she had

done warranted this treatment. And knowing what she did about Bill and June, she wondered how he could be so hypocritical. He punctiliously avoided looking in June's direction or, when the meal was over, going anywhere near the Naughtons. But he had something up his sleeve, Gail was sure, and she felt uneasy when he handed her some coffee, and said:

'Let's move over to the fireplace and talk to Dalmuir.'

She threw a fleeting glance at Ian. Their eyes met. Then Ian turned to the Brigade Major, who was lighting a cigar and said something to him. She knew that he wanted to talk to *her,* just as much as she longed to speak to him. Since the early arrival at the Waverley Station this morning, they had only caught a glimpse of each other during lunch, and had not spoken.

She said:

'I'm a bit tired, Bill. I didn't sleep very well in the train last night. I think I'll go upstairs.'

Bill gripped her arm. His fingers were like iron and made her wince.

'Oh, no you won't,' he said between his teeth, 'you'll stay down here. Don't try any of that rushing away into a corner business. I'm sick of it. It's time you came into the open, my girl.'

She stared at him blankly.

'Really, Bill, I think from the way you're

271

treating me, you must be out of your mind.'

He ignored that and walked with her across to the fireplace. She was forced to go with him, otherwise he would have dragged her there.

The Brigade Major moved away from the fire.

'Must say a word to the Brigadier,' he said.

Bill, Gail, and Ian were a trio alone now by the great open fireplace. Ian stood a little stiffly, and almost to attention, as Gail and her husband joined him. He thought how wretched Gail looked this evening. Lovely in that black velvet dinner-dress with the long tight sleeves, but he had never seen her look quite so pale. There were deep shadows under her eyes. Poor little darling, he thought. She was so obviously miserable, and he could do nothing to help or comfort her. Nothing except pray to God that he would soon be sent to France.

Bill was, as usual, over-cordial.

'Well, well, how are you, sir? I've just been telling my wife that if the Loch Castle is to be our billet for the duration, then let the war roll on!' he added with a laugh.

Ian barely echoed the laugh.

'Oh, my Castle is very attractive,' he said, 'but personally, I would like to find myself a bit nearer the Maginot Line.'

'M'm. You're rather fond of France, aren't you?' said Bill.

Ian stirred his coffee. His dark, brooding eyes were no longer fixed upon Gail. He could

272

scarcely bear the expression in her eyes. It hurt him too much. He said:

'Yes, I'm very fond of France.'

'Where was it you and Gail first met? Paris? You've never really told me,' continued Bill.

Now Gail felt distinctly uneasy. What was the matter with Bill and what was he driving at? Why was he referring to her past friendship with Ian all of a sudden?

Ian said:

'Yes, in Paris, wasn't it, Mrs. Cardew?'

'Oh, I say, I say!' came from Bill with another over-hearty laugh, 'there's no need for all this formality, is there? Surely you two got to the Christian name stage in Paris. One usually does, in Paris, what? Ha-ha-ha!'

Silence. Gail felt as though her heartbeats were doing double time. Ian's eyes were upon her now and she knew that the blood scorched her face in a blush which she could not control. And now, Ian Dalmuir too was a little uneasy. But he gave Bill a cold stare.

'Maybe we did. I've really forgotten, it's so long ago.'

Bill raised an eyebrow.

'Three years? That's not so long. How did you first come across Gail? Did you see much of each other? I've always meant to ask, and never had time. There's so much to think about these days.'

It was Gail who answered now.

'Captain Dalmuir and I were both friends of

my French girl friend, Simone and her brother André. I *did* tell you, Bill, in Edinburgh that evening when Captain Dalmuir first came in for a drink.'

'You didn't tell me much,' said Bill pointedly.

'Sorry, but if you don't mind, Cardew, I must leave you. I've promised to take a hand at bridge,' said Ian in the coldest of voices, put his cup down on the mantelpiece, and moved away.

Wrung though his heart was with pity, with love, for Gail, he dared not even throw her a parting glance. He only knew that he disliked Cardew with all his soul. Disliked him and did not mean to remain here to be cross-questioned by him, whatever the fellow was driving at.

Gail looked after him, her eyes tormented. She felt a chill as of death itself envelop her. Then Bill said:

'I've changed my mind about going upstairs. I'm going up myself. I want to talk to you.'

She clenched both her hands.

'No, no,' she said to herself, 'not another scene tonight. I couldn't bear it. I'll break down altogether if he goes on . . .'

Bill had left her, strode across the big hall and disappeared from sight. She stood irresolute. A little wildly, her gaze wandered round the room. How happy, how normal everybody else seemed. The Naughton family, chatting with two of the subalterns. Almost with envy Gail regarded June Naughton. Not an enviable character, but it must be fine to be so *stupid* and so heartless. Not to care about anything or anybody except oneself. She stood there, fair and radiant in a rose-pink dress, showing her teeth in a dazzling smile at the young officer 'Pop-eyes' who was supposed to be head over heels in love with her. And Joyce Fenton, *there* was a lucky girl! Drinking coffee and talking to her husband about the golf they were going to play the next morning he could get off. Stolid, unimaginative Joyce. Just a good sort, but, oh, so pleased with life. On the best of terms with the man she had married and what more could any woman ask, Gail thought wretchedly.

Through a kind of haze she saw Ian Dalmuir's tall soldierly figure approaching her. He reached her side and spoke rapidly in an undertone:

'Gail, darling, what was that all about? Is Cardew suspicious? What the devil did he mean by that peculiar spate of questions?'

'I don't know, Ian. I just don't know. He's been peculiar all day.'

'Well, don't let it worry you, darling. He can't find out anything, and quite honestly I'm not going to stand for any nonsense. If he makes your life unpleasant, he'll have to answer to me.'

There was a lump in her throat and her eyes

misted over. She fought fiercely with a desire to break down there in front of him and the whole room.

He added:

'I don't want to stay and talk to you. There are too many eyes on us. Chin up, darling. Things will be all right. Remember that I love you.'

He moved away again. For a moment, she stood silent, eyes shut, trying to get a grip of herself. Remember that he loved her! God, that was the one bright star, the only star, in the darkness. That knowledge of his love.

She supposed that she had better go up and face Bill. Face another sordid row. Or a reconciliation. She wondered which would be worse! As she moved across the room, Joyce Fenton approached her. Joyce did not share Mrs. Naughton's antipathy for Gail, nor did she know anything about the trouble between Gail and the Major's wife. She said:

'I say, Mrs. Cardew. I believe we are getting the car into Edinburgh tomorrow. Will you come with me to Jenners and help me buy some more wool for our knitting party, and we might have a cup of coffee together.'

The invitation sounded so wholesome, so sane, and yet so trivial in the sea of her troubles, that Gail was glad to accept it.

'I'd love to come with you,' she said.

'You're not looking too well,' said Joyce sympathetically, 'your trip down South hasn't done you much good.'

'No, it hasn't,' said Gail with a short laugh.

Then, reluctantly, she bade Joyce good night, limped up the stairs toward her private suite. When she walked into the sitting-room, she found Bill engaged on a curious task. He had all her suit-cases open and was feeling in the silk pockets and linings. As she entered, he paused only for an instant to throw her a baleful look, then continued the search.

With her heart beating quickly, she said:

'What do you think you're doing?'

'Just amusing myself,' he said.

'Why are you going through my luggage like this?'

'Looking for evidence,' he said coolly.

She shut the door and stood with her back to it.

'Evidence of what? Honestly, Bill, as I said downstairs, I think you've gone suddenly out of your mind.'

He pushed the suit-case which he had been rummaging on to the floor. It fell with a bang.

'Not at all. I've merely come to my senses at last. Everyone in the Castle seems to guess what you've been up to—except myself, and now I'm merely looking to see if you've added to your indiscretions by writing or receiving letters.'

She breathed hard and fast, her large grey eyes hunted.

'Letters from whom—to whom?'

277

'Dalmuir,' he said, 'it's now quite easy for me to jump to the conclusion that Dalmuir is the gentleman you favour, my dear Gail, and the reason for your handing the frozen mitt to *me*.'

So it was out! Gail felt hot and cold in turn. She clasped her hands together behind her back, her fingers nervously working. Now, she thought, was the time for her to keep calm. To lie if need be, although not because she wanted to. With all her heart she wished to be done with prevarication and to tell Bill the whole story. But since it so vitally concerned Ian, she could not. She said:

'You *are* out of your mind.'

He came up to her and caught her by the shoulders, his fingers pressing through the velvet of her dress into her soft flesh.

He said:

'You're a first-class liar, my dear little wife, but you can't get away with it. You had an affair with Dalmuir in Paris. I'm pretty confident now. I've been putting two and two together. And when I was away in Glasgow, you thought you'd be clever and carry on with the affair. The only thing which seems to me to be crass stupidity on both your parts, is the way you flaunt the affair in public by coming back together on the night train. Tired after your long journey, are you? Perhaps you didn't sleep, because—'

'Be quiet,' she broke in, 'don't dare say

278

another word. If you do, you'll be sorry for it, Bill. I'll put on my things and I'll go back to Kingston and stay there. I'll never live with you again. You've no right to insult me and if Ian heard you—'

'Ian!' It was Bill's turn to break in with a laugh, 'it's "Ian" now when the mask's off, is it? Downstairs, it was Captain Dalmuir! You make me laugh—the pair of you.'

'Be quiet, I say,' came from Gail in a low shaking voice, 'you'll drive me so far but no farther, Bill. I'm not going to be bullied by you like this, not a moment longer.'

'Do you deny that you were having an affair with Dalmuir?'

She flung back her head, her eyes dark and enormous in her deathly face.

'Yes, I deny it—absolutely.'

'Do you deny that you didn't deliberately travel up with him last night?'

'I do. It ought to be plain to you that if I were carrying on an intrigue of that kind, I'd be a little more intelligent about it. It ought to be obvious that it was by pure coincidence that we caught the same train.'

'And do you deny that your attitude to me isn't because of Dalmuir?'

She looked him straight in the eye. She answered with honesty:

'Whatever my attittude toward you may be, Bill, it is not because of *any* man, but because of your own hateful behaviour toward me.

279

You're unkind, inconsiderate *cruel* . . .'

And she might have added 'disloyal' but still forbore to throw that at him. She could so well have used it as a lever in this moment, and yet her sense of justice forbade her to because of what had happened in Paris, and because she knew she could not tell Bill the complete truth.

Bill's hands fell away from her shoulder. He said sullenly:

'Well, I haven't any proof about Dalmuir, but I must say I'm suspicious, and I think I have the right to be. And I tell you this . . . whether he's my superior officer or not, if I do get hold of any proof, I won't hesitate to let Dalmuir and everybody else in this Castle know about it. I'll ruin him . . . that's what I'll do!'

She began to shake. Mentally she was strong . . . strong enough to fight for Ian like a tiger. But physically, her strength was deserting her.

She had been through too much this last twenty-four hours. At this very time last night, she had been enduring that painful scene with Ian, renouncing him . . . her love for him . . . bidding him 'good-bye,' even though they must still live under this roof together.

She tried to regain full mastery of herself. Clearly and distinctly, she said

'You have no cause whatsoever to attack Ian Dalmuir or attempt to take away his character. He has done nothing to warrant it. Nothing at all. And I want you to understand that for good and all.'

Bill eyed her through his long fair lashes, his face still red and angry. Compunction suddenly seized him. She looked very ill, and perhaps he had gone too far, he thought. After all, he had no proof . . . only June's insinuations. In a softer voice he said:

'Well, whether it's Dalmuir or some other man, it's time you showed me a little affection. If you love me and you're faithful to me, why the hell don't you prove it?'

The world was swimming around her. This, she knew was the price that must be paid in order that Ian's character should be cleared. She tried, rather pitifully, to smile at her husband.

'I will prove it, Bill. I will if you'll only be kind . . .'

He made a movement to take her in his arms. But when he held her, he held a dead weight. Her brown curly head fell back against his shoulder. He realised with consternation and some self-reproach that she had fainted.

## TWENTY-THREE

It was typical of Bill Cardew that rather than fetch help for his wife and risk there being some talk about it in the Castle, he allowed Gail to recover from her fainting-fit under his own clumsy ministrations.

281

He lifted her on to the bed, squeezed a sponge in cold water and dabbed at Gail's forehead, patted her hands, and spoke to her with some real anxiety.

'Are you all right, Gail? I say, old girl, wake up. I didn't mean to be beastly. Open your eyes, Gail. Come on, old girl, come on . . . !'

Gail very soon opened those large wounded eyes of hers and realised that Bill was trying to do his best to make up for the hours of bullying and criticism. She whispered:

'I'm all right now. Leave me alone, please.'

'Shall I fetch you some eau-de-Cologne, or some brandy?'

She shut her eyes, and put her laced fingers across them, because the light hurt her. Her head was swimming and she felt sick.

'No, I don't want anything. Just leave me alone, please, Bill.'

He looked at her awkwardly. Damn it all, he thought, she *was* pretty white, and she had given him a bit of a scare, fainting like that. He supposed he had been a bit tough with her. Knowing Gail as well as he did, he could not really be suspicious about her actions, nor about Dalmuir, who was one of these chaps who'd believe in the theory of: 'I could not love thee dear so much, loved I not honour more.' And if they *were* having a sort of eye-to-eye flirtation, let them get on with it. He had little June behind the scenes and she amused him, and a bit more than that!

282

Awkwardly, Bill tried to be nice to his wife.

'I really am sorry, darling. I lost my head a bit, just jealous of you, you know. Now let's be friends. We don't want to squabble, you and I.'

She opened her eyes again and gave him a long look which held a great deal of bitterness.

'No,' she said, 'we don't want to squabble. There's nothing on earth I loathe more than this state of bickering between us. We're married, and even if it hasn't been a success, we'd better try and make the best of it.'

The familiar scowl drew Bill's thick fair brows together. 'Oh! So you don't think our marriage is a success!'

She drew a long sigh.

'Don't let's start another fight.'

'Well, if it isn't a success, it's your fault more than mine,' said Bill huffily. 'You don't seem to care—'

'Please,' she broke in, '*don't* start another argument. I just can't stand it.'

He pulled a packet of cigarettes from his tunic pocket and lit one, snapping his lighter with an irritable gesture.

'Have it your own way. Say it's all my fault. So what?'

'So nothing,' said Gail with a short laugh, and turned her face to the pillow.

He eyed the slim, prone figure in a surly way.

'Do you want anything?'

'Nothing, thank you. I'll have my bath in

283

a moment.'

'Sure you're all right?'

She turned and gave him a smile which all the world might have found touching because of her very endeavour to show a friendliness which she could not feel toward this man with his moody, shifty, irascible temperament. She said:

'Thanks, Bill. I'm okay now. You go down and play some bridge.'

He moved toward the bed and, bending, dropped a kiss on her hair.

After he had gone, she switched off the light and lay there fully dressed in the darkness, feeling that she had not the strength to take off her clothes. Her exhaustion was not merely physical. Hers was a sensation of mental fatigue which was almost stupefying. It was as though she walked like one lost in a vast maze and could not find the way out. It was an agonising struggle, and in the maze with her was Bill and they were always meeting, always fighting, never helping each other. For how could they, when the love that had led them to marry was dead; had been proved no love at all, but merely one of those flaming infatuations which can fade out overnight! And beyond the maze was Ian, always Ian somewhere there in the tranquil distance with the sun on his face. The Ian whom she loved better than life itself. His hands were outstretched to help her, but she could not take them. His love, like hers, was undefeated by the years, yet must be stifled. It was a hopeless business and it needed a strength of will and a courage which tonight she felt far from possessing.

The whole situation was really too difficult and tense for her to deal with at any time. It would have been bad enough with Ian far away. But to know that he was here, downstairs at this very moment, for instance, and in a state of mind which was possibly only one whit less wretched than her own, was intolerable.

'If only I could go home again and stay with Mummy and the others', she thought. And while she lay there in the darkness the tears dripped slowly down her cheeks and soaked into the pillow and she did not even stir to wipe them away.

Things were not much better in the morning, but Gail supposed that she could congratulate herself that they were no worse. When Bill was working, he was always better, anyhow. She could at least grant him that he was a good soldier, and that nothing was allowed to interfere with his job. And once he and Ian were out at gun-sites, away from the Castle, she felt a little better, a little less strained.

She went with Joyce Fenton by car into Edinburgh. Joyce was a nice, jolly, easy-going girl and did most of the talking, and

285

Gail was glad of the sane and wholesome companionship. Not for the first time she envied Joyce the lack of complication and emotional strain in her life. She was in love with her husband and he was in love with her, and they were together, and what more could any human being ask of life?

The girls walked down Princes Street together and went into Jenners to buy their knitting wool, and have a cup of coffee.

Out of the wide window Gail looked up at the Castle. It was white-rimmed with frost this morning. The great red cross painted over the roof looked a lurid scarlet against the pallid, wintry landscape.

'It's grim and yet splendid, isn't it, that old Castle?' she said to Joyce. 'And to think what those old walls must have seen in their time. All the historic episodes of Scotland. And what a long stretch between the pageantry of Mary, Queen of Scots, and—today—with wounded German airmen lying up there in a hospital ward—in the second greatest war the world has ever known.'

Mrs. Fenton glanced at the Castle and smiled.

'M'm,' she said and added: 'Don't you think those silk stockings at six-and-eleven are jolly dear?'

And that made Gail laugh because it was so natural. Joyce couldn't be bothered with analysis of the Castle. She was much more interested in the price of silk stockings and not ashamed to show it.

The two 'Army wives' became more intimate as they drank their coffee. Joyce said:

'I hope you don't mind me mentioning it, Mrs. Cardew, but you have looked awfully rotten lately. We've all thought something was wrong with you. I do hope it isn't.'

'Nothing's wrong,' said Gail. 'Just private affairs . . . You know . . . things don't always go quite right.'

'Poor dear,' said Joyce sympathetically. 'I know they don't. My mother's maid who's been with her twelve years has just given notice.'

And that made Gail laugh again. And passionately she envied the woman whose trials and tribulations could be measured by the price of a pair of stockings and the loss of a servant. She wondered what on earth the jolly and simple Joyce would have said had she blurted out the whole story of Ian Dalmuir.

And then Joyce suddenly brought up the name of their host at the Loch Castle.

'I admire Captain Dalmuir awfully, don't you? I think it's splendid the way he has given his Castle over to us for billets. My husband thinks he's grand in every way.'

Gail looked into her coffee cup and her lips curved into a little secret smile.

'Yes, I think he's grand, too,' she said softly.

'I wonder if he has any girl friends. He

never seems interested in women and yet he's so fascinating to look at.'

Gail did not answer. It was a dangerous subject and she would have liked to have stopped it, but Joyce continued.

'Between you and me, I think that little piece of nonsense, June Naughton, has had an eye on him. But then she's got an eye on your husband and my husband, all the husbands. She's a public menace and I wonder Jean Naughton doesn't keep her under control.'

'I don't know that the modern girl accepts the word "control," ' said Gail, feeling rather matronly all of a sudden.

'So it's said,' said Joyce. 'But if I have a daughter and she behaves like that, I'll smack her.'

Suddenly they both stopped talking. Everybody in the restaurant sat quiet. For through the frosty air came the shrill warning note of the siren. Up and down. Up and down. That eerie and sinister note to which the people of Scotland and England were becoming accustomed.

'Air raid,' said Joyce. 'Do we go on with our coffee or go down to the shelter?'

'Go on with our coffee,' said Gail.

'Agreed,' said Joyce.

The two girls lit cigarettes. Down in the street they could see people hurrying off the roads and into the public shelters in the gardens below the Castle. Air-raid wardens with shrill blasts of their whistles held up cars, stopped bicycles, warned people off the streets. The trams and buses had come to a standstill. It was as though the whole of Edinburgh was suddenly galvanised, bewitched into a strange uncanny stillness.

Just one or two loiterers insisted upon standing outside, looking up at the sky, waiting to see the raiders.

'They won't drop any bombs,' said Joyce cheerfully. 'Our men are waiting for them. We've got 'em taped. I'm not moving till I've finished my coffee.'

Gail wondered where Ian was at this moment. Somewhere with Bill, possibly watching the anti-aircraft guns prepare for action. The droning sound of planes made both the girls look out of the window. Three British fighters, like black gigantic birds, raced across the grey sky, heading eastwards. And that was all there was to see, and all that happened until the 'All Clear' of the sirens sounded again. Then the big shop woke up and Edinburgh was plunged into its customary noise and activity once more.

On the way back to the Castle, Gail said to Joyce:

'Bring your husband up for a cigarette to our room tonight. It would be nice.'

Joyce said that she would love to. And Joyce felt rather a warm and friendly feeling toward this girl of her own age who had such a pale little face and looked so tired and wretched. She did not quite understand what was wrong with little Mrs. Cardew. And certainly she did not share Jean Naughton's antipathy for her. But one thing she did know . . . and she and her husband had often mentioned it . . . that young subaltern, Bill Cardew, wasn't good enough for her. He was handsome enough and clever at his job, but he was a bit of a bounder and everybody in the Castle knew it.

# TWENTY-FOUR

The Naughtons had only intended that their daughter should remain at the Loch Castle for a fortnight, but as time went on June pleaded and cajoled with her parents to allow her to remain up in Scotland. She was 'having such a marvellous time' she said. She didn't want to go back to her aunt in the country down South, and she was sure Captain Dalmuir wouldn't mind how long she stayed, she said.

So the Naughtons, only too pleased to have their one and only child with them, gave way. When the Major mentioned the matter to Ian, the latter was forced to be polite and say that Miss Naughton could remain as long as she pleased, although secretly Ian would have liked to have got rid of June whose presence he felt was a disturbing element in the Castle.

However, June had her way, and when December came, she was still at the Castle.

She was also still continuing her secret and unashamed affair with Gail's husband.

By this time, the inconsequent and egotistical young girl was as deeply in love as her shallow nature allowed, with the handsome Bill. He held her ardour in check just far enough to keep her interest alive and make her anxious to conquer him afresh. June did not like a man to make it too obvious that he cared for her. She was contemptuous of the young subaltern 'Pop-eyes' who hung about her begging for crumbs of favours. She had lost all interest in Ian Dalmuir, whom she now called 'Snooty.' And she never paused to look at things from Gail's point of view, because it was not in June's nature to worry whom she hurt so long as she got her own way.

She knew that both father and mother adored her and were completely blind to her faults and follies. She was quite aware that her father, in particular, would have been shocked and heart-broken if he thought that she was indulging in a love affair with one of his own subalterns, and a married man at that. And she knew that every time she met Bill she took a risk. But so long as Bill encouraged her, she found the risk worth while.

But Bill Cardew was fast discovering that he had bitten off more than he could chew, so far as June was concerned. She had reached a point where a few secret kisses and caresses were not enough for her. She was mad about him, she said. She would like him to leave Gail openly and run away with her. Let Gail divorce him, then marry her, June.

That was not in the least in Bill's calculations. He kicked himself for not having married June instead of Gail. (He would have done so had he met her first.) But he did not respect or admire her particularly. She was just very satisfying to his senses and as she was Major Naughton's daughter, she would have been a good 'catch.' But divorce was not in his line. He had too much to lose, and he valued his reputation as a soldier. Besides, he was not unaware that what he felt for June was passion in its most heady form—but merely passion. Gail would always hold what heart he possessed.

He felt particularly annoyed with June for being indiscreet when, one day after lunch, she cornered him in the big hall, while coffee was being served.

'I haven't seen you alone for days, and I've *got* to meet you somewhere this afternoon,' she whispered urgently.

He cast a quick nervous eye round the room. Gail was talking to the Brigadier. She was looking a bit better and they had been fairly friendly these last few days. Dalmuir was at the far end of the hall. Nobody was within earshot. Bill said:

'For God's sake, don't concentrate on me in front of everyone.'

June flushed an angry scarlet and gave an irritable jangle of her many bracelets.

'You can't talk to me like that, Bill,' she began.

He interrupted her.

'Everyone's looking at us,' he said through his teeth.

'Nobody's looking at us, you old meanie.'

'Well, what is it?' he asked weakly.

'You're off this afternoon, aren't you?'

'Yes, and I'm taking Gail for a walk.'

'Oh, no, you're not. You're coming out in the car with me.'

He scowled. He liked to make his own running. He disliked it when June became possessive. But she was telling him in no uncertain language that she expected him to meet her and she wasn't going to stand for a refusal. Her father was busy and he had given her the use of his car. Bill was to meet her at the bottom of the drive outside the gates, and they would go along the road toward Selkirk and turn off somewhere where they could be quite alone. She was tired of half-hours in the woods or park where they were always in danger of being found by the gamekeeper or Ian, himself. She had *got* to see him alone, and for a whole afternoon.

Bill protested. But June was insistent and a

rather ugly look came into those limpid blue eyes of hers. Her red underlip pouted like a child's. She said:

'I've a good mind to tell Mummy exactly how I feel about everything. It's getting too much for me and I'm miserable . . .'

'Now wait a minute,' said Bill, with another nervous look about him.

'Are you going to come out in the car with me or not?'

Bill caved in. After all, he wanted that hour with her. She was deucedly attractive and when that eager red mouth of hers was against his, it sent him pretty crazy. He didn't want to throw June over so long as she behaved sensibly. But there must be an end to this 'tell Mummy' business.

He promised to make an excuse to Gail and take that car ride with June.

At the other end of the big hall Gail finished her conversation with the Brigadier and found herself suddenly face to face with Ian.

For days now she had done no more than exchange smiles with him and those long hungry looks which left them both so hopelessly unsatisfied. She had been trying so desperately to keep to her resolution to put aside her love for him, and treat him only as a friend. She thought that he looked very worried and wondered how long it was since she had heard him laugh, that gay boy's laughter which had so often joined with hers in France.

'How are you?' she asked wistfully.

'Just ticking over,' he smiled down at her.

Those dark magnetic eyes made her catch her breath. 'That's how I feel,' she said unsteadily.

'You haven't had any more trouble . . . with *him?*'

'No. I think I've managed to make him understand that he can't bully me. And we haven't had any scenes lately.'

Ian frowned.

'How I hate the thought of you being involved in scenes.'

'There's only one thing that worries me,' she said. 'And that's Bill and . . .'

She did not finish that sentence. Something stopped her. She had been about to mention the name of June. She longed to confide in someone . . . and most of all in Ian . . . about Bill and June. Perhaps nobody else in the Castle noticed that they were 'carrying on.' But Gail knew it. She was well aware that they met secretly and often. And she did not know how to put an end to it. She could not bring herself to speak to the younger girl. It would be too humiliating. And she dreaded risking a scene with Bill on the subject, since he would only drag up the name of Ian and threaten him again. She was in a horrible position where Bill was concerned. At the same time she dreaded him making a fool of himself, not only for his own sake as an officer and a gentleman, but for the sake of his mother. Any scandal about Bill and that old lady down in Kingston would break her heart.

'What is it, darling?' Ian asked.

He did not mean to call her 'darling.' It just came naturally to his lips. And with all his heart he longed to lead her out of this room to some quiet place where he could put his arms around her and kiss the colour back into that white young face and the light back into those eyes which used to shine so brilliantly with love and happiness. Suddenly he said:

'Thank God I think this *ménage* will shut up very shortly. There's some talk of us all being moved. And I, for one, will be going over to France.'

That made her quiver. She felt as though a chill wind blew through the firelit hall and froze her through and through. She said:

'Oh, *Ian.*'

'It'll be better that way, Gail.'

She bit hard at her lip and clenched both small hands together.

'Must it really be France?'

'Yes. I hope so. I want to go.'

'You would. It's like you. But I shall never know a moment's peace ...'

He smiled at her with all his love in his eyes.

'I shall hold the thought of you as a shield. And anyhow, my dear, I don't think there'll be much of a flare up out there till the spring. So don't worry too much.'

'When do you think you'll go?'

'Any moment. I'm waiting for orders to come through.'

'Where will Bill be sent?' she asked hopelessly.

'Well, his course will end by Christmas, and then it'll mean some attachment for him to an anti-aircraft brigade somewhere, I should think. And that might mean anywhere in England, or Scotland or Wales.'

'Not France for him?'

'I very much doubt that. He'll be on instruction work here for a bit.'

There was no time for them to discuss the future further. Mrs. Naughton was advancing with that unpleasant look on her face which betokened to Gail that the good woman felt quite certain Captain Dalmuir and Mrs. Cardew would be better with a chaperone.

Gail moved away and left her with Ian. But Ian had work to do, and no time for Mrs. Naughton.

It was one of those intensely cold winter afternoons when a fog comes down suddenly and without warning and blots out the landscape.

About three o'clock the Loch Castle was shrouded in a yellow veil and the lights were all on. The parkland was barely visible from the Castle windows. Mrs. Naughton went from one Army wife to another, expressing her anxiety about her ewe lamb. Darling June had gone to Edinburgh shopping in her father's car. Mrs. Naughton was furious with herself for not going with her, but the girl had said she would be quite all right, and Mrs. Naughton had been so busy doing a bit of dressmaking this afternoon, and the fog was unexpected, anyhow.

By half past three most of the officers had returned to the Castle from work, with the exception of Bill, Ian Dalmuir, and Joyce's husband, Kenneth Fenton.

Bill was supposed to be out on some special job and Ian and Fenton had gone together in a Government car to look at new gun-sites, on which Ian had to make a report.

Ian was, at this moment, actually on his way home. He was driving. It was a slow journey because the roads were not only slippery, but the fog was growing thicker and thicker every moment.

'I think we'll give up the good work and get back to a dish of tea, don't you?' Ian suggested to his companion.

Captain Fenton agreed.

'All for it, old boy.'

Ian knew the road well and turned off the main Selkirk–Edinburgh route, up a narrow by-road which was a short cut to the Castle. Suddenly there loomed out of the fog in front of them the shape of another car. Ian had to pull up with a jerk. The car was so badly parked that it left little room for another to pass. Ian said:

'Some people are infernally stupid. Just get out, Fenton, will you, and see if there's anybody in that bus. If so, they can drive on and make room for us.'

Kenneth Fenton got out of the car and walked briskly up to the vehicle which was blocking their way. It was growing dark now and he had to bend down and peer through the glass windows to see the driver. The driver's seat was empty. Fenton could just make out two shapes at the back. And now he chuckled to himself:

'So that's it,' he said.

He walked back to Dalmuir. He was a cheerful soul and easy-going. He grinned at Ian.

'I say, old boy, there's a bally party going on in there. Damned shame to interrupt it. They're all in a huddle on the back seat. What'll I do, sound the horn?'

Ian smiled.

'Sorry to break in on love's young dream, but we must get ahead, old boy.'

Fenton, whistling, returned to the other car. He pulled the collar of his military overcoat well over his ears. The cold was piercing. He knocked on the glass and said:

'Hi, you there. Sorry to interrupt, but we want to get by.'

There was a deathly silence. Kenneth

Fenton knocked again.

'You there . . . would you drive your car on so that we can get by?'

Still no reply. Fenton's amiability evaporated, and he opened the car door.

The next moment he was staring amazed and dumbfounded at the pair who were no longer embracing, but sitting up in an attitude of acute embarrassment. Their faces were both revealed to him. The man's foolish and ashamed, the girl's defiant.

Without a word, Kenneth Fenton turned and walked back to Dalmuir.

'Well, of all the lousy things,' he said in a tone of disgust. 'Do you know who those two are?'

'No, who?'

'Cardew and that Naughton girl, June.'

Ian, who had been about to put a pipe in his mouth, left his hand suspended in mid-air, and stared at his brother officer.

'Cardew and June Naughton! You mean *they* were . . .'

'Yes, old boy, fairly locked in each others' arms when I first looked in. And Cardew with that nice little wife, too. It's a bit steep. As senior officers, I think we ought to say something to the fellow about it. In fact, I think he ought to be hauled up before the Brigadier. One can't do that sort of thing with one's Major's daughter. He ought to be kicked.'

300

'Yes,' said Ian Dalmuir, slowly, 'I rather agree with you. He ought—to be—kicked!'

## TWENTY-FIVE

For a moment the two officers looked at each other gloomily. Neither of them cared much for this situation. It was too sordid. Each felt as though the honour of the Regiment had been besmirched. Then Fenton said:

'They're off!'

Ian put his head out of the door. The sound of an engine being revved up was coming from the car in front of them. Then it moved slowly away and vanished like a phantom in the mist.

With a grim smile Ian sat back and stuck a pipe in the corner of his mouth.

'He wasn't going to face us, and I am not surprised.'

Kenneth Fenton took his place back beside the driver and slammed the door. And now they, too, moved slowly down the road. Every moment it was growing darker. Very soon the yellowish fog would have the whole countryside wrapped in an impenetrable blanket.

'Look here,' said Fenton, 'we can't let things rest at this. I'd say something to that lousy swine myself, only you're the senior captain, old boy. How about it?'

'Don't worry,' said Ian. 'I'll say something to him all right.'

'Have him up before the Brigadier.'

'I wonder if you realise what this would mean if it got to Naughton's ears.'

Fenton positively blushed.

'Old Naughton's daughter! It's a lousy business.'

'I'll deal with it,' said Ian briefly.

Fenton stole a glance at the senior captain. He was a great admirer of Dalmuir. Ian was popular with the whole mess and not without reason. But Fenton had never seen Dalmuir quite like this before. He looked white . . . as though he had received a personal shock. Of course, it was a shock to anyone, thought Fenton, to have discovered a brother officer in such an invidious position. But it seemed to have had more than an ordinary effect on Ian Dalmuir.

Only Ian knew how much this incident *had* affected him personally. It was horrible to him to discover that Gail's husband was having an intrigue with that young girl. He had always known that Cardew was a second-rate fellow. That Gail had made an immense mistake by marrying him. But he hadn't realised that Cardew was quite as bad as this. It was such a disgrace for Gail. That poor child who was doing her utmost to make Cardew a good wife and who was clinging to every shred of honour and decency for his sake. Hadn't he,

302

Ian, also forsworn his love, his all-consuming need for Gail because she was married? And the man to whom she was married had no compunction in sneaking out behind her back to an assignation with the daughter of one of his commanding officers. Of course, the fellow was a fool as well as an outsider.

When their slow journey through the fog ended and they reached the Castle, Fenton said:

'I shan't speak to Cardew. And I shan't mention anything until you've seen the Brigadier.'

Ian, stepping out of the car, gave Fenton a queer look.

'It won't be so pretty for Mrs. Cardew if there's a big scandal. Rather tough on her, isn't it?'

'Damned tough,' agreed Fenton, 'but one can't let a thing like this happen without doing something about it.'

'Quite,' said Ian, curtly.

As they walked into the agreeable warmth of the big hall where tea was in progress, Ian told himself that it was going to be no easy matter to put things right for Gail's husband, even for Gail's sake. Fenton was an easy-going fellow in a way, but he was a bit of a stickler for Army convention and good form, and Cardew had gone beyond all the bounds of honour. What he had done would be, in the eyes of all the rest of them, unforgivable.

Major Naughton himself would be so furiously indignant at the thought of a married man carrying on even a flirtation with his daughter that he would not hesitate to see that the junior officer suffered for it.

Ian took the cup of tea that was handed him and drank it gladly. He was cold and tired. Feeling altogether worried and dejected, he looked round the hall. Everybody seemed to be here, eating heartily of the excellent scones and buns which were always provided. Both butter and honey came from the estate, and food rationing held no terrors for this billet.

Cardew and June were back. No doubt they had come in separately, but here they were. The girl was laughing and talking to her mother. She did not seem concerned, but when Ian caught her eye she looked away quickly and nervously. He felt nothing but contempt for her. She was nothing more than a nymphomaniac in his eyes, but he was sorry for her parents.

As for Bill Cardew . . . Ian felt his gorge rise at the mere sight of Gail's husband. He, too, gave Ian a quick nervous look and then continued some conversation which he was having with his wife. Ian's heart went out to Gail. Poor darling, she faced a wretched future, married to a man who was utterly unworthy of her, faithless within a few short months of their marriage.

She had nothing to reproach herself with,

he thought tenderly. Her love for him, Ian, had blossomed long before Bill came into her life, and it was not her fault that that love had come back into her life later. But since it had happened, she had done her level best to uproot it. And to what purpose? Cardew wasn't fit to lick her shoes.

Ian could not trust himself to speak to Gail at this moment. Beyond a quick smile, he ignored her presence. But after tea he walked deliberately up to Bill and said:

'I'd like a word with you in my study, if you don't mind.'

A wave of scarlet ran up under Bill's fair skin. Gail saw it and was amazed. What had Bill to blush about like that, and why did Ian want to talk to him? She could see that Bill didn't want to go, but it was virtually a command from a superior officer rather than a request.

He mumbled: 'Yes, sir.'

Gail put a hand against her heart. It was beating quickly. As the two men walked out into the hall, she followed them with anxious gaze. What had happened?

Gail's husband and Ian Dalmuir faced each other in the room which Ian had made his study. A small room with a beautiful turret window. The walls were hung with oil paintings of the hunters which had belonged to the old Laird. Over the door there was the head of a particularly fine moose. On the mantelpiece stood a glass case, containing a great stuffed trout whose silver scales caught the light and shone proudly. Ian's uncle had been a great sportsman in his day.

Ian did not, as would have been his custom, offer Bill either a cigarette or a drink. Ice-cold, very much master of himself, he addressed the younger man.

'You know what I want to see you about, Cardew.'

For the second time that afternoon Bill flushed crimson. He shifted awkwardly from one foot to the other, hands in the pockets of his trousers.

'I suppose so.'

'Well, I'd like to know what you've got to say about it.'

Bill set his teeth. He had never liked Dalmuir. He had always been jealous of him, of his wealth, his position and his popularity with the other men, and recently, of his friendship for Gail. But now, with all his soul, he loathed him. He found himself in an abominable position. He hated the knowledge that Dalmuir and Fenton had found him out. It made his position with Dalmuir impossible. And it made him look a fool as well as a cad. Being found out always made a fellow look a fool.

Parallel with his hatred of Dalmuir, ran a seething fury against the girl who was in this show with him. It was typical of Bill that he

306

did not blame himself for the indiscretion and folly. He blamed the girl. His passion for June had run out with the sands of time. He realised that he had made love to her for the last time this afternoon. And the little devil had got him into this fix with her blandishments. It was she who had dragged him out in that car this afternoon. He hadn't wanted to go, but, of course, he had thought they were safe in the mist on that lonely road. It never entered his head that Dalmuir and Fenton were looking at new gun-sites in that direction.

When he had left June, the girl had been in a state! Scared stiff, of course, because they had been found out. Threatened him that she would tell her mother and make him leave Gail and marry *her*. But he wasn't having anything like that. He had made this one big mistake in his career and got himself into the hell of a jam, but he wasn't going to let it ruin him. No, not even if he had to crawl to Dalmuir.

Of course, he knew that there had been something funny up between Dalmuir and Gail and that June Naughton knew about it. But it wouldn't do to start blackmail or any hanky-panky of that sort. Dalmuir wasn't the chap to stand for it.

Bill had no alternative, in his own mind, but to throw himself on Dalmuir's mercy.

He began, sheepishly:

'I daresay you and Fenton were a bit

staggered, but I assure you there's nothing in it. It's just a bit of nonsense. The girl was what I call a bit adjacent and . . .'

'I think you can cut out all that,' broke in Ian, with a look in his eyes that made Bill squirm. 'You know as well as I do that there's no possible excuse for your conduct.'

'Oh, look here——' began Bill.

'You're a married man, Cardew,' broke in Ian again, 'and your marriage is only about three months old, isn't it? I repeat that you have no possible excuse.'

Bill set his teeth.

'Oh, very well.'

'In addition to this, Miss Naughton is the daughter of your second-in-command. You young fool! Do you want to be asked to resign your commission?'

Bill made no answer. He was enveloped by a sickening sense of futile rage. God, how he hated being spoken to like this and by Dalmuir of all men. How he would like to accuse Dalmuir of fooling round with Gail. But he dare not. He hadn't sufficient proof.

Ian continued:

'I may say that Fenton and I both consider this should be reported to the Brigadier.'

Bill went a bit green about the gills. His round blue eyes goggled.

'Oh, I say, sir, it isn't as bad as all that, is it? After all, you know what the girl's like. There was no harm, I swear. I made a fool of myself,

308

I admit, but you don't know everything.'

'What is there to know?'

Bill stuttered:

'I mean I . . . There were personal reasons
. . . I'd had a bit of a dust-up with my wife . . .
Just a fit of pique . . . Very indiscreet and all
that . . . Just the heat of a moment . . . nothing
more to it, I swear to you.'

Ian clenched his hands. He felt sick, just as
he had felt in the car when he had heard what
Fenton had to tell him about those two in the
fog. He had never felt a deeper contempt or
antipathy for any human being than he felt for
Bill. And he felt, too, that he now had Gail's
husband in his power. He could ruin him if he
chose. He could get him hounded out of the
Loch Castle and possibly out of the Regiment.
War or no war. Naughton would see that
Cardew didn't go unpunished. *If* it got to
Naughton's ears. *If!*

There rose before Ian's vision the pale, sad
little face of Gail. Those sweet eyes of hers
looked as if they were heavy with lack of sleep.
Those lips which had been made for laughter
were drawn with pain and repression. A sense
of complete frustration weighed Ian Dalmuir
down like a monster that crushed him. The
old bitterness against the mother who had
betrayed his trust and done this thing to him
and to Gail struck him afresh. He could even
regret, today, that he had not thrown up his
military career, his future, his family's wishes

and married Gail in Paris three years ago. Anything rather than that this situation should have come about.

And now it was within his power to ruin Bill Cardew. It would be pleasant to destroy the man who had hurt Gail so badly. And yet, would it not hurt her as well? She would have to share his disgrace. He knew her nature. She would be kind and merciful and she would stand by her husband. She might be reduced to still further misery through him and for him.

Bill was speaking:

'I should be very much indebted to you, sir, if you would overlook the indiscretion. As you know, I'm fond of my job, interested in my work. I wouldn't like to say good-bye to it.'

Said Ian briefly:

'I grant you that you are good at your job. But that isn't enough in the Army. If you can't behave as an officer should, you are not fit to have charge of troops.'

Bill licked his lips.

'I feel rotten about it, sir. I know Gail would be very upset.'

Ian did not look at him. He stared blindly at the antlers of the moose against the oak-panelled wall. The fellow was whining. Despicable. And the name of Gail conjured up fresh regrets and a grief which was always new, always a sword in Ian's heart. For Gail's sake alone, he could scarcely ruin this fellow. He must give *her* a chance. She had to live

310

the rest of her life with Bill Cardew, the poor darling! If he showed Cardew no mercy, which was what he would like to do, their marriage wouldn't stand an earthly hope of happiness. Already Ian felt remorse because of his own share in making Gail unhappy, so now he believed it was up to him to help them both.

He said:

'You're a b— fool! But I won't waste time telling you that. It seems you know it. I wouldn't like it to reach the ears of your wife or the Naughtons. Fenton thinks you ought to be hauled up before the Brigadier and so do I. But this isn't a time when we want scandal. There's a war on and we want to get on with it. I'll do what I can to hush the matter up if Fenton agrees.'

A great weight rolled off Bill's shoulders. He went quite white with relief.

'That's very decent of you, sir.'

'I don't want to be thanked,' said Ian, curtly. 'Just let it be a lesson to you to behave yourself in future. There's a job in your line going up at Scapa and I think I can get you transferred up there by wangling things with the Brigadier.'

Bill swallowed. He didn't particularly want to be sent to Scapa. It sounded damned isolated and damned cold. And, of course, Gail wouldn't be able to follow him. But anything seemed, better than the disgrace that had threatened him half an hour ago.

He felt neither friendly nor grateful toward

311

Dalmuir for saving him, but he assumed an attitude of contrition and thankfulness. Ian dismissed him abruptly.

'If you take my advice, you will inform Miss Naughton that your affair is over finally, and that she had better find some excuse for leaving the Castle tomorrow, unless she wants to be asked to go.'

'I'll see to that,' mumbled Bill.

After Bill had gone, Ian sent for Kenneth Fenton. While he waited for the young captain to appear, he asked himself bitterly what Bill would have to say to his wife. Doubtless he would never tell Gail the truth. As for him, Ian, he had gained nothing by this condoning of Bill's offence except the satisfaction of knowing that he had saved Gail's marriage from complete ruin. And perhaps after he had gone to France, Gail would manage to put the broken pieces of her marriage together and make it something of a whole. But he, Ian, must never see her again.

That was what he had really done by saving Bill. He had lost Gail for ever.

He would explain to Fenton that because of Bill's brilliance at his job he had decided to give the fellow a second chance, besides which, none of them wanted a scandal in the Castle. Fenton, of course, would agree, so the matter would be dropped.

When June Naughton left the Loch Castle suddenly—it seemed that she was in a bit of a hurry—nobody appeared to notice it with any concern, except, perhaps, the faithful subaltern, Pop-eyes, who had pursued her in vain.

The first thing Gail knew about it was when Bill gave her the information after lunch one day when they were in their sitting-room.

Gail, to please Bill, had been making a list of the women whom she wished to ask to lunch at the 'Aperitif' in Edinburgh next week.

When she mentioned June (only because she felt she had to ask the Major's wife and daughter), Bill gave her a queer look and said:

'June left Scotland this morning.'

'She didn't come and say good-bye to me,' said Gail, surprised.

'You didn't want her to, I don't suppose,' was Bill's short observation.

Gail, who was darning a silk stocking, paused, and looked reflectively into the fire. She felt decidedly glad that the girl had left the Castle. She had loathed being a silent witness to the affair which she knew had been going on between June and her husband. At the same time she wondered what had happened. One or two things had been going on lately which perplexed her. Ever since that evening when Ian had called Bill into his room, Bill had been strangely altered. He had never been more gloomy or depressed, but his manner toward Gail had been irreproachable. He was not only polite, but considerate. Naturally

313

she was thankful for this change in him, but she wondered what had effected it. What had Ian said to Bill? Another thing which she noticed, and which had upset her, was that that nice Captain Fenton seemed so altered in his manner toward Bill. He almost ignored him. And Joyce the other day, looking rather embarrassed, had turned down an invitation from Gail to come up and play bridge. It was pretty obvious that Fenton disliked Bill.

And now June had gone! Well, so much the better.

Gail supposed that she had better be grateful for small mercies and ask no questions.

When Bill had gone to work that afternoon, she took Ian's setters out for a walk. Coming back from the kennels, she met the young Laird of the Castle. As his tall graceful figure advanced toward her through the violet-blue winter dusk her heart leapt, but sank again almost at once. Useless to let her heart-beats quicken for Ian Dalmuir.

He saluted her and fell into step beside her.

She tried to make impersonal conversation.

'I nearly lost Morag just now, chasing a rabbit.'

'Did you?' he said vaguely. Then stood still a moment, looking down at her. Her cheeks were pink from the exercise she had just taken, and the cold. She wore a woollen cape with a little hood which he found enchanting. His heart yearned over her and he felt intensely grieved at the thought of the utter waste of her youth, her beauty, her sweetness, on Bill Cardew whom she did not love.

He said:

'I'm glad we've met out here. I want to say good-bye to you, and I'd rather say it alone than formally in front of all the others.'

She caught her breath. Her cheeks took on a deeper burning hue and then grew as white as the frost which rimmed the naked twigs of the trees.

She said:

'You're going to France?'

'Yes. I travel south tomorrow and cross over ... well ... shall we say, one day this week.'

She felt a lump in her throat and an aching tearing pain in her breast. Utter desolation descended upon her.

'Of course, I was expecting it,' she said.

'Don't be upset, Gail. It is much the best thing really, and I want you to know that I *want* to go.'

'I understand that.'

'There'll be a change here, of course. The Castle billet will close down. The Brigade's going to move anyhow. And although he doesn't know it yet, Cardew is being sent to Scapa. You can't go with him, so you'll be able to go home.'

She drew a long breath.

'I am glad of that. I'd rather be alone with

315

my own people once you go across the water.'

'Well, as long as you're happy, I shall be happy,' he said abruptly. 'I couldn't bear to think of you being miserable . . .'

'You needn't think that,' she broke in quickly. 'I'll be all right. As a matter of fact, Bill has been much nicer the last day or two. Ian, I don't quite understand, you must have said something to him. What did you say? Will you tell me?'

He turned away and looked up toward the Castle. The servants were pulling the blinds. It was 'black-out' time. One by one the orange oblongs of light which were windows vanished until the Castle was shrouded in the mist of the twilight. A profound sadness and darkness settled upon the Celtic soul of the man who stood there beside the woman he adored and must never see again. For he knew that it would be better, once they parted like this, that they should not meet any more.

'Don't ask me what was said between Cardew and myself. But *you* didn't come into it. That's all. It was something else. Gail, dearest, just promise me that you'll try to be happy when I go.'

'I'll try,' she whispered.

'I leave early in the morning. I shan't see you before I go.'

Those words struck a dismal chord in her own soul. She would not have been human had she not broken down a very little, just a little,

316

the hot tears welling into her eyes and the muscles in her throat working. And he would have been less than human had he not caught her in his arms and embraced her, as they stood there in the fast gathering darkness.

'Good-bye, my dear, my darling. I'll never stop thinking of you. Don't remember the pain . . . only the happiness that we knew in France.'

'You said that once before,' she wept and kept her face pressed against his shoulder, her hands holding him tightly to her. 'Darling, precious Ian, I love you. I'm not ashamed to say it. You take the whole of my heart with you tomorrow. I'll do my best for Bill, but I love *you*. I always will. I shall pray that you'll be safe.'

For an instant their lips clung in passion and a poignant tenderness greater than they had ever before experienced. But it was too much for Gail. She felt the great burning tears forcing their way under her lids. She hated this parting more than she had ever hated anything. It seemed so awful that she had not the right to kiss him good-bye, to write to him when he got to France, do all the hundred and one things a woman wishes to do for the man who goes to fight for her.

She gave him a last convulsive hug and then broke away and ran blindly through the dusk back to the Castle.

She did not leave her room again that night. She could not face them all downstairs, make

317

light conversation, hear this person and that discussing the fact that Ian Dalmuir was going to France tomorrow. She could not bear to see Ian himself again, and perhaps, she thought, it would make it easier for him if she absented herself. So she pleaded a violent headache, took aspirin, and went to bed in a darkened room. It was a black night for her. A night which she believed to be of irrevocable parting from the man she adored, and it was made no easier by Bill's presence and his somewhat clumsy attempts to be solicitous for her when he came to bed.

That seemed in her opinion one of the worst parts of marriage to a man one did not love. That enforced intimacy of his presence, which on a night like this, for instance, was merely an intrusion on her private grief.

But she tried not to show her distaste for him. When he took her hand and held it she let him do so without protest. She thought: 'I must do my duty to Bill. It would be wrong of me if I didn't.'

And in the midst of her choking sense of frustration and sorrow, she remembered what Ian had told her today. Soon Bill would be going to Scapa and she could go home alone. Never before had she so sorely needed the peace, the familiar surroundings of her childhood's home.

But that day on which Ian Dalmuir left his native land and journeyed on his way to join the British Expeditionary Force in France became memorable to Gail for another and more vital reason.

She had remained in bed that morning. Unusual for Gail, but she felt so utterly worn out after her sleepless and miserable night. She had her breakfast in bed and tried to sleep again with the aid of some more aspirin, and drawn blinds. She just could not bring herself to go downstairs. The Castle would seem so empty, so changed, without the presence of its Laird. She wanted to sleep and forget, for a little while longer, how empty the whole of her life would seem in future without him.

It was Joyce Fenton who burst rather suddenly and unceremoniously into Gail's darkened room, switched on a table lamp and sat on the edge of her bed.

'My dear,' she said breathlessly. 'My dear, are you well enough to listen to me?'

Gail roused herself and sat up. Her head was still aching and she felt heavy-eyed, but she became immediately aware that something was wrong. Something unusual had happened. For Joyce Fenton's face was without its usual healthy colour, and her eyes looked frightened. She took Gail's hand and said:

'My dear, I'm afraid it's bad news.'

'What, Joyce? What is it?'

'Well, they've asked me to tell you,' said Joyce clumsily.

Gail's heart missed a beat.

'For heaven's sake, tell me what?'

Joyce looked as if she was about to cry.

'It's so awful. I hate to do this when you're not well, too.'

For a moment Gail's brain felt too stupid to work clearly and she had a sudden awful feeling that something had happened to Ian. That was her first thought. But Joyce was telling her another story altogether. There had been a raid that morning over the Firth of Forth. There was no warning here, but Edinburgh had known about it. One of the ships lying there by the bridge had actually been struck and there had been some loss of life. But the worst of it was the falling shrapnel from the anti-aircraft guns. There had been some damage to civilians, Joyce said, and Gail's husband and the young subaltern, 'Pop-eyes,' had been there this morning on a job, and had actually been involved in the raid. A piece of shrapnel had caught Bill. Struck him in the head. He had been taken to Edinburgh Castle. They had just telephoned for Mrs. Cardew to go at once to him.

Gail, listening to this jumbled story, stared at Joyce Fenton, a completely fatalistic feeling enveloping her. Her brain refused to work clearly. She could not really digest what Joyce had just told her. But she heard her own voice as from a distance, asking:

'Is Bill—dead?'

# TWENTY-SIX

'Of course,' said Joyce Fenton, 'if you don't feel fit enough, you musn't go to the hospital. I mean, if you have a temperature or anything, it would be very unwise, as it's very cold.'

Gail looked at her blankly for a moment. Joyce was crying. Joyce was a kind-hearted girl and she cried easily. But Gail was too shocked for tears. Both mind and body worked mechanically from that moment onwards. All thoughts, all emotions, were at a standstill. It was as though she stood outside herself and, in a detached way, watched everything. Then she realised that Joyce had not answered her question. She was beginning to roll up her stockings. She looked up at Joyce, and said:

'Is he still alive or not? I'd like to know at once.'

'I don't know,' said Joyce. 'Nobody seems to know. The Brigadier told me and asked me to tell you and all he said was that Mr. Cardew had been seriously injured.'

Gail went on with her dressing. She shivered violently with nerves rather than cold. Joyce made one or two kindly efforts to help her, handed her her clothes, found some shoes—took her coat from the wardrobe.

'The Brigade car is waiting with the Brigadier,' she said. 'Would you like me to come, too?'

'Thank you,' said Gail.

Joyce wiped her eyes and looked a trifle curiously at Mrs. Cardew. She was a strange little thing, but Joyce had always liked her. But she knew that if she had heard that Kenneth had been badly injured in an air raid and was lying there in Edinburgh Castle, she would have had an absolute *fit*. She couldn't possibly have taken it so calmly. But then, of course, she *adored* darling old Ken. Nobody seemed to think that Gail and her husband got on very well. And so queer, too, since they had so recently been married. But Gail looked very white and no doubt this news had come as a great shock to her.

It was in a state of shock that Gail journeyed into Edinburgh in the car, sitting between the Brigadier and Mrs. Fenton. The Brigadier, tall and grey-haired, a man who had won distinction in the last war, did his best to be kind and tactful, but he could not disguise from Gail the fact that the report which he had received from the M.O. was a bad one.

'First real raid, you know,' he said, with a cough, 'and Cardew was doing his duty, of course. Very bad luck that he and Mr. Peters happened to be in the thick of it.'

Gail heard herself asking dully after Mr. Peters. That was poor 'Pop-eyes.' Young Peters apparently hadn't been hurt. But the Lord Provost's house in Edinburgh had been

322

struck and a woman injured in the head.

The Brigadier and Mrs. Fenton continued to talk together. Gail sat silent, staring ahead of her. She knew intuitively that Bill was dead; that she would never see him again. She did not wish it to be so. But she knew it. Greatly though he had disappointed her and acutely though she had suffered over the return of her heart's love, it was not in Gail's nature to wish harm to a living soul, let alone the man she had once cared for and married so short a time ago. But when she reached the Castle she was fully prepared for the tragic news that was given her. Bill was dead. He had succumbed to that wound in the head whilst they were trying to operate and remove the fragments of shell.

They were very kind to her there, the matron, the nurses, the doctor in charge of the case. They asked if she wanted to see Bill, but she preferred not to do so. 'I'd rather remember him as he was,' she said.

They sympathised. The sister in charge assured her that Mr. Cardew 'looked beautiful.' His face had not been injured. Gail's imagination was vivid enough to allow her to picture Bill's face sculptured by death into carved ivory. He would be very handsome. It was positively frightening to think that anyone so young and so virile as Bill could die like this. It brought home to Gail with shocking suddenness the fact that there was a war on. It was the war that had killed Bill. But it was the sort of death that he would have been glad to die. With all his faults and his failings, Bill had been a good soldier. Everybody was telling her that now. His end had been in no way glorious or distinguished. Just falling shrapnel. In an air raid over the Firth of Forth. But it had been whilst discharging his duty that he had received the fatal wound. And, of course, he would be buried, they told Gail, with full military honours.

She sat in the matron's room very still, very calm. The breakdown was yet to come. She listened to all that was being said to her, and just nodded, smiling faintly in acknowledgment when they praised Bill. The Brigadier assured her that Mr. Cardew had served his country to the best of his ability. Back at the Loch Castle they would all say that. It was forgotten now, that a few hints to the Brigadier had resulted in a transfer for Bill from Edinburgh to Scapa, out of the Brigade. He was a hero now, a hero because he had died in the war, and Gail, his widow, must wear the laurels for him.

She did not want to wear them. She felt that any great show of sorrow would be hypocritical. The loss of Bill was not as dreadful and overwhelming to her as it should have been, and she knew it. But in this immediate hour of his death she scarcely allowed her thoughts to dwell on the fact that his end had set her free . . . and that Ian, who was 'somewhere in France,' would be astonished and exhilarated to learn that she was free. She was too shocked and too genuinely sorry for Bill to think of Ian just now. And her whole compassion went out to his mother. Poor old Mrs. Cardew would be the one to suffer through Bill's sudden and calamitous end. Hers would be the broken heart. For, casually though he had always treated her, he had remained her darling and her pride.

Gail was bordering on collapse before she left the Castle, but she insisted on going down to Princes Street in the car, buying a great many flowers and taking them back to the hospital.

'Put them there with him,' she said to one of the nurses. 'It'll make everything seem less grim.'

The nurse took the flowers away, and now suddenly Gail's eyes filmed over with tears, and she whispered:

'Good-bye, Bill. Good-bye, poor Bill! You loved life and I'm sorry it's ended for you. I'm sorry, too, if I hurt you in any way.'

And it was with self-reproach, rather than any remembered antagonism toward him, that she left that hospital where lay an English officer who had died of wounds.

The collapse came when she stepped out of the car at the Loch Castle. During the drive back, she had not spoken, only allowed Joyce's firm young hand to clasp hers in silent sympathy. During that drive, her imagination had full sway. She thought of Bill as she had last seen him this morning. She was glad that they had not parted in anger, in misunderstanding, which recently they had often done. She remembered that he had been depressed, but that when he had bent over the bed and kissed her good-bye, he had been quite normal and affectionate, talking about his work and saying that he would not be back from Dunfermline till the afternoon. He had told her that he was going across the river with young Peters. Top-eyes' was probably the one person in the Castle who got on well with Bill. She had seen Mr. Peters at the hospital. He had seemed unnerved and upset after the raid and the sudden death of his brother officer. But he had paid a glowing tribute to Bill's courage and coolness during the raid. She was glad to think that the last few hours before Bill died had probably been pleasant ones for him, spent in the company of a man he liked, and in the interest of his job.

It was impossible to think that he would not return to the Loch Castle; that never again would she see him put on his uniform, brush that fair glistening hair of his, show his white teeth in that winning smile which he could muster at will. It struck her now, in the midst of her stupor, how death can change one's feelings. It wiped away animosities. It softened opinions and memories. She could only recall the Bill she had been fond of, and whom she had married, believing that Ian Dalmuir was for ever lost to her.

Then Mrs. Naughton met her at the door of the Loch Castle. The death of Bill had also wiped away Jean's hostility and suspicions. Like everyone else who had known Bill, she was ready to think kindly of him—and his widow.

She held out both hands to Gail, who, supported by the Brigadier and Mrs. Fenton, walked up the steps, 'looking dreadful,' as Jean afterwards told Major Naughton, with that relish of morbid detail which women, rather than men, display at such times.

'You poor dear . . .' she began.

Somehow it was the changed and kindly attitude of her former enemy which proved too much for Gail's resistance. She realised in earnest what had happened. She hid her face in her hands and burst into floods of tears. Mrs. Naughton and Joyce took her upstairs.

In the days that followed, Gail refused to allow herself any consolation in the thought or memory of Ian. She did not even write to tell him of Bill's death. She could not. It would not have seemed to her right and proper. The time would come, of course, when she would get into touch with him. The time would come when at the back of her mind she knew that life would recommence for her gloriously; be completely changed.

But for the present she gave herself up to the duties which, as Bill's widow, she wished to discharge as faithfully as she had tried to discharge them during his lifetime.

When she wept, her tears were genuine, not tears for herself but for him, and for his mother. Her own parents hastened North in order to be with their daughter in this tragic crisis. But Mrs. Cardew collapsed and remained at Kingston in charge of doctor and nurse. The old lady had been hard hit by the loss of her son. At the same time, her pride in him helped to soften the keen edge of her grief. She wrote pathetic letters to Gail. She had always known, she said, that Bill was a splendid soldier. She was thrilled by the photographs of him which appeared in the daily papers, and the widespread reports of his death.

Somehow or other, Gail brought herself to a state of mind and body when she could attend Bill's funeral, but it was too much for her in the end. Those muffled drums and the plaintive strains of the Last Post, tore one's very heart-strings. She was led away by father and mother, and there were many sympathetic eyes that followed that slim-looking young figure in black. Such a young widow and so sad!

Sad for *him* was what Gail thought repeatedly. And yet how he would have loved his own funeral, the pomp and pageantry; the fact that he, '2nd Lieut. William Cardew,' was the name on every lip, and that he was the figure of the hour.


## TWENTY-SEVEN

Christmas had come and gone. A strange Christmas which seemed almost unreal to Gail, so altered were the aspects of her life by the loss which had plunged her into widowhood.

She spent that Christmas in her old home at Kingston with her parents, and Chris and Scampie who were overjoyed to find their cherished sister at home for the holidays, having anticipated that she would be in Scotland, and unable to see them.

During the school holidays they made things as gay as possible for Scampie's sake . . . holly, mistletoe, crackers, hanging up stockings, all the customary paraphernalia, still dear to the childish heart . . . And at moments Gail had felt as though her marriage had been a strange interlude in her life, an episode which had little to do with the past and nothing with the present. They were months which had turned her into a Gail which was not really Gail. A neurotic creature who was the result of a rash war marriage . . . a crazy mistake. A Gail who had suffered unbelievably, once Ian Dalmuir reappeared on the scene.

329

But now that interlude with all its sufferings and disappointments was over. Gail found herself strangely at peace, and she believed that it would have been Bill's wish that she should not go through a period of intensive mourning for him. She wore sober colours, but not black. She was quite sure he would have disliked her to dress entirely in black. There was a war on. There was plenty of suffering in the world and no one had the right to be a depressing figure, parading grief. More especially in her own case, Gail felt it would have been a hypocrisy to make too great a show of sorrow. For once the whole thing had passed over, and she was back at Kingston with the family, she became very much aware of her new freedom, and all the rich promise of happiness, of love's reward in the future.

She had written to Ian and had her first letter from him. It had taken a long time to come. 'Passed by the Censor,' giving her little information about himself other than that he was in a comfortable billet, and that it was bitterly cold.

It was not a love letter in any sense of the word, but merely to express shocked surprise at the news of Bill's death, and to ask her to give his sincere condolences to old Mrs. Cardew.

*'I know how you must feel it, too, my dear,'* he wrote, *'and being the tender-hearted person*

*you are, it will mean much pain for you. You will never be out of my thoughts and I will write again very soon. There is no need for me to tell you that I am at your service, now and always . . .'*

That had been very comforting to Gail and she had appreciated in full the delicacy which had prevented him from mentioning their own personal reactions to Bill's death. It was enough that he should tell her that he was 'at her service, now and always.' It had been enough for him that she had written to say that *he* was never out of *her* thoughts.

Both were content to wait for a more appropriate hour in which to tell each other what they really felt, and what they both knew, deep down, awaited them.

It seemed to Gail as though her love for him, and his for her, was hiding warm, and alive in some secret place, biding its time. There was a tremendous muffled thrill in the knowledge that it would, eventually, like a delicate and lovely bud, break into full flower.

Gail enjoyed the family Christmas. It was good to be with her own folk at a time like this. And none of them spoke about Bill. Only once Chris mentioned his name to Gail. It was after the parents and Scampie had gone to bed, and brother and sister sat before the dying fire. They had been roasting chestnuts and defying indigestion. Then Chris suddenly said:

331

'I say, Gail, old Bill dying like that . . . sort of wipes out everything, doesn't it?'

Gail looked at the fire and nodded.

'Yes, of course it does.'

'He had a pretty decent end, doing his duty and all that,' said the boy.

She realised that her young brother was paying a tribute to the man he had so cordially disliked and mistrusted in life. She thought it very sweet of him. She, too, had tried to pay many tributes to Bill's memory, and for Bill's sake, she never failed to pay a daily visit to the lonely old lady down the road, who had a huge portrait of him in uniform over her mantelpiece and whose memory, for her at least, remained unsmirched.

'What'll you do, Gail?' Chris asked her, 'when Scamp and I go back to school.'

'I've been offered work at the Hospital Supplies Depot and I shall start there as soon as possible.'

'I say, Fish-face, that chap who writes to you from France, is he a particular pal of yours?'

Then a deep pink stole into Gail's cheeks and at the thought of Ian her heart beats quickened. She answered:

'My greatest friend. You'll meet him when he next comes home on leave.'

And that was the day to which she looked forward more eagerly than she had ever looked forward to anything in her life, Ian's first leave, when she could meet him, talk to him, be with him, knowing that there was no barrier between them.

Now their letters grew more frequent and a warmer note was creeping into his, an almost proprietary note which was a thrill for her. He took it for granted that as soon as he arrived she would meet him and they would see as much of each other as they could.

*'We have many things to talk about,' his last letter said, 'so many plans to make. Gail, I feel you very close to me these days. Stay close to me always, won't you?'*

And she had written back:

*'I shall always be close to you, Ian. I am trying to forget those years that separated us. It would be so wonderful if we could just start again, from those days in France when we were so divinely happy. I want to feel that the rest has been just a kind of dream . . . an experience which I shall try not to regret, because I don't believe in regrets. One must look forward and never back. I am trying to learn your philosophy, Ian—"to remember the sweetness and not the pain" . . .*

Toward the beginning of February she had a letter from him on an even more possessive and eager note than usual. And it was to give her, also, the news that he was due for leave at any moment, and would wire her. He wrote:

*'Would it be impossible for you to get a permit and come to France? Somehow I have a great desire to meet you again in our beloved Paris. You could bring your mother with you if she wished to come and you would be my guests. You must tell her all about us. It's no good keeping it from people now. I know that we must wait a decent interval before we can be married, but you belonged to me long before you married Bill, and I feel somehow that I have the right to your love now. And don't, please, darling, feel at all embarrassed about me standing the expenses of the trip if you can make it. You know that I am able to afford it and that it will be for* my *pleasure. I get very short leave and somehow I would rather spend it in France than in Scotland, just for the moment.*

*'The time will come when I shall want to go back to the Loch Castle, but it will be to take you there as my wife.*

*'I love you, Gail, with every drop of blood in my body, and I will love you until I die.'*

She was tremendously thrilled and exalted by that letter. It seemed to bring him there before her very eyes; the tall familiar figure in uniform; the sleek dark head; those dark, poet's eyes, the tenderness of his smile. Incredible tenderness mixed with strength. A man for a woman to adore, and she knew that she adored him

It was the first time that he had actually mentioned their marriage and that, too, gave her enormous pleasure. To go to the Loch Castle as Ian's wife . . . Could any prospect be more wonderful? Then inevitably came the reaction . . . An awful horror that he might be killed out there in France before he could get back to her. War was a hungry, greedy monster. It might take Ian from her as well as Bill, and if it took Ian, then it would take her own life's-blood, she thought.

With all her nerves on edge, she went to her mother and told her everything about Ian. For the first time Mrs. Partner was to have unravelled to her the mystery which had surrounded Gail when she first returned from France, three years ago.

Gail sat on a stool beside the fire at her mother's knees, just as she used to do when she was a child. Mrs. Partner listened to her, gently stroking the brown curls of the daughter who had always been so dear to her. Her first and perhaps her best-loved child.

'You needn't tell me anything more than you want to,' she said, 'but what you have already said makes me in a way happy rather than unhappy. It explains a good deal which has worried me in the past. I only wish you had told me before.'

'I didn't want to worry you,' said Gail in a

low voice.

Mrs. Partner sighed.

'That's what mothers are meant for, dear, and I might have saved you from all these months of misery. I would have warned you that you should never have married Bill, feeling as you did about this other man.'

Gail echoed her sigh.

'Maybe, I wouldn't have listened to you, Mum. That's what daughters are like! And I thought I *did* love poor Bill for the time being. I know now that it was just infatuation and the glamour of the war. And, of course, I had no idea that Ian would come back, and that it was his mother who had put an end to our affair.'

'She did you both a great wrong, Gail.'

'I suppose she loved Ian, and thought it was for the best for him.'

'Tell me about Ian.'

For the next hour Gail spoke about Ian. She had so much to say. It was as though a torrent broke loose in her heart and poured forth . . . A rhapsody of love, of admiration for Ian to which her mother listened with a little smile and a deep sense of satisfaction, because this she recognised was no infatuation but a deep love which had withstood the difficulties and disappointments of years. She saw plainly that she would soon lose her girl again. But this time it was not going to be with any sense of misgiving or doubt. If Ian Dalmuir was all that Gail said he was, then it looked as though Gail had found the right man at last.

Gail read extracts from Ian's last letter, and discussed with her mother the proposed trip to France.

'I don't think I shall go, darling,' said Mrs. Partner, 'I'm not as young as I was and I don't much feel like crossing the Channel, and I don't *much* like the idea of you doing it. But I understand your point of view—and Captain Dalmuir's. Naturally you would like to meet again in surroundings where you used to be so happy.'

Then Gail said, laughing:

'Oh, Mummy, don't call him Captain Dalmuir. Call him Ian!'

'Ian, then,' said her mother.

'You'll adore him.'

'I'm sure I shall.'

'Do you think I could go to Paris alone?'

'Darling, you'll have to discuss it with your father. How about Simone? Does she still live there? Could you go to her?'

Gail's heart leapt. Simone! That was an idea. It would be perfectly wonderful if she could go back to Simone and her people . . . back to that house in which she had first met Ian.

She had not heard from her French friend since the war started. Doubtless she and her family were evacuated from Paris to their country house, but she could send a wire and find out. As far as she knew, it was permitted for English people to cross the Channel in order to visit their friends.

Another twenty-four hours and Gail knew exactly where she was. A wire to Simone proved that the family were still in Paris; that Simone was working as a secretary in the Censor's Department but would be delighted for Gail to pay them a visit and stay there as long as she liked.

A letter from Simone added, further, that André, her brother, had already been in action, received the Croix de Guerre for gallantry shown whilst leading his company in a night reconnaissance; that he would be at home shortly on leave, and they would all like to see their old English friend.

Gail was almost too excited to sleep that night. Could anything be more heavenly than the prospect of meeting Ian in Paris? With Simone and André . . . the old foursome . . . who had laughed and danced and picnicked together in that glorious summer of three years ago. If it was so, it would seem that her dreams would indeed come true and that she and Ian might pick up the golden threads which had been dropped there, and weave the old familiar pattern, cutting out all the mistakes, forgetting the griefs, obliterating the tears.

She sent a telegram to Ian informing him that as soon as the date of his leave was fixed, she could join him in Paris and would be staying with Simone. He wired back:

*'Glorious! Bless you!'*

And after that Mrs. Partner found it a task to make Gail rest or sleep, she was in such a state of nervous excitement. She was never still for a moment. When she was not working at the Supplies Depot, she was shopping, sewing, writing long, long letters to France. She did not want to wear any of the clothes she had bought for her trousseau when she married Bill. Extravagant though it might seem, she had a fetish about that. With the help of the little local dressmaker, who had many a time 'run up' a dress for the two young ladies of the Partner household, Gail made herself a new outfit in which she would go to France for that perfect reunion.

Long afterwards, she looked back tenderly upon these days and realised how fraught they were with emotion . . . surcharged with a warm, secret understanding which flowed like waves of sheer electricity between Ian and herself, until the day they met again.

That day was in early February and following the severest winter that Paris had known for twenty-five years. It was an almost mild day. A day when the sun shone down from a pale blue sky flecked with clouds. Not a very hot sun but just enough to hint that spring was approaching and that there would be an end to the bitter winds, the ice and the snow that had devastated Europe.

Gail did not go to the station to meet the train that brought Ian to the capital. He had advised her not to. He was uncertain of his time of arrival and stations were cold, draughty places, besides being very public. He wanted to be alone with Gail for that first meeting and her wishes synchronised with his. Wishes easily granted with the help of kind little Simone, who was enchanted by the idea that her friend should recapture her great romance of the past; a romance in which she, herself, had been so concerned at the time.

At midday a Paris taxi deposited the tall Scots soldier in his military great-coat, luggage, gas mask, all the paraphernalia, at the door of Simone's beautiful home, in the Boulevard Suchet.

Simone was at her depot, working. Gail was alone. She stood at the window watching that beloved figure emerge from the taxi, her heart beating so fast that she could scarcely breathe. When Ian rang the bell, she ran breathlessly to the gilt mirror over the mantelpiece to look at herself. Was she all right? Would he like her new dress? Would he be disappointed?

The reflection in the mirror showed a girl who looked the same young and radiant creature whom Ian Dalmuir had loved when she first left school. Nobody would have dreamed that she had been already married and widowed. The new dress, which was of soft woollen material, of a dark, almost violet blue, with a wide belt, made her look very slim, but she was not as thin as she had been in Edinburgh. Her cheeks were glowing with colour, and her eyes were star-bright, under the dark silky lashes. Simone's clever hairdresser from the Rue St. Honoré, had curled the chestnut brown hair sleekly and smartly in an aureole about her head. She had pinned a small bunch of violets and snowdrops on one shoulder. She wore no jewellery except her wedding ring—which would soon be changed for another.

She stood there a moment staring at herself in a stupor of happiness, of excitement. Then the door opened and she swung round, both hands pressed to her breast. The old manservant who had been here for many years announced:

'*Monsieur le Capitaine Dalmuir.*'

The door closed behind the servant again. Ian stood looking at Gail and she at him. Both were speechless in the poignancy of that moment.

Then Ian let the gas mask slide from his shoulder, flung gloves and cane on a chair and held out his arms.

'Darling! Darling! *Darling!*' he said huskily.

She could not answer but ran to him and clung deliriously, the greatest joy she had ever experienced sweeping her from head to foot.

His arms held her close, and his kisses were warm and passionate on her upturned mouth. This was their real reunion, this was where they could begin again and forget all those dark days which had existed between their last meeting in France, and now.

When she did speak it was only to utter his name again and again, with all the old endearments, whilst her hands lifted the glengarry from his head and caressed the dark smooth hair.

'Ian, my darling, my sweet. My *precious* Ian!'

'God, it's good to see you, to hold you again,' he said.

'Heaven,' she said.

'Heaven's the word, my darling angel!'

She found him looking well, and of course, undeniably happy. Never before had she seen Ian look quite so boyishly pleased with life, and with reason. For when they had first loved each other, there had been so much against that love and the possibility of their marriage. And later they had known nothing but suffering and regret. But now there were no barriers, no difficulties. They had only to wait a little while and they could be together always.

He took off his coat and belt and they sat together on the comfortable couch . . . very French with its stiff, red and grey striped-silk cover and masses of cushions . . . facing the wood fire which was always burning in this,

342

the library. Old Jacques brought in sherry and biscuits for *le Capitaine* and for the next hour they were uninterrupted, unable to tear their gaze from each other, sitting there, arms about one another, talking of many things, exchanging news, making plans. Ian found little time for the sherry and biscuits.

'I only want to go on kissing you and kissing you, my darling love,' he said.

'I am all yours,' she said, 'I always have been and always will be, now.'

Neither of them alluded to the past. Bill's name was not mentioned. Nothing was to mar the perfect rapture of this meeting. Ian did not even speak much about Scotland and the Castle.

'We'll go back there together when we're married,' he said, 'and perhaps when this war ends we'll make it our home.'

'I love it, as you know,' she said softly. 'I should adore to live there with you.'

He looked down into her brilliant eyes and sighed a little.

'It's been a long time, Gail beloved, but everything now seems so well worth while. You're never going to be unhappy again, are you?'

'Never. Even when you have to go back to the Front I won't be unhappy. It'll be an awful parting and I shall worry dreadfully, but I shall be happy in the thought of you and our future together.'

He lifted her hand to his lips, kissed each finger in turn and then the palm. With that soft palm still against his lips, he smiled at her.

After a moment he said:

'You're a wonderful person, Gail, and very beautiful. I've never seen you look as beautiful as you do today.'

'I expect that's because I'm so happy.'

'It does me good to hear you say that. Ah, Gail, if only it was later in the year, I'd like to pick you up in my arms and carry you through the woods at Fontainebleau like I did before.'

'You don't know how often *I've* remembered those moments at Fontainebleau.'

'They'll come again. I'll get leave for my marriage and we'll go there and recapture the spirit. It's so very much alive.'

Suddenly he remembered something, put his hand in his tunic pocket and drew out a little box.

'Do you know what this is?' he added.

She caught her breath as she looked at the small leather case.

'It looks like—a ring—'

'That's what it is. I found it in Amiens when I had to go there one day recently. It's very old and will have to be made smaller for your little finger, but I thought you might like it. You see, we're sort of engaged, aren't we?'

They laughed together. It sounded so funny, being engaged, after all they had gone through. Funny, and rather sweet. The ring

344

enchanted Gail. It was dark blue enamel and marcasite, in an exquisite design.

As he slid it on her finger, Ian said:

'I have all the family jewels, darlingest, locked away in the bank at Edinburgh. They will all be yours, and we'll find something better than this in Paris during my leave. I bought this because it just took my eye.'

'I love it,' she said and held out her hand in order to regard the little ring from a distance.

Ian said:

'This is the sort of thing a man dreams about before he comes home on leave. This room, this fireside, and you in my arms. Darling, my darling, how happy I am!'

Then he held her in silence. With her head against his shoulder she closed her eyes, listening to the crackle of the wood on the fire, the muffled roar of traffic, those sharp squeaking taxi horns which were essentially Paris.

Then turning, she put her lips against the khaki sleeve of his tunic, giving him her heart's silent adoration.

# EXTRACTS FROM GAIL'S DIARY, WRITTEN A FEW WEEKS LATER

'I don't know quite what persuaded me to begin another diary. They are supposed to be out of date. Some people consider it old fashioned and a waste of time to keep one. But somehow I like to put down in words what I feel and what I do. Especially when it is something wonderful, because in years to come it will be a pleasure to read it all again and be able to go over, in detail, the loveliest episodes of one's life.

'Perhaps, also, it is in memory of that other pathetic little diary which I burned the night before my marriage to poor Bill. I wish now that I had kept it, because in it I chronicled all the mixture of ecstasy and pain which I knew when I first met and loved Ian. But those pages, many of which were blotted with such bitter tears, are now in ashes. And in these pages there must not be any tears. Only ecstasies. For this is the story of my reunion with my darling and the unbelievable thrill of the days which followed his return from the Front.

'When I saw him again that morning in that house in the Boulevard Suchet which will always be dear to me, I was conscious of a much deeper love for him than that which

I felt in the first days, To that other Me, the schoolgirl, he had been wildly attractive. Nothing could compare with the enchantment of his companionship and the thrill of him as a lover. But to this Me, the woman who had lost him, suffered, then found him again, he is more than a friend and a lover. He is a god to worship. I felt from the moment that he took me in his arms again after our long parting that I would willingly die for him.

'I knew, also, that henceforth his wishes would be mine, and that I wanted to do nothing without him, but just to live and breathe for him. So, of course, when he suggested later on that day, that we should not wait the conventional time before getting married, I agreed with him absolutely and without argument.

'We discussed the matter alone, then later with Simone. Simone, who had, with the years, developed into a dear, sagacious creature with a very sensible head on her young shoulders. In fact, it was she who asked us why we bothered to wait.

'We all knew that my marriage to Bill had been an error of judgment. And a marriage which would never have been contracted, let alone dreamed of, had I still been in touch with Ian. Simone pointed out that I was being unfair to myself to have it on my conscience that I *had* married Bill, and that if I allowed what was known as 'the right thing'

347

to influence me now too strongly, I was wrong. It was 'the right thing' to wait a year before I married again. But in whose eyes? Not ours. Only in the eyes of the world. A world of shibboleths and proprieties which were riot always by any means fundamentally right. So often they were carried out in hypocrisy, and thereby lost their virtue.

'In our hearts, Simone said, Ian and I were longing for a legal union. We had in virtual fact belonged to each other years ago. Fate had parted us then. Fate and Ian's mother, with disastrous consequences. But we still belonged to each other. And it would be nothing less than hypocritical for us to wait for our marriage just in order to placate Society.

'We both told Simone that we did not wish to be selfish or callous to the memory of Bill. To that, she replied that she felt sure if poor old Bill could see us and hear us on earth, he would be only too pleased for me to do as I wished in the matter. His poor spirit could not have any delight in maliciously desiring our continued separation. As for being selfish, the only people to whom we owed consideration were those directly concerned. Bill's mother, for instance, who would be deeply shocked if her beloved son's wife, with apparent lack of feeling, married again within a few months after his death. Poor old soul! Naturally, she would not understand, because she did not know the facts. Then there were my people.

348

Mummy might understand, because she was very broadminded, but Daddy was different. It might hurt him to think that his daughter had completely disregarded the conventions, and he would think it bad as an example for Chris and Scampie.

'Then again, there was Ian's side of it. He had no family to care what he did, but there were his brother officers. People like Major Naughton and the Brigadier, those who had been at the Loch Castle with him and Bill would fail to understand it, if Captain Dalmuir suddenly, and speedily married the widow of his late subaltern.

'No, there was every reason why there should not be a public union between Ian and myself. But none, said Simone, why we should not be married secretly and keep it quiet until some future date when we could announce it without qualms.

'Why, Simone asked us, did we not get a special war-time permit and be married in Paris before Ian returned to the Front. And if I wore a new wedding ring, who would notice it? Except for my mother, whom I would tell, no one else need know. Ian must content himself with writing letters to me, using my former name . . . It would all be a bit difficult and a bit of a strain, but, in Simone's opinion, we would both be happier to know that we were actually man and wife, and to make the rest of this leave a brief and very sweet honeymoon.

'Ian agreed with Simone, and I was naturally only too anxious to give my consent. I wanted more than anything in the world to become Ian's wife and to feel that there was nothing to keep us apart, now or ever. It would make the leave perfect for Ian, and I argued with myself that I owed it to him. He had been robbed of something by my marriage to Bill ... robbed of long weeks and months when we could have, and should have, been together. There was a war on and he was in the thick of it, risking his life. It was up to me, the woman he loved, to give everything in the world to him that I possibly could. Although I hardly dared to allow myself to think it, there was always that faint but sinister shadow of a thought in the background ... the fear that he might be taken from me. I felt that I must belong to Ian as his wife before *that*.

'So the forty-eight hours that followed Ian's arrival in Paris were unimaginably exciting and crammed with happiness for both my darling Ian and myself. Simone's parents were kind understanding people and they gave us every assistance. Simone had explained the whole position, and they, too, thought it only right, with this awful war on, for us to take our happiness while we could, and away with conventions! So long as we hurt nobody else, like that poor old lady in Kingston! . . . what did anything matter.

'A special licence was procured. André was

best man . . . André looking marvellous in his uniform of the French Army, with the Croix de Guerre on his breast, and Simone supported me . . . and so Ian and I were married.

'Writing this, as I am, in my little bedroom in Kingston, that whole day in Paris seems like an unearthly dream. Something snatched from Paradise itself and almost too exquisitely happy and tender to be true.

'But it is true enough. Here is Ian's wedding ring on my finger, replacing Bill's. Another little platinum circlet, very similar, and yet how different . . . And how different was the second marriage! Incredibly so! No church, no bridal attire, no swelling organ, no reception, cake, party, all the fuss and pomp of that first wedding in Kingston. No doubts and apprehensions, no disappointments or tears. None of the swift disillusionment which had come upon me during that honeymoon spent on the Thames.

'My wedding with Ian was the acme of perfection, and, so it seems to me as I look back now, the fulfilment of the dream we had once dreamed together in Le Touquet. God knows I was happy then, but with a feverish happiness which was, in a way, transparent. Through it I could see the pain, the sorrow of the inevitable end. I knew then that I had committed a sin and would have to pay for that sin. But this time it was all so *right*. The same thrill, the same passionate love was there, but it was built on the security of marriage, and that just made all the difference!

'Of course, as a rule, one has to give fifteen days' notice before a marriage can take place at the *"Mairie,"* but because Ian was serving at the Front he was exempted from doing this under special War Regulations. He just produced word from the Military Authorities that it was all in order, and it was all arranged.

'I can see that *"Mairie"* so vividly. The rather imposing room with its large table on which stands the "Civil Code." There were two large gilt chairs rather like thrones for Ian and myself, and four ordinary ones at the back for Simone, André, and their parents. I felt rather thrilled by the large tricolour flag on the wall opposite us and those stirring words *'Liberté, Egalité, Fraternité'* carved above the flag. It was so much more dignified and full of atmosphere than an English Registrar's office. The stained-glass windows, the thick carpet, the large group of palms and flowers on either side of the Mayor's table made it seem almost like a church.

'We were ushered into the room by a Beadle with a mace of office, and then the Mayor came in in his ceremonials which consist of evening dress, tails, white waistcoat, white tie. He beamed upon us in friendly fashion as though approving of this bridal between the tall Scots officer and myself. He was a bit pompous and rather funny but I shall always remember him with affection. He put on his wide tricolour sash with its heavy gold fringe and our marriage service began.

'I was in such a daze of happiness that I hardly heard the words of the Civil Code which dealt with matrimonial rights and obligations. Then Ian and I signed the book, the witnesses added their signature and it was over.

'But that was not all. We had to go on to the British Consulate and there we went through yet another ceremony performed by the Consul. So after that double marriage, as Ian said, we felt so very *much* married.

'We walked out of the British Consulate to the car which waited for "the bride and groom." I was almost suffocated by my sense of happiness and of pride, because I was no longer Gail Cardew, but Mrs. Ian Dalmuir, and I daresay I *did* look my best. My darling Ian said I had an "angelic" look, which rather made me laugh, because I am not really the angelic type. But if a woman doesn't look beautiful for her marriage to the man she loves, she never will.

'I just wore the simple violet blue suit that the dressmaker in Kingston had made me. But there were two new additions to my toilette which I am sure helped the "angelic" appearance. A perfectly marvellous fur coat which Ian had bought for me as a wedding present. I had never had such a coat in my life before. It is hanging here in my wardrobe in my little bedroom at home. I often look at it and touch it and feel my heart miss a beat at the memories it conjures up.

'It's a sort of cocoa-coloured ermine, beautifully worked; so rich and soft to touch, and divinely warm. On the collar I wore a big bunch of lilies-of-the-valley, which of course Ian had sent me, and which rather added the "bridal touch." And the coat was by no means his only present. During the twenty-four hours that we waited for our licence, he just heaped presents on me. I couldn't stop him. I've never known anybody so generous. It just seemed that he couldn't give me enough; at least, that is what he said. He kept finding things that he wanted me to have. A new hat; I wore that for my wedding too. It was Paris with a capital "P," an absurd little velvet thing, perched on top of my head, with a long soft veil which tied under my chin. Simone said I looked *"ravissante."* I hope I did, for Ian's sake. What he said about me when I turned up for my wedding would fill my diary. Bless him!

'It seems to me that my top drawer is full of presents from Ian. Another "engagement ring" . . . well, it can hardly be called that now . . . but it's a heavenly emerald, and cost Ian a fortune. When I told him not to be extravagant, he just laughed and said he had far too much money, and some one to spend it on now. When I reminded him that Income

Tax was going up and that soon he would hardly be able to keep up the Loch Castle, he just laughed at me and said, "Who's the canny little Scot? Not Ian Dalmuir but his wife!" '

'He gave me two new bags and a new cigarette case, with his regimental badge on it in diamonds, and a leather-bound book of poetry which we both read and loved, and I felt rather out of it because I had no money of my own and could only give him a very modest wedding present . . . a new tobacco pouch, which he said he would use daily and which was "just what he wanted." Darling Ian! He didn't really need it at all.

'Well, after that simple wedding, we had champagne and sandwiches with our dear French family to whom I owed so much. And then, Ian and I moved to the "Edward VII," which was the hotel at which Ian always stayed and which he liked best.

'We had decided that owing to the shortness of his leave it would be ridiculous to attempt a honeymoon anywhere other than Paris. We should have liked to visit Le Touquet, to stay at the "Hotel Picardy" there. But in war-time everything would be closed and it would be bitterly cold there at this time of the year. So we stayed in Paris, where we could fill in the moments and be gay together when we wished to be so. Paris is less severe with its black-out regulations and early hours than dear old London. And everywhere there were officers,

355

both English and French on leave, lunching, dining, dancing, with wives or sweethearts.

'And so I lunched, dined, and danced with my husband—glorious word! And every heavenly night that I went to sleep in his arms and woke up in them again, it was to feel that a miracle had taken place for me. I was his, all his, then, and that other poor, pathetic marriage was as though it had never been. I never thought of Bill during that week with Ian. I hardly had time to think at all—only to *feel*, one ecstatic emotion after the other.

'Of course, it had to come to an end and I dreaded the day that a miracle had taken place for me. I was his, all his, then, unhappy and he was marvellous about it. Not a grumble or a moment's depression. It was his job and he had to do it, and there it was.

' "It'll be hell leaving you, darling," he said one night toward the end of that blissful week, "but to brood over it will only make it much worse. We must just be thankful for these days and look forward to our next leave together." '

'I agreed with him absolutely, and I admired his philosophy. It is mine, too. I always think when there's an unpleasant fact to be faced, grumbling only makes it a lot worse, and I didn't want to be one of these wives who hang on to their husbands and moan about separations which cannot be avoided.

'We had an unforgettably lovely evening before he left. A cocktail at the 'Georges

"Carpentier" bar, a perfect little dinner at the "Cremaillere." I like to remember just what we had since Ian ordered it. Oysters, truites-au-bleu, chicken done with cream and mushrooms, and a perfect red wine with it. We both of us prefer wine to champagne. We couldn't linger too long over our coffee because Ian had seats for a Sacha Guitry play, which we loved. Afterwards we had meant to dance, but by mutual consent, instead, we went straight back to the hotel. I can remember Ian's words in the taxi:

' "It's a waste of time dancing in public when I might be alone with you just quietly holding you in my arms. My darling beloved."

'How I adored him for that! A woman likes to feel that the man she loves prefers to be alone with her and is not bored with her. Then, only then, did I have a flashback to the autumn and remember how hurt I'd been because poor Bill wanted to take me out and spend one of those "showing-off" evenings rather than have it with me alone.

'I can remember getting back to the hotel and being quite cheerful until I had my bath, then lying thinking in the hot scented water (Ian had thrown extravagant handfuls of Guerlain's *Vol de Nuit* into it); a sudden depression came over me. A sort of reaction. I knew that there, in the bedroom, Ian was waiting for me, smoking a last cigarette. But this time tomorrow I wouldn't be in this luxurious bathroom and he wouldn't be anywhere near me. I would be back in England and he in his billet "Somewhere on the Western Front!" There was no knowing when we might meet again. No knowing *if* we might meet again. This hateful beastly war! And it had been a hateful waste of years for Ian and me since we first fell in love with each other. I felt angry and miserable and suddenly very afraid. I hurried out of my bath, and put on the grey chiffon night-gown with the cherry velvet sash, which was his favourite. It had an enchanting chiffon coat to match; it couldn't pretend to be warm but it was certainly attractive. Then I literally ran into the bedroom, and threw myself into Ian's arms. He saw the expression on my face and understood. Ian is such a marvellous person for understanding. He wasn't going to comment on the fact that there were tears in my eyes, because he knew how proud I was about not crying. He just reached up a hand and switched off the light over our bed. The room was dark then, except for the red glow of the electric fire and I was glad of that darkness and oh, so glad of the warmth, the strength of Ian's arms, and the soothing tenderness of his fingers threading through my hair. Very gently his lips touched my eyelids and charmed away the tears. He kept saying: "It will be all right, my sweet. It *will* be. I know it. Don't worry . . ."

'We lay there together in the warm

darkness, whispering, cheek to cheek. I was very soon restored to calmness and my old philosophy about being "the cheerful wife." And an hour later we were both laughing. It's good to laugh as well as to love. Ian has a divine sense of humour and I think I have always had one, so we will always get through our bad times together by finding something to laugh at, thank God!

'I don't think there was very much sleep for either of us that night. We both of us realised that as soon as it was over it must be good-bye. Ian was to catch an early train and would only just have time to put me on one for Calais as I was catching the midday boat. I could have stayed another day or two in Paris with my friends. Somehow, Paris without Ian would be too empty a place. There is a marvellous song by Jack Strachey called *"Paris Is Not The Same."* I bought the record when I got back to London, and it just fits in with my present sentiments.

'Lovely and unforgettable that last night of Ian's leave, and we didn't let the misery we both felt at parting spoil a moment of it.

'By mutual consent we both got up early and had our *café et croissants* in the sitting-room. After which I sent for the *femme de chambre*, got her to bring me some metal polish, and a cloth, and I polished the buttons of Ian's khaki tunic, and rubbed up his belt. I was feeling definitely a little sick, with that awful sinking sensation in the pit of one's stomach when one knows that something wretched is going to happen. But I wouldn't show it that morning. Nothing would induce me to shed a single tear before Ian left. I must have looked rather white and grim, sitting there, vigorously rubbing up the belt. Ian put on his tunic, and looked down at me and said: "You're a damned good batman, darling. I've never had such lovely bright buttons!" And he stooped to drop a kiss on the top of my head. And I set my teeth and answered cheerfully: "I'd give my soul to be your batman, darling, then I could go with you. Couldn't I?"

'I handed him his belt and he buckled it on and gave me his sweet quick smile. "You will be with me all the time, darling," he said. "You'll be in my heart and mind—always very near me."

'Then I had to finish some packing and afterwards we stood together arm in arm a moment on the balcony of our hotel and looked down at Paris.

'It was a cold morning and rather foggy. But Ian wouldn't let the depression of the weather get him down. He said that it reminded him of Scotland. He asked me if I remembered those autumn mists that used to curl round the Castle and blot out the heather-covered moors. Indeed, I remembered it. And I thought of the Castle and the peace of it all up there without a war on. And I pictured Ian and

360

myself wandering through the grounds with dear old Dougal and Morag bounding in front of us. I remember saying to Ian: "We will be back there together quite soon. Somehow I *feel* it. Perhaps on your next leave."

'He smiled and said that was a grand idea. And that on his next leave we would announce our marriage, and let the world know that we love each other.

'I hardly like to write about the hours that followed. It was just one perpetual strain trying to be cheerful and not cry, and really, I was almost glad when the dreaded moment came for Ian to see me on to the boat-train for Calais. I took a last look at him as he stood there on the platform before me, with his great-coat buttoned to his chin, and the glengarry at its usual rakish angle on that dark, much adored head. Just for an instant I hugged him close and told him how much I loved him and how much it meant to me to know that I was his wife. And we both clung and kissed, and nobody cared. It was Paris and it was war, and there were lots of other men in uniform, both French and English, saying good-bye to wives or sweethearts. Women who loved, perhaps, as I loved, and felt the anxiety, the pain that I felt.

'A last kiss and the train moved out of the station. The last glimpse I had was of Ian standing at the salute, smiling at me. I smiled back and waved at him out of the window as long as I could see his darling face.

'It wasn't a very good crossing from Calais. I didn't mind it being rough because I am a good sailor, but I hated the thought that I was being taken further and further away from *him*. But at least it was better than that other crossing from Boulogne years ago, when I didn't belong to him as I do now, and everything was so much more ephemeral. I knew that this love, this union between us was a secure, steadfast thing which would endure as long as life endured and, perhaps, after that.

'They were all so kind to me when I got home. Particularly Mummy. She understood what I was feeling and she didn't fuss me or reproach me for having married Ian suddenly and secretly. She just suggested that I shouldn't keep it a secret from Daddy or from Chris. They would both understand, she said. Neither of them had cared for Bill. And both could be told about Ian and the way his mother had originally parted us. Mummy said that she would rather everyone knew, except Scampie, who was too young to understand. We could wait for Ian's next leave and then tell her, when we meant to make a general announcement of our marriage.

'Daddy was much more sympathetic about it than I thought he would be. And I had a perfectly sweet letter from Chris, once I sent the news to Shrewsbury. I don't think there are many boys of his age who are so understanding and sympathetic as my young brother.

'It is nice not to have to keep it a secret from my family and it means that my letters can come from France addressed as they should be to *Mrs. Ian Dalmuir*. I have just written a long letter to Ian telling him everything that has happened since I got home. And, as I wrote to him, I posted my heart with that letter.

'Tomorrow I start work at the Hospital Supplies Depot again. That's what I shall do until Ian comes back. Work and work for the war and not give myself too much time in which to be miserable or worried. It's no use. I know I've got to be a fatalist. If Ian is meant to be taken from me in this cruel war then it will be. But I believe down in my very bones that he will come back to me.

'*God keep you, Ian, my darling, my darling . . .*'